LAST SEEN BREATHING

The market town of Tawrbach is deeply shocked at the accidental death of ex-actress Rhonwen Spencer Griffith, rich widow, local cultural leader and leading light of the Operatic Society. The strange death of her failed son Elwyn soon after is less remarked, and it's at first assumed he may have died from natural causes. But Chief Inspector Merlin Parry takes a different view when he receives, anonymously, a copy of the memo Elwyn sent just before he died to the three male members of Madam Rhonwen's Operatic Committee demanding they pay him an outrageous sum for his mother's secret, explicit and uninhibited diaries.

So what had really been going on at Madam Rhonwen's intimate house parties? Why is the rector, amongst others, so concerned when he learns about the diaries, and why didn't Elwyn's pregnant wife even know they existed? All is uncovered when DCI Parry, and portly DS Gomer Lloyd, solve the mystery with a combination of solid police work and intelligent deduction.

In **Last Seen Breathing** David Williams provides a refreshingly original duo of Welsh sleuths. The style is elegant and witty, the locations authentic, and the plot ingenious – as you would expect from the writer of the Mark Treasure stories.

LAST SEEN BREATHING

David Williams

For Mike & Mary (Llewellyn) Loxton
a story in which the Welsh
is well up to the standard
of the physiology.

Love

David Williams

July 1994

HarperCollins*Publishers*

Collins Crime
An imprint of HarperCollins*Publishers*
77–85 Fulham Palace Road, London W6 8JB

First published in Great Britain
in 1994 by Collins Crime

1 3 5 7 9 10 8 6 4 2

© David Williams 1994

The Author asserts the moral right to be
identified as the author of this work.

A catalogue record for this book is
available from the British Library

ISBN 0 00 232510 1

Set in Meridien and Bodoni

Photoset by Rowland Phototypesetting Ltd
Bury St Edmunds, Suffolk
Printed and bound in Great Britain by
HarperCollinsManufacturing Glasgow

This one for
William F. Deeck and Ellen A. Nehr

1

Detective Chief Inspector Merlin Parry, of the South Wales Constabulary, was in a tearing hurry. Even so, after locking his three-year-old, soft-topped Porsche, he paused long enough to give the roof a reassuring sort of tap. He had bought the car cheaply a month before from a redundant yuppie, and was still needing to convince himself that he'd got it cheaply enough. Someone had just told him that an open Porsche was wrong for his image anyway. Parry didn't care a toss for his image, but in a curious way it unsettled him to know that anyone else cared about it more than he did.

He crossed the road, and jogged up the sloping pavement of Church Lane, past all the other cars abandoned at varying angles along the grass verge on the other side, looking like stranded porpoises. He was pulling on his dark topcoat as he went. It was mild for mid-March, and the church would be heated, but the light grey suit he was wearing was a shade jaunty for the occasion. He should have thought of that earlier, except he hadn't seriously expected to get here at all, not on a Tuesday morning.

It had just gone eleven-thirty. The rector, the Reverend Mr Caradog Watkins, started everything on time – he'd been in the Navy where you didn't have the option not to, Parry thought, increasing his pace on the flat, going under the Tudor lychgate, along the even older, deeply worn flagstones, and on into the church through its Norman south porch – all features highlighted in the official Tawrbach guidebook. He was in luck: the service had not quite begun.

'Don't hold with cremation myself. Not proper,' squeaked the diminutive Mrs Ethel Hughes, perspiring in a venerable fur coat, her head stuffed into a black satin toque. She had made room for Parry on the back pew. It didn't seem to him that she expected a response to her comments until she dug him sharply with her elbow and demanded: 'Well is it, Mr Parry? Cremation? Proper?' in a voice loud enough, even with the organ playing, to engage the occupants of four crowded pews in front of her.

Parry leaned closer towards Mrs Hughes, where the scent of mothballs was even more penetrating. 'Well, that's debatable, Mrs Hughes, isn't it? Cremation suits some,' he answered diplomatically, in a half-whisper.

'What you say, Mr Parry?'

He had been afraid of that. Mrs Hughes was nearly ninety, with hearing at best patchy and hardly made less so with her ears covered by thickly lined satin. Parry was not going to repeat his words. Commonplace observations emerge as banalities the second time around, especially to people not directly addressed, and more especially when bellowed. Was he thinking of his image, he wondered. He squeezed the old lady's arm – an action which considerably fortified the reek of camphor – and smiled at her confidently.

Parry's naturally impassive countenance came alive when he smiled, the soft, usually searching blue eyes narrowing to slits, with small creases making star designs around the outer edges. He seemed to blink less than other people, and when he did the action was faster than a camera shutter. His oval, and presently flushed face was flattish, with a broad forehead topped by shortish brown hair. The nose was wide, and significant only in profile, the mouth long and uncompromisingly straight. He was a little above average in height with a spare figure and broad shoulders. He used his shoulders a lot in conversation, in the way some others use their hands. He was a fit thirty-eight – fit enough, at least, to turn out for the Tawrbach Reserve Rugby team if required.

Mrs Hughes's lips had begun quivering again as a prelude to further spirited comment. But her purpose was forestalled. Perdita Jones, deputy stand-by organist, switched without ceremony from an ambitious piece of Mozart, indifferently rendered, to the opening lines of 'For All the Saints', which brought the congregation to its feet – Mrs Hughes included, if a bit behind the others.

Parry had seen the awesome, recently appealed for, and massively commended little Romanesque church as crowded as this before, but only at Easter or Christmas, and never for a memorial service. It seemed the whole of Tawrbach was here – figuratively speaking that is, because the market town wasn't that small, and St Curig's only seated three hundred maximum inside its colossal stone walls. Certainly everyone who was anyone locally seemed to be present, plus a few connected outsiders – like Parry himself. He hadn't lived in Tawrbach for over a year, not since the death of his wife.

As the robed choir processed from the northeast vestry into the nave, the policeman joined in the hymn as fervently as most others in an archetypal Welsh congregation, this one, if anything, even more musically orientated than the average. The departed life the people were here to honour had been the centre of choral activity in the community – and for some distance beyond it. The late Rhonwen Spencer Griffith might not have died with a song on her lips (though there was nothing to prove that she hadn't), but there would certainly have been a song in her heart, as always. At least, this was the popular view.

At the end of the hymn, with the choristers settled in their places, the Reverend Watkins led the prayers from his stall. He was a large man, and jowly, with a shock of untamed hair, eyebrows as bushy as brooms, a voice like approaching thunder, and a steely gaze ripe, you might think, for seeking out sin.

Afterwards, the choir sang the twenty-first psalm to a special setting, and the deceased's 32-year-old, balding son Elwyn sidled forward wearing dark glasses to read a piece of scripture. His delivery was halting for a professional lecturer, even a redundant one. But people made allowances for his emotional state as well as his asthma – also because he'd taught at a polytechnic not a university, where many imagined elocution wouldn't have been so important.

9

As the next hymn was ending, the rector had moved forward to the chancel step to deliver the address. There was a much photographed fourteenth-century stone pulpit to his right, except current attitudes suggested a preacher could raise himself one foot above contention, but not six: even so, it would have taken a brave parishioner to go the whole modernist hog and try to start a dialogue with this particular preacher.

'. . . only for her to perish in a road accident, thousands of miles away in Malaysia, far from all her loved ones, family and friends,' the speaker was soon relating, pushing a massive hand grandiloquently through his hair, stout fingers spread open like the teeth of a mechanical grab.

Merlin Parry, like everyone else who had read the inquest report, knew that Rhonwen Spencer Griffith had died on holiday seven weeks ago, and that Reggie Singh (marital status unknown, but much debated), the proprietor of the Taj Mahal takeaway in Ystrad Mawr, had perished in the same accident. It was understood that the lady had put up the money for Mr Singh's restaurant in the previous year. So if conjecture was correct, she might not have expired separated from *all* her loved ones.

'A widow these ten years,' the rector continued, 'Madam Rhonwen, as she was known to us all, was the adored wife of the late . . .' he paused for effect, deepening and hollowing his voice, 'the late and revered Councillor Lloyd Spencer Griffith, OBE, JP, local legislator *par excellence*, local benefactor without compare. It's no overstatement to say he was Madam Rhonwen's irreplaceable, fairy-tale swain . . .'

And about twenty years her senior, Parry recalled, which detracted a bit from the idyll, not to mention that, judging from photos, Councillor Griffith had been a bit on the stout side for a Lochinvar. The reports had given Reggie Singh's age as forty, suggesting that Madam Rhonwen harboured an enduring affection for men somewhat outside her own age bracket. She had been fifty-six last December. Of course, it wasn't to be assumed that she and Singh had been lovers. No explanation for their sightseeing together in Malaysia had been officially requested, and none had been volunteered.

'Elwyn, her only son, did right, I'm sure, to have his dear mother's earthly remains consumed by fire in that far-off land,' the rector went on, but with not quite as much conviction in the tone as in the words. The lips and knees of Mrs Hughes stiffened in response. 'By all accounts, it was a very terrible accident, and anxious as many here would have been to pay their last respects to that . . . to that damaged body, better no doubt that we go on picturing Madam Rhonwen as she was in life – vibrant, ebullient, full of energy and beautiful with it.'

With an exaggerated arm movement, like a rider encouraging his mount, the speaker thrust his hand beneath the white surplice and into the pocket of his black cassock. The hand re-emerged clasping a billowing, if not notably clean, handkerchief with which Watkins first blew his nose loudly and then wiped an eye. The last and possibly symbolic action was even so emulated by scores of others in the congregation, where a good deal of sobbing had already broken out.

'Beautiful with it.'

Parry noted the soldierly Huw Prothero's exaggerated nod of approbation made in response to the rector's repetition. Tawrbach's most prominent lawyer was sitting, bolt upright and arms folded, at the end of the pew two along from the policeman, but on the other side of the centre aisle. His nod had been slow enough, and the head turned sufficiently to suggest that Prothero might also be gauging his wife Marged's response to the last phrase in the eulogy. The lady remained facing forwards, so that it was impossible for Parry to make the same assessment as her husband.

It was well known that the normally jolly and latterly immense Marged Prothero couldn't stand the sight of Madam Rhonwen. The dead woman had been undeniably, you could say famously, attractive, even in middle age. Mrs Prothero, her near contemporary, had been a beauty too in her time, but her looks, like her now prodigious weight, had altered considerably over the years. People had always supposed that it was basic jealousy of Madam Rhonwen's sustained good looks that had accounted for the other's distaste of her, and not, as in the case of some other older wives, a belief that

Madam Rhonwen had been sleeping with her husband: well, not necessarily.

'Beautiful with it,' the rector repeated once again, this time more slowly, with greater emphasis on the first syllable, plus a shake of the head, and a gaze so uncharacteristically glazed that Parry wondered if the cleric, mesmerized by emotion, might go on absently repeating the same words until somebody stopped him.

Abel Davies, fifty-four, and Tawrbach's leading independent estate agent, was in the row ahead of the Protheros with his wife Megan. They were both slightly taller than those about them, and both wore heavily framed spectacles. Merlin Parry had watched them exchange solemn glances of agreement at various points during the address, like a pair of assenting owls. They were doing it again now.

The middle-weight, dark haired Davies's strong tenor had been easily distinguishable during the singing. Like Prothero, he was a member of what, until six weeks ago, had been the four-strong management committee of the Tawrbach Operatic Society. But he was one of its principal stage performers too. Like a lot of amateur soloists, he had no inclination to modulate his voice for congregational singing – only an invented, pedantic concern for composition and syntax. This allowed him to show off on gathering notes, sustaining notes, and carried-over lines.

The gaunt Megan Davies was wearing her Guides uniform with hat. This showed she was present in an official capacity. Madam Rhonwen had been a generous benefactor to all the youth organizations in the town. Parry wondered if Mrs Davies's appearance was subtly intended to suggest that her relationship with the deceased had been more formal than intimate – and to indicate that her husband's had been the same.

A lot of people would ignore the implications of that last point, even a lot of wronged wives, Parry mused sombrely. In six years of marriage he had only once come close to being unfaithful to his own wife Rosemary – and unfortunately careless enough to let her witness the fact. He shifted involuntarily in the pew, and not just because it was hard and uncomfortable. The details of that piece of drunken folly inevitably flashed through his mind now – his first time in Tawrbach for months. Being honest with himself, it was that event which underlay the effort he had made to be here. Women were so unpredictable: or one he knew was.

'. . . at Woodstock Grange, in the barn where there'll be a stand-up buffet, courtesy of Elwyn Griffith and his dear wife Alison. They've asked me to say that all are welcome.'

Parry was suddenly awake to the fact that the rector was ending his address.

'And now we shall end by singing Madam Rhonwen's favourite hymn, "He who would valiant be", number three hundred and seventy-two.'

The Reverend Watkins returned to his stall, and Perdita Jones, the unpredictable woman in Parry's reflections, re-started the organ.

'Lovely service, Mr Parry? Short though. Rector went on a bit, of course,' Abel Davies was observing ten minutes later. 'Pity no one else was asked to say a few words,' he added, though everyone knew there had been so many contenders for the last role, Davies prominent amongst them, that to avoid jealousy and friction it had been agreed that the rector should be the only speaker. 'Nice wake as well,' the estate agent continued. 'No expense spared, of course. Choice bit of ham in these sandwiches, too. Well, Elwyn can afford it now. Took some pushing to get him going though. Left to him there wouldn't have been a memorial service at all.' He moved slightly to a position that allowed him to pick up edibles with less effort from the plates on the long table nearby. His wife, Megan, looked disapproving, though whether of her husband, or of the shortcomings of Elwyn Griffith, or because this was her normal expression, it was, as always, difficult to be sure. Her small, tight mouth with a receding lower lip suggested she was on the verge of issuing a reproach most of the time.

The policeman wrinkled his nose amiably. 'If anything there seem to be more people here than we had in the church,' he said. 'More room, of course.'

'You're keeping up your cello, I hope, Mr Parry?' said Mrs Davies, a touch severely.

'Not really, no. The incentive's gone, d'you see? No one to play duets with. Not in Cardiff.' He glanced at Perdita. It was quartets they'd played originally, of course, she and her ex-husband Gavin, and Rosemary and himself – and trios after Gavin had deserted his wife.

'Pity,' Mrs Davies replied, more severely. 'Everyone should have a cultural interest, don't you think? Like my husband with the Operatic.' It was another oblique indication that it was culture not Madam Rhonwen that had kept Abel Davies committed to his art.

'Ah, the cello. Epitome of mourning accompaniment,' put in Davies, who prided himself on his lyrical asides. 'That's M-O-U-R mourning,' he spelled out, for fear anyone had missed the topical allusion.

'I did take up evening classes this winter,' Parry offered, ending a short silence. 'Welsh history. Always been inter-ested in that. Trouble was I fell behind with the lectures. Well, it was inevitable in my job. Can I get either of you ladies another drink?' He looked first to Megan Davies, and then to Perdita Jones who, to his surprise, had earlier agreed to drive with him the half-mile from the church – though she had done so with some diffidence.

Both women refused the offer of more to drink. 'We've all known happier times in Woodstock Grange, haven't we?' said Perdita, smoothing back a wisp of the long, corn-coloured hair which she wore gathered into a ponytail. Parry's quizzical glance in response to her comment made her look down sharply into her glass. She was slim, attractive and twenty-six, with unusually clear skin, high cheekbones and widely spaced, hazel eyes. Apart from being an inexpert organist – but a competent pianist – she was a physiothera-pist, her poise and supple movements offering a kind of advertisement for her professional abilities: at least, Parry had always thought that.

Woodstock Grange had been Madam Rhonwen's home. It was a substantial stone pile – mid-nineteenth century Gothic, built on the site of a demolished farmhouse. It stood in five landscaped acres, southwest of Tawrbach, and half way to the village of Quintinmawr where the Protheros lived.

The wooden barn close to the house was a good deal older than the main building, although it had been restored, and adapted as a small theatre by the late Councillor Spencer Griffith in an effort to please his wife. Under stout open rafters, at one end it had a balcony with stepped seating, and at the other a permanent, sprung stage with dressing rooms and other brick-built backstage appendages behind that. It was used regularly for the Operatic Society's musical productions, and for rehearsals, concerts, and dances. This was the first time it had been used for a funeral wake. The wake for the councillor had been in the main house; it was more fitting that the one for his wife should be in the building that would now become her monument.

Abel Davies adjusted his spectacles delicately with thumb and forefinger applied at one side, the remaining three fingers of his hand pointing ceilingwards like a stage duchess taking tea. 'Anybody heard whether Elwyn Griffith has made up his mind about selling the Grange?' he inquired lightly – too lightly for conviction. He was plainly anxious to know why a potentially large transaction and commission which, if they went to anyone, should rightly come to him, hadn't shown signs of doing so yet.

'Can't you ask him now, Abel?' asked his wife, stating the obvious when no one else had volunteered anything. She was continuing to nurse a practically empty glass of orange juice – which was fitting, Parry supposed, for a senior Guide.

'Funny chap, Elwyn,' said Davies, half to himself, but by way of answering his wife's question. Her directness hadn't seemed to bother him.

'You mean asking him might put him off giving you the business, Mr Davies?' Parry suggested.

Davies cleared his throat. 'Something like that, yes. I was too close to his mother, d'you see?' He and the others noted that his wife stiffened. 'I mean he's not naturally going to patronize people who er . . . who worked with Madam Rhonwen, is he? They didn't get on at all, you know.'

'But were they actually estranged?' asked Parry.

'People used to say so, yes. His wife Alison for one. You've been away of course, Mr Parry.' Davies moved closer and his voice dropped a little, though only a little. 'Mark you,' he continued, after gulping some wine, 'they weren't estranged when it came to Elwyn accepting her money. For the cottage she bought him and Alison last year. And that cost a pretty penny I can tell you.' The estate agent nodded knowingly as the man most likely to have the true facts of that particular transaction, and who was constrained from sharing them with everybody only by another disapproving glance from his wife. 'And there was no problem about him accepting an allowance from Rhonwen. To keep him till he got another job. Or got something published. That's common knowledge,' he completed firmly, while looking at his wife.

'He's written two novels,' said Perdita in a more spirited tone than before, in Elwyn Griffith's defence. 'With a good chance the second was going to be published. Well, till quite recently,' she ended, assurance a bit diminished.

'I wonder if Madam Rhonwen put up the capital for Alison Griffith's interior design shop?' asked Parry. 'That must have paid off if she did. Someone told me it's doing very well now.'

'She put up some of the loot. I put up the rest,' said a gravelly male voice from behind the policeman. 'It's a joint venture between Alison and Sally, my wife. So how's life, Merlin bach?'

The speaker was Tony Lovelaw. He was a few years younger than Parry, though with the same build, and with an avuncular presence that seemed a bit in advance of his years. He was local area manager for an animal feedstuffs company. The two men shook hands warmly.

'You haven't been playing this season?' said Parry.

Lovelaw was also an occasional member of the Tawrbach Reserve Rugby team. 'Neither have you,' he replied, 'except for that one match before Christmas. Sorry I missed it. Getting too old, boyo, and bloody lazy with it, that's my trouble. You're looking all right. Living in Cardiff now, is it?'

'Yes, a lot closer than Tawrbach to where I work, in the Rumney nick.' The policeman smiled.

'And closer still to the Arms Park. I'm told you've bought a posh flat in Westgate Street,' said Lovelaw. Cardiff Arms Park is the Welsh National Rugby Stadium set in the heart of the capital city, a solid indicator of where priorities lie in the principality. The main entrance to the ground is in Westgate Street.

'It's a modest flat, on the fourth floor, and it's rented – '

'No need to apologize, boyo,' Lovelaw interrupted, gazing round at the others. 'Sally and I'll look forward to getting an invitation next season. Say hello to her before you go. She's here somewhere. You're still on serious crime then? I tell you, if all the criminals – '

'Mr Parry. Very glad you were able to come.' It was Lovelaw's turn to be interrupted – by Huw Prothero who had now joined the group. He spoke as though he were hosting the occasion. His accent was perceptibly less Welsh than any of the others and his words were offered in a more penetrating and higher key than Lovelaw's. 'We miss seeing you in the town since you left. And at the Operatic. Settled down again all right, have you?' The lawyer levelled his chin, hollowed his back and tweaked the end of his moustache.

'Yes. It's been some time now.' Parry was looking at Perdita Jones as he spoke. 'And to be honest, the job keeps me too busy to do much else. Even to get here occasionally.' This was true, but it was largely his own doing. He had immersed himself in work since his wife had died. It was also true that for some time after her death he hadn't wanted to spend time in Tawrbach. And it wasn't nostalgia that had drawn him back today, though the memorial service had been the excuse.

'Very sad about your wife,' said Prothero, in a tone that was more dismissive than involved. He was looking about him as though there might be others whose presence he should be acknowledging and who would no doubt wish to acknowledge his.

'Sad about Madam Rhonwen too,' said Parry, making conversation. 'Big turnout today.'

'As you'd expect, of course,' the lawyer replied abruptly, returning his gaze to the policeman. 'Not that young Elwyn

17

has done much to organize anything. Left it to the rest of us. Abel Davies here, Evan Cromwell-Evans, and myself. As usual. The Operatic Committee to the fore. Less, of course, the late beloved Rhoñwen herself.' The end of his nose rose a fraction, and the bristle edges of the well-trimmed moustache rose with it.

Parry looked at the time. 'If you'll all excuse me, I ought to be going. Can I . . . can I give you a lift, Perdita?'

'No thanks, Merlin. I'll walk back later.'

It didn't sound like a brushoff – except to Parry. So that was that. Well, he'd made contact, which had been his purpose in coming – meaning no disrespect to Madam Rhonwen whom he had genuinely enjoyed.

'Not leaving already, Mr Parry?' It was Evan Cromwell-Evans who, a moment later, grasped his arm tightly as he passed. The dynamic owner of Shevan Electric Markets, short and swarthy, with a head that seemed too big even for his bull-like, hairy body, had turned from speaking with Elwyn Griffith.

'Afraid so,' said Parry.

'That's a shame. Bought a new stallion I wanted to show you after. Sure you haven't got another minute? The Lexus is outside. I could run you down to the house and back straightaway.' The house in question was a new one, in the village of St Joseph, a mile south of Woodstock Grange.

'No, really it'll have to be some other time. I'm late already.' Cromwell-Evans had always been sure that Merlin and Rosemary Parry had shared Rosemary's devotion to horses. This had not been so, but Parry had given up trying to explain as much years ago. 'Nice to see you again though.' He turned to Elwyn Griffith – plain Griffith, he recalled, not Spencer Griffith, because the one-time, left-wing academic had considered the Spencer an affectation. 'Well, once again, Mr Griffith,' he said, 'I'm deeply sorry about your mother. And thank you for the lunch. And you, Mrs Griffith.' He smiled at the vivacious young brunette standing beside her husband who was talking with the slightly older and differently vivacious Mrs Cromwell-Evans. Parry had spoken earlier to both women.

'Glad you could come.' The young man fingered what was left of his hair – an unkempt and lengthy crescent growth at the back of his head. He was only a fraction shorter than Parry, but slight and stooping, with hollow cheeks, sunken grey eyes, and a handshake as limp as a retriever's paw. Earlier it had been impossible to gauge much from his eyes. They had been hidden behind the dark glasses which were seldom removed – except the wearer removed them now. For a moment Parry saw Madam Rhonwen's face in her son's, but it was a diluted version and the resemblance was fleeting. It served at once, though, to emphasize the femininity in Elwyn's face, and the absence of the mother's strengths.

'Any chance we can entice you back into the Operatic this autumn, Mr Parry?' was Cromwell-Evans's parting question. 'We badly need more baritones.'

Parry shrugged. 'We'll have to see later.' Then he added as an afterthought: 'Will rehearsals still be here in the barn, Mr Griffith? Are you keeping on the Grange?'

'We haven't decided yet. Takes a lot of upkeep, this place.'

'Of course.' He'd done his best, but it seemed Abel Davies would have to possess his soul in patience a bit longer yet.

Parry nodded a final farewell to Madam Rhonwen's only offspring. He got a pallid, hardly animate stare in return. Even so, the stare was not nearly as pallid and inanimate as the next time Parry was to look on that face – but by then its owner was fated to be extremely dead.

2

Evan Cromwell-Evans gave Panther, his new horse, a touch with the whip. He took the final, downland furlong at a fast gallop. It was the day after the memorial service. He had ridden nearly five miles, starting at six-thirty when it was still almost dark. There was plenty of open riding country beyond the house: hunting country too. It was why he had bought the land, and called the place he had built on it Ridings. Cromwell-Evans had recently joined the local hunt and was intending to end up as its master: not bad for a coal miner's son.

'Good outing, was it, sir?' asked the flat-capped Dai Sugden who was waiting in the brick-paved stable yard. There, a row of three looseboxes and a tack room faced a longer range of garages. 'You and Panther go lovely together, you do,' he added obsequiously, looking humble while holding the reins, scratching a long sideburn, and generally playing the part allotted to him by an employer keen to play the country squire while being a bit short on supporting peasants. Sugden was only thankful that the spirited Panther wasn't giving trouble. Mr Cromwell-Evans was too ambitious as a rider, for someone who hadn't been at it long.

'Feels magnificent, I can tell you,' said Cromwell-Evans dismounting from the sixteen-hand horse with gusto, if not much style. It was a long way down for a five-foot-four rider. 'He'll do all right. Worth the money I paid. Got balls he has. No question.' He patted the black horse's rump, while his gaze concentrated on needlessly affirming the last observation.

'That's all right then, sir.' The scrawny, badger-faced Sugden was groom and gardener at Ridings. He had been a lot of other things in his time, including apprentice jockey until he had grown too tall. His wife was cook and house-keeper at the house. They were both in their fifties, childless, lived rent free in the flat over the garage, and they were well paid on top of that.

'Needs a good rubdown,' said Cromwell-Evans, watching as Sugden led the horse into the first of the looseboxes. At the moment there was only one horse, but Cromwell-Evans was negotiating the price of another, again for his own use. Sheila Cromwell-Evans didn't ride. The children had ponies, but for the time being they were stabled down the road at the local riding school. 'You'll get on with the paddock fenc-ing today, Dai,' Cromwell-Evans ordered later, as Sugden helped him off with his riding boots and on with his brogues. Then he made off towards the house. He had an energetic style of walking, bent arms working hard, fists clenched, shoulders dead level.

Built in stark red brick, Ridings was post-Modernist — meaning that it was neither neo-Gothic, nor neo-Classical, nor imitation Georgian, nor wholly covered in glass. A cacophony of steep pantile roofs of varying lengths and heights, and set in many directions like irregular compass points, it had been dubbed Hollywood Tesco by a local archi-tect who hadn't been given the job of designing it, and his description had stuck. There were eight main bedrooms and bathrooms, and four large reception rooms, plus a study, a billiard room, and a conservatory of winter-garden pro-portions overlooking the south terrace. The indoor swim-ming pool and sauna were in the semi-basement where the proud owner of this extravaganza was hurrying now.

Cromwell-Evans did most things in a hurry. He told people it was why he had done as well as he had, and why he would continue to do even better in the future. Twelve years before this he had been an ex-TV repairman who, with the help of a large mortgage, had acquired a run-down electrical shop with a flat above in one of the least salubrious parts of Cardiff. Today he was the titular owner of six substantial electrical discount stores in shopping developments in South Wales and bordering Hereford and Worcester, with a further large one planned in the new Wenville shopping centre, two miles outside Cardiff on the road to Tawrbach. He was still heavily mortgaged, but he had long since learned to call this being highly geared.

Along the way, Evan Evans, as he then was, had added Cromwell to his surname. This was to help with his social advancement, and in deference to the partly Welsh Oliver Cromwell with whom he claimed remote kinship (on the strength of their both having forebears called Williams), whom he fancied he mildly resembled and whose working methods he deeply admired. He had also discarded one wife and acquired another, called Sheila, who was younger and more glamorous than the first. Sheila had provided him with two children, a girl, Catrin, now nine, and a boy, Gareth, now seven. He had also acquired a new and prosperous father-in-law, Stanley Johns, a successful West Wales building contractor.

Johns's initial distaste for Cromwell-Evans had gone further than a father's predictable aversion to a 39-year-old, divorced suitor for his adored, eighteen-year-old daughter. As well as finding him too old, he had considered Cromwell-Evans pushy and too ambitious by half. But Johns was a realist, and also, importantly as it transpired, a devout Catholic. When Sheila had announced that she was three months pregnant, and that her lover was ready to change his religion (nominal Methodist) so that they could marry with the church's blessing, all had been accepted, if not immediately forgiven, by Stanley Johns.

Forgiveness had worked its way in later, along with the building contracts for several of the Shevan Electrical Markets – the name Shevan being a tactful put-together of the names Sheila and Evan. By the time the new Wenville development was on the drawing board, Johns was not only contracted to do the building of the Shevan store there, he had also pretty well agreed to put up half the substantial capital cost in return for loan capital shares in the business – of which he had quite a lot already.

After swimming ten lengths of the pool before showering and shaving, Cromwell-Evans bustled in to breakfast calling his good mornings loudly. He was dressed in a white shirt, blue silk tie, and the trousers of a sharp, blue, pinstriped suit. Breakfast was taken in the kitchen which resembled the control room in a small power station designed and furnished by Oliver Messel. He kissed Sheila and the children, and patted the bony shoulder of Claire, their earnest, bespectacled, nineteen-year-old au pair, all of whom were consuming orange juice, bran cereals and brown bread toast.

'Nice wide, was it, darling?' asked the red-headed Sheila whose inability to pronounce most of her Rs was matched with an unusually high-pitched voice that five years at an exclusive ladies college in England had done nothing to deepen, soften or improve. It was as though she was permanently providing imitations of small children with pronounced Glamorganshire accents.

'Lovely ride, yes. Bit cold at the start,' he answered.

'Bet it was, too.' She shuddered.

Sheila's voice was one of the characteristics that her husband had at first found endearing, but which he had later come to rate as irritating. Nor, sadly, had those of her other traits that he had first enjoyed proved nearly so unchanging as her voice. Her figure, which had been sexy and curvaceous, was now bordering on the fairly sexy and voluptuous. By gloomy extrapolation, it was promising to end up as decidedly unsexy and grossly plump – like Marged Prothero, and all this despite Sheila's slavish commitment to dieting. Her face was following the same downhill pattern as her body, if at a slower pace. It was still one of the prettiest faces Cromwell-Evans had ever known – bright eyed, a perfect retroussé nose, a mouth as sensuous as Marilyn Monroe's – only it was a face that had lost its innocence with thickening, and its youthful bloom from years of clogging with make-up. Since Cromwell-Evans had despoiled that innocence in the first place he could hardly complain. But he was a sensuous man who admitted to himself that his tastes had always been for younger, slender women. He had never much cared about women's minds, and certainly not his wife's mind.

That Sheila was a still ardent and unblushingly accommodating lover, as well as a caring mother to their children, were considerations actually less important to Cromwell-Evans than her father's wealth. He considered he had marital claims over his wife, but only a tenuous hold on Stanley Johns's financial resources. This last could also be said of the resources of Cromwell-Evans's bank, which lately had become an increasingly vital partner in the furthering of his corporate ambitions.

It was fortunate that over the years Johns's devotion to his daughter had strengthened. By extension, this had made him readier to indulge the son-in-law whom he believed had proved a good and faithful husband. It meant also that currently he had Cromwell-Evans firmly locked in a financial corner.

'Daddy, can Whisky and I go out with you and Panther on Saturday? After my riding lesson?' asked Catrin. Her face and auburn hair made her a nine-year-old replica of her mother before time had taken its toll. Whisky was the name of her pony.

'Expect so. If you're good,' Cromwell-Evans replied. After absently eyeing the post set beside his place, he had picked up a blue envelope with a typed address below the heading 'Confidential', and was now slitting it open with his bread knife, after pulling his coffee cup nearer to him.

'And me?' pleaded Gareth who was dark like his father.

Cromwell-Evans sniffed. 'No, not yet.' He paused as he began reading. 'I've told you, not till you're eight.'

'But Daddy, I'm —'

'That's enough, Gaweth,' his mother cut in. 'Something wong, is there, Evan?'

Her husband's cheeks had drained of their earlier outdoor glow. 'No, no. Nothing,' he offered gruffly, still staring at the typed sheet in his hand, but not reading it any more. 'Business, that's all,' he added, but blinking uncontrollably. He folded the sheet, and on the second attempt succeeded in stuffing it blindly into his shirt pocket. 'Got to make a phone call,' he barked, getting up, making for the door, and dropping his napkin behind him which Claire quickly retrieved.

It was an episode that Sheila found surprising. Her husband seldom received business correspondence at home and, so far as she could remember, none that had ever upset him, certainly not enough to make him sugar his coffee twice.

Breakfast at the Davies home was a less elaborate event than it was at Ridings, though it was conducted in the more formal atmosphere of a conventionally furnished dining room.

Abel Davies only took coffee. He had drunk his first cup while standing before the window, scanning the pages of the *Daily Telegraph*, an exercise he shared most mornings with a grey and languorous Siamese cat. The animal was named Selina, after a deceased great-aunt of Mrs Davies's. Selina, like the paper, was spread out on the walnut sideboard, beside the silver coffee-pot. Davies was dressed in a red check wool shirt, cricket club tie, and trousers made of a bluish Welsh tweed.

The house was at the top of Church Lane which ran south at right angles from the centre of the High Street down to the river bridge. A hundred yards short of St Curig's Church, it was one of four town houses in a three-storey terrace. The houses, originally substantial dwellings for well-to-do merchants, dated from the late eighteenth century. In those days Tawrbach had been a staging post for West Wales cattle drovers on the way to and from England. Davies, at heart a romantic, thought of that time as Tawrbach's first great era of prosperity. So far as he was concerned, the second great era had begun ten years ago and had continued into the present. It had been a period when property in the town had improved in value beyond his most optimistic expectations – even allowing for a two-year slump in the middle. He had done well throughout. For he was not simply a prominent estate agent. Less publicly, he was a speculator in property on his own account, and even during the recession he had done well by buying up repossessed properties at knockdown prices, tarting them up, and selling them on.

There was a formal walled garden at the rear of the house that Davies was now contemplating through his heavy bifocals, while stroking the importuning Selina, and sipping a second cup of coffee. His wife, in a severe grey wool dress (a shade darker than the cat), was sitting at the mahogany, oval table behind him, engaged with a pot of decaffeinated tea, a bowl of muesli and the *Guardian*.

The couple exchanged little general conversation at this time of day – and not much at any other time, but breakfast in particular was conducted in near silence by long standing if, appropriately, unspoken agreement. Taking the meal with their backs to each other served to underline the point. It wasn't that they exhausted topics for discussion in the bedroom earlier: they had separate bedrooms and bathrooms and hardly saw each other until they were downstairs. BBC Radio 4, set at a volume that allowed for comprehension but not necessarily rapt attention, had just supplied them with the eight o'clock news. A woman presenter was now quizzing a defensive Minister for Education about the alleged increasing illiteracy amongst children of all ages. The subject was of no interest to Abel Davies, but socially aware, if childless, Megan Davies was half listening.

'Early tulips are showing well. They'll be out soon,' said her husband suddenly, and paying no tribute to the early daffodils out already in the borders skirting the scallop-edged lawn. He preferred tulips. 'You should tell Stan to put more peat round the azaleas and rhodies,' he added. Timely instruction was not covered by the silence pact, and the prior observation about the tulips had been no more than the equivalent of throat clearing.

Stan was the gardener who came on Friday mornings. It wasn't a large garden, but it was more than Megan cared to handle alone, even if she could have made the time between applying herself to good works. Her husband wasn't interested in manual work of any kind. His leisure activities centred on cricket in the season, and the exercising of his singing voice at all times of the year.

'Leaf mould not peat,' Megan responded in a reflex way, without looking away from the paper which she had propped against the milk jug. Nor did her husband's interjection prevent her registering and then rejecting the Minister's claim on the radio that illiteracy was *clearly* being reduced, thanks to the Government's increase in the education budget *in real terms* year on year.

Davies sniffed. He knew that peat bogs were now supposed to be protected. But how a hundredweight of peat dug up in Limerick and put down in Tawrbach could rate as a net reduction in world peat reserves was beyond him. He shrugged, then jerked back his head when Selina coquettishly flipped the end of her tail under his nose. 'Leaf mould, then,' he agreed resignedly, allowing that it was no one else's fault if the Irish lacked his logic and economic wisdom, but still conceding a point to green political correctness. 'Was that the mail?' he added, after a clatter from the hall letter box indicated it was unlikely to have been anything else.

Without verbal acknowledgment, Megan rearranged her own reading glasses on her nose, got up, smoothed the grey dress, and headed for the hall. Letters delivered to the house were usually for her, or addressed to the two of them and customarily opened by her in what she termed her business corner of the large kitchen. Most of her husband's correspondence was directed to his office, which was just around the corner in the High Street.

It was several minutes before Megan reappeared, moving slowly, and carrying a clutch of correspondence. She had opened all the letters already and was scanning the contents of an appeal from the Shipwrecked Mariners Association, one of her less predictable charities. 'Oh, this one was for you,' she said, looking up over the glasses after pulling an envelope from the others in her hand. 'Sorry, I opened it by mistake. That's the colour the Philharmonic uses.' The envelope was blue, and similar to the one that had been addressed to Cromwell-Evans.

'What's it about?' Davies inquired, putting down his cup and turning towards her from the sideboard. The cat dropped silently to the floor, stretched its rear legs, then stalked over to the still-open door into the hall.

'What? Oh . . . it's from Elwyn Griffith, I think. Didn't take it in properly,' Megan responded, her initial hesitation caused, it seemed, by her having returned to her own reading.

Davies pulled out the letter which, for some reason, his wife had reinserted into its envelope. The frown he adopted when starting to read was shortly replaced by a scowl which just as quickly turned to a look of outrage. 'Bloody hell,' he exclaimed involuntarily, and not quite under his breath.

'What?' His wife, now seated again, looked around.

'Well, did you read this?'

'Not really. I told you. Something important?'

'I'll er . . . I'll just get my jacket,' he said, without answering the question. 'Then I'll be off round to the office. Heavy day,' he completed, moving towards the door.

Megan didn't appear to register his departure. She was gazing at another letter but her mind was elsewhere, and certainly not on the words of the Shadow Minister for Education now being interviewed on the radio. He was insisting that illiteracy was rife *clearly* because the Government was failing to increase the education budget *in real terms* year on year.

Quintinmawr, a mile from Tawrbach, was a hamlet consisting of a green, a pub called the Cricketers, an assortment of insubstantial dwellings, and a manor house. It had no church. The Manor House was a squat, whitewashed building in the Welsh farmhouse style, a good deal less imposing than its title might suggest. It was much smaller than Woodstock Grange or Ridings, and while it may well have been older than the Davies house in Church Lane, it had the appearance more of decrepitude than venerability. The house was long and faced directly on to the green with only the road and a scrap of unfenced garden in between. The grey slate roof was sunk in the centre, the woodwork needed repainting, the outhouses renewing, and the driveway resurfacing.

Huw Prothero, the owner of this appallingly neglected property, staunchly defended any charge that he had allowed it to decline. The place, he often averred, was waterproof, structurally sound for a building of its age, and adequately heated – allowing for the prohibitive price of fuel and the fact that he and his wife were used to donning extra woollens when needed. He was sure that a conspicuously well-maintained building attracted burglars – quoting the fact that Ridings, for instance, had been broken into twice since it was built, despite its being protected by a sophisticated alarm system. Prothero believed alarm systems were expensive and useless. Marged Prothero was in broad agreement with these sentiments. Like her husband, she was frugal by nature – though not nearly so mean.

Prothero was shaving in the only bathroom in the Manor House. This was a very large room. The present white enamel fitments were installed by the lawyer's equally penny-pinching father when he bought the place, for a song of course, in 1934. The room faced north and the only heating was a minute, painted towel rail normally, as now, buried under wet linen. The morning being cold, Prothero was wearing a Jaeger wool dressing gown over striped flannel pyjamas, with the sleeves of both rolled back to the elbows. As well as scraping his face hard with a safety razor, the blade of which was long since past its expected commercial life, he was repeating the gentle back exercise that Perdita Jones had taught him recently when his doctor sent him to her for treatment. This entailed his making a kind of levitating movement from the standing position, moving his weight forwards on to his toes, hollowing his back, and stretching his chest onwards as if, Perdita had explained brightly, he was a ship's proud prow.

'D'you want your tea in there or in the bedroom?' Marged Prothero demanded amiably if breathlessly in a chesty contralto. She was outside the open doorway where she had arrived singing a snatch of something by Ivor Novello – or Ivor Novello Davies as the composer is more accurately identified in his native Wales.

Marged was a prodigiously large woman, although her ears and eyes were so remarkably tiny as to be almost doll like – the eyes deep-set behind plump cheeks that were more bloodshot than merely ruddy. She had just ascended the stairs with both hands grasping a tray of tea things. She was dressed, top to toe, in a quilted garment, the collar of which was pulled up around her uncombed hair. To her husband, glancing back at her through the dim light of the landing, she looked like a large, upholstered armchair with the stuffing bursting out at the top.

'Bedroom will be fine. There in a jiffy,' Prothero replied before once again moving his chest onwards, humouring himself that he looked less like a ship's proud prow than he did a potent Welsh lawyer. Then he rinsed the razor under the cold tap, watching the water run away down the green encrusted plughole. He was having loin-moving thoughts about Perdita Jones and his next appointment for physiotherapy. It was not that Perdita had provided him with anything but strictly professional attentions the first time, only that he found the prospect of stripping in front of an attractive young woman a deeply satisfying contemplation.

Of course, in Madam Rhonwen's day he hadn't needed to indulge in fantasies . . .

'The post has come. Got it here,' Marged offered, interrupting her husband's fairly harmless, erotic ruminations, as she shuffled towards the main bedroom, taking up 'We'll Gather Lilacs' where she had left off, and dragging her slippers across the polished wood floor.

The Protheros had often thought of buying tea-making equipment to use on the upper floor but had never been convinced that the expense would be justified. One of them had to go down to the kitchen early every morning to stoke the Aga — Marged on weekdays, her husband at weekends — and it was no trouble to put the kettle on there at the same time.

'Anything interesting for me in the post?' Prothero inquired when he joined his wife in the bedroom. His question related to the appearance of the envelopes and not to their contents. The two had a strict rule about not opening each other's correspondence.

'I think that one's from the Philharmonic,' Marged replied, still humming under her breath while fingering the envelopes, her already tiny eyes narrowed to even tinier slits so that she could see things adequately without putting on her glasses. She was seated at her untidy dressing table, placed before one of the two south-facing windows. The table was a heavy, wide Victorian piece in stained oak with three mirrors on top, and drawers below in two bowed pedestals with a kneehole between. This matched the monumental wardrobe and the tallboy set to face each other on opposite walls, as well as the high, steel-framed double bed with its decorated head and tailboards. The plump, indented feather mattress with a mountainous disarray of bedclothes in the middle might have looked as though it had been the scene of a spirited orgy, but was merely witnessing the effort required before either Prothero could emerge from its depths each morning.

Marged continued to sip her tea, whilst summoning the courage to discard the quilted housecoat and the nightdress beneath it. Her undergarments for the day were spread on top of the bulbous decorated cast-iron radiator set between the windows.

Prothero selected the blue envelope from the three placed beside the tea tray on one end of the dressing table. He noted that it was marked 'Confidential'. 'This isn't from the Philharmonic,' he commented, after slitting it open with his finger.

'Looked like it.' His wife gave a chesty cough, selected a cigarette from a packet of Marlboro, gazed at it accusingly, then lit it. She blew out smoke, and coughed again, but more loosely than before. 'That's better,' she observed, inhaling again from the cigarette. 'Best smoke of the day.' She picked up her glasses, then reached for her hairbrush.

Huw Prothero was in the centre of the room as he finished reading the letter.

It happened that his wife caught sight of him in the mirror as he did this. 'Bad news, is it?' she asked.

It was just then that the telephone by the bed started ringing. The upstairs instrument was a luxury Prothero had installed some years before. Unlike an electric kettle, it was classified as a necessary professional tool, and was tax deductible.

3

'Elwyn Griffith must have taken leave of his senses. That's all I can say. Gone round the flipping bend,' said Abel Davies from his swivel desk chair. Nor was this scorching judgement a result of his having heard Griffith might be offering Woodstock Grange for sale through a rival firm in Cardiff. That was still only rumour, and there were bigger considerations at stake now than a two-and-a-half per cent estate agent's commission.

'It's not as if he's in need of money, either,' Huw Prothero insisted flatly, not to say enviously, from a seat on the other side of the desk.

Evan Cromwell-Evans stopped his pacing abruptly in mid-step, swinging around dramatically to look at the others. His leading shoulder stayed lower than the other, his chin pulled in, his arms bent, his fists clenched and level like a boxer's. 'Well you're not suggesting we're going to pay the bugger, are you?' he demanded fiercely, shouting the words. 'Because I can tell you, I'm not paying, for one.' With that he went on pacing.

'Not so loud, Evan. Dilys might hear you next door,' Davies hissed. Dilys was his secretary, but he was being overcautious since he knew she wouldn't be arriving before nine.

The three were in Davies's private office. It occupied most of the upper floor of the estate agency in the much restored Tawrbach High Street. They had met here just after eight-thirty at Cromwell-Evans's insistence on the telephone.

The two-storey building was in a now protected terrace of shops dating, it was broadly suggested, from mid-Georgian

32

times. The room, with a low and bulging ceiling, was furnished in an entirely functional manner, most of the lower wall space occupied by metal filing cabinets that matched the metal desk. Above the cabinets were unglazed picture frames with coloured photographs and details below of some of the better properties currently being offered for sale.

'Naturally I'm not saying we should pay,' said Prothero shaking his head. 'In any case, I don't know why Elwyn Griffith should think I have that kind of money. That's if he does think so,' he added darkly.

The other two exchanged understanding glances. In the circumstances they had expected Prothero to plead poverty. It was his standard reaction to any burgeoning claim on his personal fortune – a fortune most people assumed was substantial by any standards.

'What he's thinking is, we owe for past services from his mother. That's it clear enough,' said Cromwell-Evans coming to a halt at the end of the desk. 'Well he's got another think coming.'

'And whether any of us can find the money or not is irrelevant, Huw,' offered Davies. 'For the moment anyway. You're sure he doesn't need money?'

'I'm positive he doesn't,' answered the late Madam Rhonwen's family solicitor. 'You know what was in the will. Everybody does. It was in the *Western Mail*. Elwyn gets everything. Well, good as everything.'

'So perhaps we've missed something relevant in the memo. A . . . an underlying motive,' Davies suggested next. 'Perhaps we should read it again.' He sucked in his cheeks.

'I don't need to read it again to give you an opinion on –' Prothero began, but Cromwell-Evans interrupted him.

'Half a mo. Abel could have something there,' he said. 'You read it out loud then, Abel. Slow now.'

'All right.' Davies picked up the typed blue sheet that had been lying on the desk in front of him and wobbled his glasses about on his nose. 'It's dated yesterday, and it says, "Memo to Messrs Evan Cromwell-Evans, Abel Davies, and Huw Prothero."'

'That's alphabetical, of course,' said Prothero who had

produced his own copy of the document from his pocket. His observation had been addressed to no one in particular and was intended to mark that as a qualified lawyer he had been wrongly placed after a shopkeeper and an estate agent. He was a stickler for rank and proper procedure.

'So what?' Cromwell-Evans questioned impatiently. 'Get on with it, Abel.'

Prothero's eyebrows lifted, but he said nothing more.

'Right you are,' said Davies, continuing to read. ' "In view of the importance of the illuminating, handwritten diaries, now come to light, which my mother kept during the last ten years of her life —" '

'Illuminating, he says,' Cromwell-Evans cut in, pausing in his stride, nodding his head and folding his short arms across his barrel chest. 'There's a key word, if ever there was one. Well, illuminating is what I'll be doing to young Elwyn's backside when I catch up with him.' He moved off again sharply to stand in front of one of the framed advertisements. 'Illuminating it with a bloody horsewhip,' he added.

'Yes, well . . .' said Davies, looking up.

Prothero sighed, leaned his head downwards, and clasped his hands between his knees as though he were praying. That the diaries were handwritten, in Rhonwen's unmistakable bold script, was the key and damning factor so far as he was concerned.

' "As her only son and literary executor," ' Davies returned to the reading, ' "I propose to offer the diaries for publication, uncensored. Through their explicit and frank contents, they provide an uninhibited commentary on social and cultural life in an important part of Wales, by the dynamic personality who did more than anyone else to guide it through the period." '

'You wouldn't know from that he's supposed to have hated her guts, would you?' said Cromwell-Evans, now sitting himself on the corner of the desk. 'Hypocritical bastard,' he added, 'with snide words like uncensored, explicit and . . . and what's that other one?'

'Uninhibited,' Prothero provided immediately with another sigh, carefully enunciating each syllable and matching Davies for clear diction if not studied mellifluousness.

'That's the one. Bastard.'

'It goes on,' said Davies, '"I have a book publisher in mind who I am confident will want the diaries. In addition, I have reason to believe that both the *Sunday Times* and the *Observer* will be interested in bidding for the serial rights."'

'There he goes again with his confident, and his reason to believe. That's all bluff, of course,' said Cromwell-Evans with crisp certainty.

'Well, let's hope it is. Let's hope he hasn't actually shown the diaries to anyone,' Prothero entreated, bowed eyes still studying clasped hands. He had put his copy of the document back in his pocket some moments before, as though it had been paining him to look at it.

'It's not likely, is it?' Cromwell-Evans responded. 'It's obvious we're being offered first refusal or there's no point, is there?'

'I suppose not,' answered the lawyer dully.

'"As an alternative,"' Davies continued, '"if, as the three remaining members of the Tawrbach Operatic Society Management Committee, and more experienced in business than I am, you wish to buy the copyright of the diaries with a view to having them published yourselves, I would be glad to consider an offer for them. Naturally —"'

'Glad, he says! He'd be bloody ecstatic,' Cromwell-Evans chipped in.

'"Naturally,"' Davies repeated, '"any such offer would have to be substantial, and certainly not less than three hundred thousand pounds. This is what I believe would be the minimum price I could expect from an interested publisher. All subsidiary rights would be included, of course, and I understand no VAT would be payable." It's signed Elwyn Griffith,' Davies completed, removing his spectacles and putting one of the earpieces between his teeth.

'That's rich, isn't it? That he doesn't think VAT would be payable. Bloody nerve. Wanting a hundred thou from each of us,' Cromwell-Evans expostulated, while energetically swinging the foot that wasn't touching the floor backwards and forwards in a potentially dangerous manner.

Prothero lifted his head sharply. 'No, that's not exactly what he's saying, Evan. He wants three hundred thousand pounds altogether. That's not the same thing,' he said pointedly, while studying the expensively shod, swinging foot of the owner of Shevan Electrical Markets.

'Split three ways it's a hundred grand each,' said Cromwell-Evans, ignoring Prothero's clear implication that he, Cromwell-Evans, might be expected to pick up the whole cost himself. 'And split any way you like it's blackmail, so we could report him to the –'

'It's not blackmail, Evan. Not put that way.' Prothero leaned back in the chair as he spoke, the fingers of both hands meeting across his middle, his expression and tone now that of a learned legal adviser correcting a client as backward as he was misinformed.

'Amounts to blackmail, doesn't it?' asked Davies.

'No it doesn't,' Prothero insisted. 'It's simply an offer to treat.'

'Some bloody treat,' said Cromwell-Evans. 'Huw, you're nearly as bad as he is with the jargon.'

'I'm sorry, but he's done nothing illegal so far. He's simply invited us to buy a manuscript.'

'At a fancy price. And a manuscript he knows we'll want destroyed before it can write off our reputations,' Cromwell-Evans completed, blinking furiously and rubbing one side of his face as if he was trying to make it hurt.

'Oh, come. I think you're overestimating –'

'Overestimating my fanny,' the other interrupted vehemently. 'There's things she could have put in that diary that'd crucify me in business. Harmless enough happenings . . . well, to men of the world, but they'll look bloody terrible in print.'

'Ah, but I think Huw could be right,' said Davies. 'We still don't know what's in the diaries, do we? Not for sure?'

'But we can use our imaginations, can't we?' Cromwell-Evans countered.

'And not necessarily be right,' Davies put in quickly.

There was silence for a moment, broken only by the sound of a motor horn outside.

'So you think he could be bluffing about what's in them?' said Cromwell-Evans quite slowly, his tone suddenly less belligerent. He shifted his position a little on the desk, and absently scratched his crotch. 'You think they could be harmless? I mean from our point of view?'

Prothero frowned. His conscience was as guilty as the others'. 'It's always possible. Our first requirement will be a sight of the manuscript. Or a copy of it, at least.'

'Wouldn't that be suggesting we're serious about buying the diaries?' asked Davies.

'Not at all.' Prothero hollowed his back, which made him taller in the chair, and aware of it. 'But if he refuses to let us see the text after inviting us to buy, as Evan says, at a fancy price, we could most probably get a court injunction to prevent publication.'

'And all the publicity that'd go with it?' said Davies, more firmly than questioningly. 'Wouldn't that defeat our purpose?'

'It could do, yes,' Prothero agreed, grudgingly, because the consequence hadn't occurred to him first. 'But I'm sure he'll agree to show us the text.'

Cromwell-Evans got to his feet, went to a window and looked down on to the street. 'Going back to what Abel said just now, about an underlying motive,' he said, 'could it just be the bastard's not out to ruin us at all? That all he wants is to spoil his mother's lily-white reputation? Or else get paid to keep it intact, like? And he knows we're the people most likely to do the paying, even if we don't in the end, which is something that won't bother him anyway. Am I making myself clear?'

Another spell of thoughtful silence followed this convoluted theorizing.

'That may be wishful thinking,' Davies offered eventually. 'Of course, we can't know everything there is to know about Rhonwen. About her private life. Not everything.'

'Like we never knew she kept a poxy diary, for a start. Telling about the budding actresses she had down to stay for training in . . . in stagecraft.' Cromwell-Evans uttered the last word as if it were in quotation marks and associated with something sinister. 'And about the late-night Jacuzzi parties we –'

'We don't want to hear about any of that, Evan, thank you,' a reddening Prothero interrupted, breathing fast as if he'd been running. 'Not from anyone. Not that the occasions weren't, as you say, harmless. As amongst men of the world,' he ended with less acerbity, as though he was trying to keep his spirits up.

'Except that's not what they'll look like in print,' said Davies. 'We've got to face facts. Because it's those things we're worried about. What she wrote about the girls she had staying, and what happened those times after the committee meetings, and –'

'And who got invited to the parties besides lover boy Reggie Singh,' Cromwell-Evans followed on, turning from the window to look at the others. 'And the rest. Because that's not the half of it, is it? There were other little parties. Ones we weren't at. Except it'll all be the same to people who'll think we were.' With elbows bent he did two sharp arm-stretching movements, before adding: 'Abel's right. We have to believe it'll all be included.'

'But we can't know till we've seen the diaries,' insisted Prothero. 'Evan, you might have the real motive in what you said. Elwyn could be asking us for money as a sort of smoke screen. We know he doesn't need money, but if he pretends he does, and we refuse to pay, he'd have an excuse for allowing his mother's reputation to be spoiled. Inadvertently.'

'Inadvertently?' Davies questioned.

'Yes. The diaries can't be all bad. On the contrary, most of what's in them may be good – culturally enlightening even. Everything she did for music and the arts will be in there, no doubt. It's what's left that could er . . . hurt her reputation.' Prothero cleared his throat. 'And ours.'

'The bit that's uncensored, explicit, frank and . . . uninhibited,' said Cromwell-Evans.

'I see what Huw means, though,' Davies offered. 'By including everything in a published version, Elwyn could plead he was only being scrupulously honest. Objective, like.

Except at the same time he'd be doing down his mother.'

'Apart from that, the dirty bits are what'd sell the thing. It's always the same with those kind of books.' Cromwell-Evans, the realist, dropped into a chair as he spoke, but moving from side to side in it as though the perch was tentative.

'So at best we're saying we may not be mentioned in any embarrassing way. But if we are, perhaps we could persuade Elwyn . . . well, pay him to er . . . just tone it down, like? Leave us out,' said Davies, but without solid hope registering in his voice.

'Not a chance. Well, not for less than what he's asking for at the moment. No, we've got to see the diaries, and take it from there,' Cromwell-Evans summarized, pushing up his sleeve to look at his watch and exposing a wrist as hairy as a satyr's. 'Look, it's gone quarter to nine already. Alison Griffith has probably left for work by now. Time to ring Elwyn. So what are you going to say, Huw?'

'That we've received the memos, and that he had better come to see me in the office. That'll be enough on the telephone.'

'You're not saying we won't pay?' Cromwell-Evans demanded, sitting well forward in the chair, and slapping his knees with his hands.

'Not on the telephone, no. Give it here, Abel, will you? That's your private line, is it?'

Davies nodded, and while he was pushing one of the two instruments on the desk towards Prothero, the lawyer looked up the number in his pocket book. There was silence from the others as he dialled. 'Hello? . . . Oh, oh, hello, Alison. This is Huw Prothero.' He frowned at the others and plucked at his moustache. 'Yes, very well, thank you, and you? . . . Good . . . Yes, lovely service. Very fitting and reverent. Tell me, is Elwyn at home? . . . He's not? . . . All day? Dear me, I was hoping to see him.' His frown deepened, and the moustache plucking increased furiously as he listened to the voice on the other end of the line with rapt concentration for some seconds. 'I see. Arriving Cardiff Central tonight at eight minutes past midnight? Yes, I know the train. Leaves

Paddington at ten ... No, I'm sure there isn't a bus to Aberkidy that late ... Look, there's no need for you to do that. I'm in Cardiff myself this evening. Let me meet him instead. Drop him off on my way home ... No, no, it's no trouble at all. Give us a chance to discuss some urgent business. To do with Madam Rhonwen's literary estate ... You didn't?' His eyebrows lifted as he glanced around at the others. 'He didn't mention it to you? ... Oh, it's not at all significant, but one likes to expedite these things promptly ... Right then, you can leave that to me. And er, there's no way I can reach him during the day? ... No, I understand. Well, thanks very much. See you soon, I expect.'

'In London, is he?' asked Cromwell-Evans immediately after Prothero put down the phone.

The lawyer nodded. 'Left on the five to seven from Cardiff Central this morning. Gone to see some publishers, she said.'

'Oh God,' said Davies.

'Which ones?' Cromwell-Evans pressed.

'She doesn't know. Nor what he's seeing them about, well not specifically. I imagine he's going to the *Sunday Times* and the *Observer* since he mentions them in the memo.'

'Should we leave messages with them, d'you think?' asked Davies.

'No way,' said Cromwell-Evans immediately.

'I think that's right. Too risky,' said Prothero. 'Anyway, Alison didn't know Rhonwen had left any literary works.'

Davies sighed loudly. 'So he hasn't mentioned the diaries to her.'

'Definitely not. She just assumes he's seeing publishers about his own writing.'

'I wouldn't bet on it,' said Cromwell-Evans. 'He hasn't finished anything new for a year. He told me that yesterday at the wake. So what's to discuss? His second novel's been the rounds already and come back. Months ago.' He got up from the chair. 'It's the diaries he's up there trying to flog. Must be. What was that about you meeting him?'

'I didn't think there was any time to waste. Not in the circumstances. The new circumstances.' Prothero swallowed awkwardly. 'I'd forgotten he doesn't drive. Someone dropped him at the station this morning. Alison had arranged to meet him tonight. I've said I'll do it instead. She was very grateful.'

'D'you want us to come with you? I'd have to alter some arrangements,' said Davies.

'I can't be there,' Cromwell-Evans put in sharply.

'No, that's not necessary. I'm at the Angel tonight, as a guest at the Portia Society dinner. It won't be over much before half past eleven.'

Nobody spoke for several seconds, then Davies said: 'Looks as if he's serious, doesn't it?'

Cromwell-Evans was pacing again. 'Well, if he's leaked anything libellous about me to a newspaper,' he said, 'I'll murder the bugger.'

4

'It's very late, Merlin. You should have let me come in my own car,' said Perdita Jones, buckling up the seat belt in Parry's black Porsche.

'My late father, he always said,' Parry began quietly, and as always, breaking the words into short phrases, 'a lady worth taking out should be collected, and brought home. And that was the minimum. Well, according to my dad. He never mentioned a maximum.' He closed his lips tightly, producing good-humoured furrows on either side of his mouth as he urged the car up the ramp from the tenants' car park under the long block of mansion flats on the south side of Westgate Street, Cardiff.

'Whose home? Hers or yours?' She put a hand out to squeeze his arm, then quickly withdrew it. She had made similar gestures during the evening – but they had been no more than tentative blandishments. He had been overly aware of all of them.

'D'you know, he never mentioned whose home? Too late to ask him now, of course.'

'Well, it's been a wonderful evening. I haven't enjoyed myself so much for ages. I mean it. Thank you.'

'Good. Nothing to thank for.'

It was just before midnight. They had been to a symphony concert, at St David's Hall – Fauré, Sibelius, and Beethoven's Fifth – followed by supper at the Four Bars opposite the castle where a ragtime quartet had been playing. They both liked traditional jazz, although she preferred blues to anything livelier. And when they thought they'd had enough

42

music for the night, they had walked the short distance back to his flat for coffee, through the then quietening city and under the floodlit castle wall.

Going to his flat had been her idea, and one she had almost instantly regretted in case he misconstrued it: he hadn't, not once he had sensed her dilemma – and he was good at things like that. He had given her coffee and played her an Elgar CD. Having got her over the first hurdle, he was determined to let her move at her own emotional pace.

Now she settled back in the car seat, allowing the long, high-collared coat to fall open over her short, tight skirt. She crossed her pretty legs. Despite herself, she knew that her perfume, her clothes, the small endearments, even the fact of her agreeing to be with him could only have been calculated to encourage Parry. But, paradoxically, she couldn't yet bring herself to engage him in any physical way. There was still Rosemary – the immovable block.

'It's such a nice flat,' she said, then swallowed. 'I'm sorry if you were expecting me to . . . to stay.' It sounded too blunt, and already she wished she hadn't said it. 'Sorry, that was a stupid thing to say. I . . . I don't suppose you were really –'

'Expecting you to stay?' His eyes had sparkled at the question. 'Oh, subconsciously hoping, probably. Most men would have done. There's honest for you. But expecting? No.' He gave a deep, rumbling chuckle, and pinched the end of his nose – a mannerism as characteristic as his clipped phraseology.

She took a deep breath. 'Well, I'm hoping. About us, I mean. And trying.' She paused. 'I can't help being so feeble. I realize I do care. I want you to know that. And I want it to come right . . . but it's something I can't hurry. It's not you. It's me. Just me. You understand?' This was the first time all evening that either of them had touched on the subject that mattered most – a rekindling of an old relationship.

'Of course I understand. And what you're going through. At least, I think so.'

'You think so?'

43

'Only because I can't feel it in the same way, that's all. Not any more.'

'I see.' She had looked away at the apparent earlier reproof. She stared ahead through the windscreen, wishing now she had kept to neutral topics, for tonight at least.

'For me what's bugging you happened too long ago,' he said.

'And to a logical mind, time should have healed, is that it?'

He hesitated before answering: 'Yes. That sounds crass, probably. But, again, I'm trying to be honest. I've told you, it's healed for me.' When she didn't respond he went on: 'And if it all comes right, I don't care how long it takes. Meantime, there's anticipation. Marvellous thing anticipation.' He had repeated the last word again quickly.

'Thanks for trying to understand, and I'm sorry.' Her irritation with herself had brought her close to tears. She felt his hand on hers suddenly – firm and reassuring. She wanted very much to respond.

'Nothing to be sorry about,' he said, his hand returning to the wheel. 'You came out with me tonight. That was a mammoth step forward, wasn't it?'

She forced a smile. 'Suppose so. At short notice too.'

'That's usual in my business. You take your pleasures when you can. Anyway, after yesterday, I thought I'd do better at the rush. Better than trying to date you long term, I mean. Like before. It worked, too. Lucky I got those concert tickets.'

She fingered the gold bracelet on her wrist, staring at it. 'I came because I felt awful about yesterday. I'm sorry I was . . . sorry about being such a bitch. At the end especially. I wasn't expecting you'd be there.' She was unburdening now, and the words came quickly. 'So you got me in a sort of permanent panic. On top of having to play the organ at no notice.' She looked up. 'That was terrible. I didn't know the music they wanted. And with all those people there.' She paused, catching her breath. 'And the last time you and I were at a . . . at a funeral, a proper funeral –'

'Was more than a year ago,' he interrupted, and with no emotion in the words. 'That's a long time, Perdita.'

'Is it? Only . . .' She finished with a shrug.

They had been kept waiting by the traffic lights at the end of the road, at the narrow angled junction of Westgate Street with Castle Street. The wedge-shaped Angel Hotel was on their right, with its imperious corner entrance and aspects on to both streets. The Portia Society dinner had ended there just half an hour ago.

'Perhaps things will start to seem long enough after tonight.' Parry turned his head to smile at Perdita as he set the car in motion again, heading west. With the medieval castle illuminated brightly behind them, they crossed the River Taff on their way to Tawrbach.

A few minutes before this, Huw Prothero had parked his new, tax-deductible Rover immediately in front of the main entrance to Cardiff Central railway station – a long, low 1920s stone building, with the title 'Great Western Railway' carved on it in such monolithic letters that no one had felt up to trying to erase them in the half-century that had passed since the company had ceased to exist.

At this hour of the night, the lawyer concluded, no one would be around to enforce parking restrictions. He locked the car, glanced about him, partly to confirm his theory, then walked briskly across to the automatic doors into the station.

He was a fairly conspicuous figure – slim, upright, steel grey hair – and more so when dressed, as now, in a hand-cut dinner jacket. Despite his being swingeingly frugal in most ways, in a very few others Prothero was overcompensatingly self-indulgent. Dressing expensively was one of those ways, and, you could even say, one of the most blameless.

He had left his overcoat in the car and was wondering now if he had done the right thing: it wasn't as warm in the station as he had expected. Even so, he enjoyed strutting about unencumbered in what he considered to be a military manner, although he had never actually been in the military.

Coming to a halt in the middle of the nearly deserted, low ceilinged, and not particularly roomy station concourse, he scanned slowly from left to right, then did so again from right to left, like some alert, if overaged, troop commander spotting for snipers.

He had quite lost the air of pessimism that had dogged him in the morning. A good dinner had helped, but before that, cooler appraisal and common sense had begun to convince him that Elwyn Griffith could be made to abandon his ridiculous plan.

The lawyer's counterplan was to appeal first to the young man's sense of filial duty, primarily towards his father, stressing what he owed to the late councillor's memory – not to say his fortune – before solemnly pointing out what the whole community would lose in corporate self-respect if the image of Madam Rhonwen was in any way clouded. Prothero intended putting things that way around since Elwyn had been closer to his father than ever he had been to his mother. It was quite probable that the boy had failed to take into account that things damaging to his mother's reputation would hurt his father's too.

By all means publish the diaries, was going to be Prothero's lofty advice, but only after any potentially defamatory passages had been expunged. Naturally, the three surviving members of the Operatic Society's management team would give every cooperation, especially with the initial editing of the text, but they would not wish to be involved financially.

Of course, in the unlikely event that Elwyn was so misguided as to ignore mature counsel from the lawyer who had been his parents' trusted adviser, he would have to understand that dire consequences could easily ensue. Prothero intended to be quite specific over this. Elwyn and any publishers involved could expect injunctions and prosecutions to rain upon them as the inevitable and expensive result of even an expressed intention to bring out private diaries that might defame living persons.

Prothero supposed the boy was headstrong – a left-wing academic unversed in the ways of the world, as well as in those of the law. That he had it in for his mother was clear enough, and perhaps he had cause, but that didn't mean he could ride roughshod over the reputations of others.

The lawyer was only glad that neither Cromwell-Evans

nor Davies would be present tonight – especially Cromwell-Evans who was altogether too hot-headed for this kind of delicate negotiation. All in all, Prothero was confident of his ability to cope with the situation unaided, and, he felt, he looked as much, as once again he began pacing the concourse.

Except for one of the four ticket-office windows, everything else on the station was closed. The Quick Snack coffee shop to the right of the entrance, and the John Menzies newsagents next to it, were both locked up. Prothero had vaguely hoped that the newsagents might have been open still. With time to kill, he enjoyed looking over paperback displays. Not that he bought many books. The public library at Tawrbach was more than adequate for his leisure-reading needs. It was simply that book-shop browsing gave him opportunities for striking up acquaintance with women. Picking up females had long been a need with him, even on occasions such as tonight when he should have been totally preoccupied with his prime purpose.

This compulsion of Prothero's was genuine, and, for that reason, it defied rational explanation. The 'sniper spotting' earlier had been a covert way of checking for possible candidates. While in the moral sense his intentions towards the women he engaged were not precisely honourable, nor were they exactly the opposite of that: anything dishonourable was in his mind not his actions. Even so, as a well-known lawyer given to foisting his company on to strange women, or trying to, Prothero took enormous risks to no satisfactory purpose. The risk was particularly acute when he was as close to home as he was now, but that only served to increase the thrill. He was fortunate that the practice hadn't landed him in trouble already. To date, the only embarrassing complainant had been a prostitute he had approached by mistake. That had been at a bus stop in Swansea two months ago. He had needed to give her money in the end, to stem her protests, with no professional favours provided or requested.

It wasn't that Prothero was against spending money on his pick-ups, only that he abhorred consorting with what he would have termed 'women of the streets'. He didn't mind treating, but he objected to paying, and the difference for him wasn't even a subtle one. Any other attitude would have impugned his conviction that personable women found him sexually attractive. That no personable woman had recently shown signs of holding such a view didn't come into it. Naturally, all of this made his sometimes pressing need for fresh female 'conquests' a good deal more difficult to satisfy than it might otherwise have been.

Again, it had all been so different in Madam Rhonwen's time: Madam Rhonwen had understood these things.

He moved now to glance at the 'Arrival and Departure' video displays to the left of the wide tunnel leading to the platforms. This was something he could have done from where he had been patrolling by putting on his glasses, except he felt that they aged him. The screen indicated that the Intercity Express from Paddington would be twelve minutes late due to a signal failure in the Severn Tunnel.

'Signal failure. Whatever next, I wonder?' said a youngish sounding, educated female voice from behind Prothero. He turned about with alacrity.

Megan Davies switched off the radio before she got into bed, looked at the time, raised her eyebrows, and reached for her spectacle case and her book. Her husband, Abel, was not yet home, but he was quite often this late, sometimes because of long operatic rehearsals or meetings, but more frequently because of business: or so he said. Tonight was business. He had called her from the office to say he'd be out for dinner. The sale of an important industrial site was imminent, and he was seeing the buyer out of office hours at the buyer's home, twenty miles away, near Merthyr. The site was one in which he was interested as part owner as well as selling agent. Megan had listened to his somewhat laboured explanation of the arrangements without giving it too much attention or credence, since she thought it was probably for the most part well-intentioned lies.

She didn't mind her husband lying to her. She regarded it as a sort of compliment that he took the trouble to invent what were often quite complicated explanations for his coming home late – or not coming home at all. The couple's relationship – or lack of any, in the marital sense – had long since licensed each to follow his or her own private devices without reference to the other, provided the outward proprieties were observed. Davies's belief that this sanctioned his own extramarital affairs and that, in practice, his wife neither exercised nor required a matching freedom showed a limited comprehension on his part. He also misunderstood the nature of her enduring sexuality which was fitful but existent.

That Megan had believed the 'outward proprieties' hadn't been observed in her husband's friendship with Rhonwen Spencer Griffith in the previous autumn had been indignantly denied by him – most particularly since he had never had the kind of relationship with Madam Rhonwen herself that Megan suspected. In any case, by the time of the lady's death, Megan's doubts about her had been expunged – which is more than Marged Prothero's had been. The lawyer's wife had also been convinced that her husband had been bedding Rhonwen, and for a good deal longer than since the previous year. The difference in Mrs Prothero's case was that she had never faced her husband with her suspicions – it wasn't her style. Simply, she had made her hatred of Rhonwen clear to the lady herself, and to everybody else. It happened though that Huw Prothero had been as innocent as Abel Davies of actual amorous involvement with the late Rhonwen Spencer Griffith.

When Selina the cat sprang on to the bed, Megan Davies's attention strayed from her book which had not yet wholly captured it. As she absently stretched out a hand to stroke the animal she returned to wondering whether her husband might really be with Elwyn Griffith tonight, and not a property buyer or a woman. She also wondered if Evan Cromwell-Evans and Huw Prothero would be with him.

Megan had read the contents of the envelope she had opened in apparent error that morning. Light blue envelopes of a hue somehow less businesslike and more feminine than those used by the Philharmonic Society, and addressed to her husband, could not be knowingly overlooked. Megan was tolerant, but she wasn't stupid. She was also a fast reader with a high acuity. Before she had left the hall she had figured that Elwyn Griffith was attempting a mixture of blackmail and extortion: it was why she had gone to the kitchen and quickly copied the memo on her machine before she had returned to the dining room.

Despite her husband's denials about Rhonwen, Megan had been sure there had been 'goings on' at the late-night meetings of the Operatic Committee. She had never been sure of their exact nature, and she certainly wasn't ready to have the facts made public by Rhonwen's evidently traitorous son.

It happened that Megan had a hold over Elwyn Griffith he didn't know about — one she had prepared the ground to exercise that morning. She smiled to herself as she stroked the now loudly purring cat. It was ironic that, as a seemingly wronged wife, she would be the instrument for saving her husband from the consequences of his sexual indiscretions. It was at that moment that she heard him coming into the house — so did Selina who had already ducked under Megan's arm, and was making for the open bedroom door.

'Oh, Lord, forgive your unworthy and penitent servant . . .'

The Reverend Caradog Watkins had been in bed since midnight. It was after two o'clock now, but he hadn't slept yet. It wasn't his wife's snoring that was keeping him awake either: for the past five minutes it had been his own silent praying as he lay there on his back sweating, his lips moving, his hands clasped tightly under his chin.

In a tangled way, it was to his credit that he had not resorted to prayer until now over the fresh horror that had been sent to assail him. What had happened in Cardiff the day before had been disastrous enough, and he had been resigned to the fact that the consequences would have to take an inevitable course, leading to an equally inevitable conclusion.

On the new devastating threat, he had looked at all the secular approaches, deciding whether, if all else failed, he could extricate himself by denying everything, or protesting innocence, which was not quite the same thing – or threatening to invoke the law's protection, if he could do that with impunity. But on all counts he had now decided the answer was in the negative, which had only left the unpromising solution he had solemnly approved in the vestry this morning. It had at least been clear then that there was nothing to suggest to others that he could be personally hurt by Elwyn Griffith's despicable plan – not so far.

'. . . keep me, Lord, thereafter in the ways of righteousness and truth,' he continued, his lips silently synchronizing the words of his remorse.

As a pious, if irrational, Christian, he was staking a lot on deserving heavenly protection over his indiscretions – particularly for one who deep down knew that he lacked the strength to avoid making similar indiscretions in the future.

There was simply no way of telling whether Rhonwen had written about him in her diaries, and, if she had, how damaging her account might be – except he had to presume the worst.

'. . . and for the soul of your servant Rhonwen, the unintentional source of my parlous predicament. Forgive her, Lord, as I have myself, and her unworthy son Elwyn who may soon come to see the error of his ways.'

Caradog Watkins hoped that his God would look less harshly on him for pardoning his persecutor, whatever he had just tried and failed to do in order to silence the wretch.

It was no wonder, then, that the Rector of Tawrbach was facing another sleepless night, and a further decline into an ever-deepening sense of abject despair.

5

It was next morning when Elwyn Griffith was found dead. The body was lying face downwards, arms straight at the sides, legs slightly bent and turned to the right. It was behind some gorse bushes on a broad verge of scrubland, a dozen paces in from an unlit, country road, half a mile short of Aberkidy. The spot was twenty yards on from a bus stop, and the same distance again from the junction with a narrow lane leading off to the left. The body was fully clothed. A dark fedora hat, a tweed overcoat and an old-fashioned, two-buckle leather briefcase lay a yard away from it. They looked as though they had been placed there, not just dropped, especially the coat which was folded in two as if for carrying. The hat was beside the briefcase, with part of the wide brim trapped under it.

By the time Detective Chief Inspector Merlin Parry arrived, with orders to take charge, a large rectangle had been staked and taped off from well beyond the bus stop, back to the hedge that bordered the verge, and along both the road and the lane. The body had been screened from the road, and a pathway up to it taped over the shortest approach from the lane. Four police cars, two liveried and two unmarked, a minibus, a police motorcycle, an ambulance, a green Range Rover belonging to the police surgeon, and now Parry's black Porsche were parked along the much narrower grass verge on the other side of the road.

The motorcycle patrolman was keeping passing traffic on the move. The road was a secondary one. It ran in a long loop that came south off the old, pre-motorway main road to Pembroke, some miles west of Cardiff. It served Aberkidy and a string of other coastal villages on or close to the Bristol Channel before it divided, with one branch heading up to rejoin the old A-road again near Tawrbach, eight miles on from Aberkidy. The traffic flow this morning was fairly light, as well as irregular – like the rain that had been falling off and on through the night.

'So who found him, Gomer?' asked Parry, looking up from where he was crouched on one side of the body, eyeing it but not touching it. The police surgeon was on the other side, kneeling on a rubber car mat he had brought with him. He had appeared just before Parry and was examining the body with care and method, his hands encased in surgical gloves. He was breathing noisily, but not saying anything. He had acknowledged Parry's arrival with a familiar nod.

'It was a Mr Arkle, boss. Elderly gent,' replied Detective Sergeant Gomer Lloyd in a voice that could scarcely have sounded any deeper if he had been standing at the bottom of a hole. He had stationed himself behind Parry.

In his early fifties, the heavily moustached DS Lloyd was shortish, amiable, Welsh-speaking, balding, and overweight. He had five children ranging in age from twenty-six to eighteen, and a jolly, plump wife who was devoted to him and who knitted him more sweaters than he would ever wear out. He had one on now under a short fawn rain jacket with large poacher's pockets. Good at his job, with a string of official commendations to prove it, Lloyd had never nurtured any ambition to move above his present rank. Like Parry, he was on permanent attachment to the Major Crime Support Unit based at Rumney Police Station.

Lloyd had arrived fifteen minutes before Parry, and just behind the now white overalled, hooded and gloved Detective Constable Glen Wilcox. The DC was senior Scenes of Crime Officer in charge of the six civilian SOCOs who had come with him – and who, like him, looked equipped to enter a space capsule.

'Mr Arkle didn't see the body from the road?' Parry asked.

'No, boss,' said Lloyd, stroking the skin below the incongruous, lively quiff of hair that sprouted above the centre of his forehead. 'He explained he was caught short, like. Stopped his car on the other side, and came across to take a leak behind these bushes, being there's no cover over there. He dialled 999 on his car phone straight off. That was at seven twenty-six. Uniform officers were here at seven-forty. They reported the bruised state of the body, and the duty superintendent at Cathays Park nick called us in just before eight. We were here at eight-sixteen,' he completed.

'So what kept everybody, Gomer?' asked Parry with a grin. He had got here pretty quickly himself, but coming direct from his flat, not from Rumney, which is two miles east of Cardiff. 'Next of kin haven't been informed yet?' he asked.

'No, boss. Since you said not to. Mr Griffith was provisionally identified from a diary in his top pocket.'

'Yes. Well, it's him all right. I know him.'

'And his house is near the beach, a mile along this lane. Called White Cross Cottage,' Lloyd continued. 'Looks like people living down there cut the corner getting to the bus stop. There's a bit of a path worn in the grass, see?'

'But he's well to the road side of it.'

'That's right.'

'Is Mr Arkle still here?'

'No, boss. We took his statement and let him carry on. He said he was due in Llandaff, at the cathedral, for an important meeting. Supposed to have breakfast with the dean first, he was. He lives near Llantwit Major. I checked him out through the station. He er . . . he was very anxious to get going.'

'I should think his bladder was bloody well bursting by then, poor old sod,' offered the police surgeon looking up unexpectedly. His name was Maltravers and he was pushing sixty himself, with hairy ears and skin like weathered buffalo hide. He was wearing an ancient black Barbour jacket, with a yellow sou'wester jammed crookedly on his head.

'Oh, he hadn't waited for that, doctor,' said the sergeant, seriously.

Parry pinched his nose and glanced at DC Wilcox who was supervising a search of the ground around the bus stop. 'Well, let's hope he didn't pee all over the evidence.'

'No, he didn't do that. Definite,' said Lloyd. 'Avoided it on purpose, he said. Used the other side of the road, after all.'

'Despite the lack of cover?' Parry grimaced.

'That's right. Sensible of him that was. Follows *Crimewatch* on the telly, he told us.'

'Good for him,' said Parry. He stood up and nodded at the uniformed PC, Roy Kennedy, who had been standing behind Lloyd. 'So it was you got here first, Kennedy, and reported a suspicious death?'

'Yes, sir.'

'Quite right too,' cut in the police surgeon, still kneeling. 'There are contusions of some kind on the back of his head, and have a look at those fingers. Flesh is damned nearly stripped off the tips. On both hands. He didn't get that from biting his nails.'

'And there's the tears in the clothes, sir,' the young constable offered earnestly. 'Like he'd been struggling, we thought.'

'I'd say he had been, yes.' Maltravers glanced up at the chief inspector. 'That may be incidental to the cause of death all the same. It's a rum one, this.'

'Meaning you don't know how he died, doctor?' asked Parry, doing up the top button of his raincoat.

'Not yet, no. Anyway, the pathologist is on his way, which gets me off the hook. I'll wait till he gets here.' Maltravers pushed himself up and on to his feet, staggering a little in the process. 'Just now you said you knew the deceased.'

'Yes, I did. Knew his mother better. He used to visit her when I lived in Tawrbach. She was Rhonwen Spencer Griffith.'

'Go on? The famous Madam Rhonwen?' The doctor was clearly impressed, or astonished, or both. 'So that's the second unexpected death in that family in a matter of months?' He made a tutting noise. 'D'you know if the son was asthmatic, by any chance?'

'Yes, from memory I believe he was.'

'Ah, well it's possible then he died in *status asthmaticus*. That's the coma asthma sufferers get sometimes. Can be fatal if it's not treated. But they'll know better when he's been opened up. See these patchy weals on the skin?' He leaned over to point to the dead man's cheek, and the skin behind the neck. 'That's probably hives, meaning he had atopic asthma. Allergy related. What's strange though, for an asthmatic, is there's no aerosol inhaler on him. I've felt his suit pockets.'

'What about the overcoat and the briefcase?' asked Parry.

'We didn't want them touched, boss. Not till they've been photographed,' Lloyd volunteered promptly.

Parry bent over and felt the pockets of the grey herringbone, Raglan-style overcoat. 'Something in here,' he said. 'Could be an inhaler. D'you want to fish it out, doctor?'

Maltravers moved across and withdrew the object with the forefinger and thumb of his gloved hand. 'That's it. Ventolin inhaler,' he said, holding it upright. He depressed the plunger. There was an audible hiss as a strong stream of vapour was propelled from the nozzle. 'I'd say it's a new one, too. Funny that.'

'And would this have stopped his asthma attack if he'd used it?' Parry asked.

The doctor frowned. 'Should have done, yes, but there are no signs he was getting relief. The opposite really.' He looked from the inhaler back to the overcoat, appeared to be about to add something, then didn't.

'But can you see any other possible cause of death besides the asthma?'

'No obvious one. There are the contusions and the finger lacerations, but nothing that looks fatal. Not from a cursory examination. But you'll need to wait till they've done the postmortem for a proper answer.'

'What about the time of death?'

Maltravers hesitated. 'At a rough guess I'd say he's been dead for between eight and . . . anything up to twenty-four hours. That's judging from the underarm temperature, and the present apparent state of rigor mortis. They'll give you a better fix when they've taken the temperature below his liver. But it's eight hours minimum since he snuffed it, and it could be longer, a lot longer, depending on where the body's been.'

'If he's been dead as long as twenty-four hours, the body can't have been here all the time. Someone would have come on it before now,' said Parry.

The doctor nodded. 'That's what I was thinking. It wasn't dark last night till around six-thirty. Plenty of traffic passing before that during the afternoon. A car driver may not have spotted him, but a lorry driver might have. Higher vantage point. Or a bus driver.'

'Or a pedestrian who got on or off a bus. Anyone who lives down this lane.' Parry paused, then added: 'So, if he didn't die here, someone brought him, and if he was brought, it's suspicious whatever he died of.'

'Photographer and the rest of the team arriving, boss,' said Sergeant Lloyd. He was watching a car and another police minibus. The drivers were being directed by the patrolman to park on the far side of the road with the others. 'And the policewoman you asked for. To go with you to the house, is it?' he completed.

'That's right,' Parry responded without enthusiasm, and wiping the film of rain off his nose. 'Time we got on with that, as well.' He looked at his watch. 'Tell Wilcox to get his photographer cracking, will you? Straight off. Better have shots of all this before anything else is disturbed. And I want to see what was in his pockets, and in the briefcase, before I meet Mrs Griffith.' He thought for a second, then looked about him: the outskirts of the village were just visible along the road. 'Is there a building close by we can use as an incident room?'

'Yes, sir.' It was PC Kennedy who had volunteered a reply. 'The old social hall. It's this end of the village, sir. It's not used much now.'

'Good. How d'you come to know that?' Parry made a point of encouraging policemen who were up on their local knowledge despite the large territories they had to cover.

'My gran lives in Aberkidy, sir. Next door to the hall, actually,' the constable replied sheepishly. 'She keeps the keys.'

Parry nodded with a grin. He looked up at the unbroken cloud in the sky. He remembered the drizzle starting after he had left Perdita Jones's house in Tawrbach at one o'clock.

'Done this sort of job before have you, constable?' Parry was asking, ten minutes later, as the WPC got into the Porsche beside him.

'Coped with the bereaved after a sudden death, sir? Oh yes. Often. All in a day's work, isn't it.' She was petite and dark, with a keen expression. Her name was Mary Norris, and she looked to be about twenty – certainly not old enough to have been involved for as long as all that with death and its consequences, or so Parry thought, unless perhaps her father had been an undertaker.

'You want me to tell the er . . . the wife, is it, sir?' the girl questioned, briskly this time, as she did up her seat belt.

Perhaps her father *had* been an undertaker. 'No, I'll do that.' In the circumstances it would be ducking a clear responsibility not to, and there was another reason besides. 'If you could just hover in the background.'

'In case she keels over, sir?' She had settled herself very upright in the seat, chubby knees tight together and no more of them showing than was strictly necessary under a regulation skirt. The raincoat she'd been carrying was draped neatly across her lap.

'Yes. But I don't think she will keel over.' Under the direction of the uniformed patrolman he moved the car out into the road, then across into the lane opposite.

'They do sometimes.'

He glanced sideways at her. 'D'you mind telling me what your father does, constable?'

'Policeman, sir,' she answered with evident pride. 'Sergeant in the Met. Retired back to Wales now.'

Ask a silly question.

He had taken directions to the Griffith cottage from PC Kennedy whose knowledge of the village had so far proved to be impeccable – thanks to his grandmother. Not that there was much of a village, and not that Griffith had lived in the centre of it which lay further along the upper road. The lane sloped steeply downwards, between high hedgerows. The mechanized surface was encrusted with old pats of cow dung, and garnished on top with newer ones: on such a narrow track, Parry hoped it was nowhere near milking time.

Half a mile on, the left-hand hedge was replaced by rusted and rickety iron fencing guarding a big fallow area where a herd of black and white cows were standing motionless, waiting, perhaps, for the rain to stop. In the distance, beyond the dipping pasture land, a graceful, tall railway viaduct spanned the view and the valley, looking as durable as it must have done when it had been built a century and a half earlier. Beyond its high arches you could just make out the grey waters of the Bristol Channel in the mist. On a clear day, Parry knew, the Somerset coast was visible as well.

They came upon White Cross Cottage on the right, shortly after they had passed a beach café and car park with a closed-for-good, not just for the season, look about them. The slate roofed, oblong cottage, with an off-centre front door at the front, was plain to the point of severity, and built to withstand gales. It was approached by an iron gate in a low rubble wall, and along a straight, brick path edged by watery, drooping daffodils. The rough-caste exterior of the cottage had been whitewashed recently and the woodwork painted.

After striking the brass door knocker – there was no bell push – Parry turned to look at the shingle beach which began on the far side of the road. WPC Norris did the same.

'Bit lonely out here in the winter,' he remarked.

'Not much better in the summer either, sir,' she answered. 'Not exactly a beauty spot, see? And it's not popular because there's nothing much doing. The punters don't go for a shingle beach when they can have sand and burgers at Barry Island or Porthcawl.'

He knew about it not being popular. He and Rosemary had driven down to the area once or twice to walk on the strand, partly because it was close when they had lived in Tawrbach, but mostly because they had wanted to avoid the crowds. He imagined that Alison and Elwyn Griffith had come to live here for the same reason. Writers were supposed to thrive on solitude, though from what he already knew of Alison Griffith he wasn't sure the loneliness of this place would have appealed to her. Of course, Abel Davies had said that Elwyn's mother had put up the money for the cottage, so the choice might have been limited despite Davies suggesting that price had been no object. Parry had doubted the truth of that: Madam Rhonwen had been pretty careful with her money.

It was as the chief inspector turned towards the building again, assessing its value, that he caught the sound of movement from within.

The door made a sticking sound as it was opened, revealing a beaming Alison Griffith on the threshold. She was above average height, with an appearance that was striking, without her being head-turningly pretty. Her bobbed hair was raven coloured, her dark blue eyes shrewd and intelligent, but with a lurking aloofness in them. Her nose was thinly chiselled like her pointed chin which she held very high, and her figure was slim without being starved. She wore some eye shadow but no other make-up. Parry had met her for the first time two days before at the service when they had been briefly introduced. She had been wearing the same blue jersey suit then that she had on now, and the same small, pearl clip earrings.

'Why, it's Merlin Parry, isn't it? Fancy . . .' Alison Griffith looked from Parry to the woman constable, her welcoming tone changing quickly to one of concern. 'Something wrong is there? Is Elwyn all right?'

'Good morning, Mrs Griffith,' said the policeman, surprised that she had remembered him. 'It's bad news, I'm afraid. Can we come in?'

Her hands went to cradle her cheeks. 'Oh God, he hasn't been in an accident, has he?'

'It'd better if we were inside.'

'Yes . . . yes, of course.' She opened the door wider and stepped away from it. Now she looked stunned, and her face had drained of colour.

60

6

The front door of White Cross Cottage opened directly on to the right-hand end of the living room. The place reflected the style of its arranger who was the part proprietor of a design shop. The walls were white, the furniture, some old, some modern, was mostly pinewood. The curtains and chair covers were made of folk weave in a mixture of autumnal colours. There were pretty scatter rugs on the polished wood floor, gleaming brass implements inside the stone hearth, some unusual lamps with attractive shades, and bold water-colour landscapes on the walls. There was a CD player, but no television set, and a log fire prepared but not lit. Heat was coming from slim radiators on both long walls. It was an interior that balanced recognition for the age and period of the building with respect for the practical needs of its occupants – a result probably achieved on a modest budget.

Alison Griffith had sat upright and in silence to one side of the fireplace, which was on the far end wall, as Parry, sitting opposite, had briefly recounted the discovery of her husband's body. An attentive WPC Norris was perched on the edge of the sofa facing the fireplace, and at the end nearest the bereaved woman.

'And he was so close to home. I could have been with him in minutes,' Alison said, as soon as Parry had finished. 'Can I go to him now, please?' So far she had maintained her composure to a surprising extent. She had closed her eyes and remained silent for a while, but when she opened her eyes again there had been no tears, and when she spoke, her voice, with its soft North Welsh accent, had been steady if subdued. Until now her hands had stayed folded in her lap.

'Of course. We can go up whenever you feel ready,' Parry replied carefully. 'But it might be more private if we wait ten minutes or so. There are a lot of police there at the moment.'

'I see, but –'

'Though we would like to have you formally identify the body,' he went on. 'Mary here will be with you. Or we can leave it till later if you want. At the . . . the hospital. There's no hurry.'

'Identify?' There was sudden hope in the tone. 'You mean it may not be Elwyn?'

He shook his head. 'I'm afraid it is. I er . . . I knew him fairly well.'

She nodded. 'I'd rather see him here, not in a hospital morgue.'

'We can go when you want, Mrs Griffith,' offered the WPC, 'but better to wait a bit, like the chief inspector says.' She knew Parry had told DS Lloyd they would try to delay returning with the widow until after nine o'clock: it was quarter to nine now.

'I understand.' Alison breathed in and out quickly. 'And you think he died of an asthma attack?'

'We're not certain of that yet,' said Parry, who hadn't mentioned the torn fingers, or the state of the clothing, or some of the other circumstances that were accounting for his own presence in Aberkidy. 'Was his asthma very bad?'

'Yes. He took pills for it every day, and he carried an inhaler.' Parry had noticed at their previous short meeting that she was given to making sharp, angled head movements – like a practised photographic model taking up fresh poses for the camera. She was doing it now, looking from him to WPC Norris or briefly in other directions, her action accentuating the slimness of her neck and the naturally forward, pliant set of her shoulders. 'Sometimes the asthma attacks were very bad,' she went on. 'He had one at the end of the reception on Tuesday. He left early for that reason. We hoped people had understood. So you think he had another when he got off the bus last night? But it must have been sudden and . . . and massive. I mean, so he couldn't manage to get here, or into the village, or even to stop a car. He's never been that bad before.' She took another breath, but slowly this time. 'I still can't believe it. I never knew people died of asthma,' she completed flatly, still without undue emotion.

'It happens, apparently,' said the policeman, believing the continued absence of tears or other signs of real distress was either because she had become remarkably self-controlled after the initial shock, or because she hadn't yet truly come to terms with what had happened. 'But as I said, we won't know definitely about the cause of death till . . . till later on,' he added.

'You mean there'll have to be a postmortem?'

'I'm afraid so. In the case of a sudden death –'

'Yes, I understand.'

'If you could let me have the name of your husband's doctor. We'll need to talk to him as well.'

'It's Dr Jago. He's in the village.'

'Thank you.' He leaned forward in the chair. 'Look, I can leave now. Go on ahead. Give you a bit of time, before . . . before you need do anything else,' he offered tactfully. He let the suggestion hang for a moment, before he added: 'Mary will stay. And would you like us to contact a relative or friend to be with you later?'

'No, that's not necessary. I'm OK. And I'll go up with you in a minute.' She swallowed, then glanced at her watch. 'It was my turn to open the shop this morning. I'd better ring Sally. She's my partner.'

'I can do that, Mrs Griffith,' the WPC offered.

'Would you? That's a great help. I don't feel up to . . .' She took a quavering breath before continuing. 'Tell her what's happened. She'll cope with the shop. The phone's in the kitchen at the back, through there. Stupid, for the moment I can't remember the number.' One hand crossed her brow. 'Oh, it's in the little orange book on the left of the phone. Under Lovelaw. Thanks.'

'No problem. Shall I make you a cup of tea at the same time, Mrs Griffith?'

Alison smiled as she shook her head, and the girl got up and left the room quickly.

'As a matter of fact, if you feel up to it, there are a few other questions I need to ask you. It'll do later, of course,' said Parry, but hoping she'd agree to answer them now.

'No, I'd rather it was straightaway. It'll fill the time till we go. And it's why you're here really, isn't it? Someone said you only deal with serious crimes.' She was looking him straight in the eyes as she spoke. 'So is there more to Elwyn's death than you've said so far? I think I can take it if there is.'

He hesitated. 'There's a bit more, perhaps. To be honest, we don't know, but we er . . . we have to cover all angles. Were you expecting him home last night?'

'Yes. But when he hadn't arrived by half past twelve I thought he'd decided to stay in London. He'd gone up originally for the day. Huw Prothero was supposed to be meeting him. Off the midnight train at Cardiff Central. Elwyn doesn't drive, you see?'

'So you weren't worried?'

'Not really. To be honest I didn't think of him till quite late on.'

'Were you alone?'

'No. Sheila Cromwell-Evans was here all evening. I'm doing over some rooms for her. We were matching patterns and wallpapers. She didn't leave till late. Sheila's always a late one. I started wondering about Elwyn when I was reading in bed later. When I noticed it was nearly quarter to one. If Mr Prothero had met him he should have been here by then. But he did stay over in London sometimes. With an old college mate in Maida Vale. They usually had supper together anyway if Elwyn was in London.'

'Would he have stayed over without telephoning you?'

'Yes.' She gave a wan smile. 'He was very forgetful about things like that. If he remembered at all, it was usually too late to ring. Only I was embarrassed when Mr Prothero rang at eight this morning. He said Elwyn hadn't been on the

64

train, or the one after. That's the last one. He met them both. Must have made him terribly late getting home himself.'

Parry frowned. 'Well it seems Elwyn didn't stay over. And he got an earlier train, not a later one.'

'How d'you mean?' Her head jerked upwards, sharply.

'We've found a bus ticket in his overcoat pocket. It seems he caught the ten past eleven bus last night from the Central bus station to Aberkidy. According to the time table, it stops at the top of your lane at twelve-fourteen. It means he could have got the train that arrives in Cardiff just before eleven. Or an earlier one, of course. If he knew Mr Prothero was meeting him –'

'But he didn't,' she broke in. 'He thought I was meeting him. We altered the arrangement after Elwyn left. Mr Prothero wanted to see Elwyn very urgently. He was going to be in Cardiff late in any case, so he offered to meet him at the station instead of me.'

'So it wouldn't have been Mr Prothero Elwyn would have rung? When he got to Cardiff earlier than expected? It would have been you?'

'That's right. But he didn't.' She shrugged. 'That was typical too, I'm afraid.'

'You mean he'd have let you drive into Cardiff to meet him, when he was already on his way home by bus?'

She gave another understanding expression. 'Most likely, yes. And hated himself after for not thinking. You see, he had a real academic's idea of time. Probably thought he'd be here before I left. Especially if he saw the bus about to go just as he came out of the station. Or he just forgot he was being met. He was very absent-minded.'

Parry wrote something in the small notebook he had taken from his pocket. 'And Mr Prothero didn't ring you last night?'

She shook her head. 'He thought of it, he said, but he imagined I'd be asleep. But that's why he rang this morning. So I wouldn't be worried. He's so considerate. Such a gentleman. He'll be devastated about what's happened.'

'And you haven't rung the college friend since? The one in Maida Vale? To find out if Elwyn stayed with him?'

'Yes. I rang him after I'd talked to Mr Prothero. But there

was no answer. I thought if he was there, they'd probably gone out for some breakfast.'

Parry looked again at his notebook. 'If we could go back to Elwyn's asthma, was it caused by an allergy do you know?'

She sighed. 'By any number of allergies. He was supposed to be allergic to all kinds of things. Chocolate, penicillin, shellfish, dogs, cats . . . hamsters even. One consultant said he was allergic to stress.' She seemed to catch her breath on the last word.

'So many causes?'

'Possible causes. It's why he'd tried so many treatments.'

'Was there anything you can think of that might have brought on an attack last night.'

The little finger of the hand she had brought to her mouth moved backwards and forwards along her lower lip. 'It's so difficult to say. It depends on where he'd been.' She paused. 'He's been very worried. About his work. His writing.'

'So you think it could have been stress that did it?'

'It's possible. If he'd had a bad day. A disappointing one. On top of the emotion from the day before. From the service, and having to meet all those people. I'm sure that upset him.'

'Why did he go to London?'

'He was hoping to see a literary agent and some publishers.'

'Did he have appointments to see them? There's nothing to indicate that in his pocket diary.'

She shook her head. 'The agent, possibly, although it's most likely he went entirely on spec. He'd given up making appointments with people, especially publishers. He said it gave them the chance to say no, or worse, to cancel at the last minute. A lot of them did too. He just sent manuscripts to people. Then called at their offices weeks later, hoping someone would have read what he'd sent. I'm afraid that didn't work either. Or not often. But he was desperate.'

Parry moved in his chair. 'Over money? Sorry, I shouldn't have −'

'No, it wasn't money,' she interrupted. 'Not any more.'

'Since his mother's death, you mean?'

'No, since before that. Elwyn needed his self-respect back more than he needed money. It's what his writing should have done for him. That's if anyone had published his books. You know he was made redundant eighteen months ago?'

'I'd heard, yes.'

'After that he tried and failed to get another teaching job. The company I worked for went bankrupt around the same time. So yes, money was a problem for a bit. Then Rhonwen lent us enough to give up our rented flat in Bristol and buy this place. And to set up my shop.'

'But Elwyn still needed a gainful occupation,' said Parry. It was a sympathetic comment not a question.

'Yes. And writing really was his best hope. The only one really. He worked so hard at it too. In the study through there.' She nodded towards the closed door on the wall to the right of the front door. 'So if he was turned down again by everyone he saw yesterday,' she completed, 'that could have brought on terrible stress.'

'I understand, yes. We found two manuscripts in his brief-case. And an address book.'

She nodded. 'The manuscripts would be spare copies of both his novels, I expect. In case he called on anyone new, a publisher or an agent who offered to read them.' Her jaw stiffened. 'Sounds as if no one offered, doesn't it?'

'The people he called on, they'd be in the address book?'

'I expect so. Will you want to know who they were?'

'Possibly. That's if we have to find out how he spent the day. Do you know what train he caught in the morning?'

'Yes. It was the six fifty-five.'

'Did he go into Cardiff by bus?'

'No, the earliest bus wouldn't have got him there in time.'

'So you drove him?'

'No, my partner's husband gave him a lift.'

'That'll be Tony Lovelaw?'

'That's right. Of course, you know Tony.' The fact seemed to please her.

'We play rugby together sometimes.' Parry matched her smile. 'Bit out of his way coming here if he was going to Cardiff, wasn't it?'

'Well, Tony's like that, isn't he? Anything for a friend. Sally and I are the same. Anyway, he saved me going all the way into the city and back again to Tawrbach, to the shop.' She sighed before adding slowly: 'Only it would have been the last time Elwyn and I had together.'

'You weren't to know that.' He waited a moment, gauging whether he should go on with the questions. When she lifted her head he said: 'I mentioned he wasn't wearing his hat and overcoat. They were lying beside him on the ground, with the briefcase. Is there any reason you can think of why he'd have been carrying not wearing them?'

She looked puzzled. 'It wasn't cold last night, but it was raining, wasn't it? I suppose he might have had the coat off in the bus. And his cherished hat. But not when he got out. He loved his hat. Said it gave him an air of sagacity. I don't think it did. Not really, poor love. Was he wearing his smoked glasses?'

'No. They were in his pocket. Would he normally have worn them at night?'

'Yes. They're prescription lenses. He was supposed to wear them all the time. He saw better with them on, even in the dark.'

Parry closed his notebook and put it away. 'You've been very good, and very brave if I may say so.'

She blinked. 'Elwyn and I loved each other very much, Mr Parry. I'm going to miss him . . . desperately.'

'Of course.'

'You lost your wife last year, didn't you?'

'Yes. I know what you'll be going through. How long had you been married?'

'Five years. We met at Reading University. I was doing design. He was finishing a history treatise. For a Master's degree.'

'And you're from North Wales?'

'That's right. From Wrexham. Elwyn and I met after he started a Welsh nationalist society at Reading. He was passionate about that in those days.'

'And I don't imagine there were that many Welsh nationalists at Reading University,' said Parry with a smile.

'There weren't, no. It's why I joined. Just to support Elwyn really. He worked very hard at it. Well, that applied to everything he did. He was a lovely man who deserved more success than he got. Much more. And better health.' Now there were real tears welling in her eyes for the first time. She took a deep breath through her mouth. 'But I mustn't break down now, must I? It's just that one thing at least was coming right for us. For the two of us, that is, but something Elwyn wanted especially. More than anything else I think.' She covered her face with her hands for a moment, then took them away slowly. 'We hadn't told anyone yet, but I found out two weeks ago I'm going to have a baby, at last.'

7

'Plucky woman, Mrs Griffith,' said Detective Sergeant Lloyd. He was sitting beside Parry in the car, sucking a peppermint, a habit he'd acquired while giving up smoking eight years before. After spending a further hour in Aberkidy, the two policemen were on their way to Tawrbach and an appointment there with Huw Prothero, at his office. 'Stood up well when she identified the body,' Lloyd went on in his resonant bass. 'Always nasty that. When it's the wife.' He grasped the front of his trousers, and levered himself up in the seat while, at the same time, giving his substantial lower half an energetic wriggle. 'That's better,' he said, resettling himself with a sigh.

'She's much tougher than you'd expect.' Parry agreed about Alison Griffith.

'And attractive with it. Not the sort you'd think would marry a bloke like that. Sounds as if he was a bit of a loner, and sickly as well. And even when he was working, he was only a teacher, all said and done. Not that I've got anything against teachers. Not really,' completed the father of five, but grudgingly, as if he might have found something given time.

'Keen member of Plaid Cymru though, Gomer. Or he had been,' Parry offered, in mitigation.

'Ah.' The detective sergeant, who was a known, non-militant supporter of the Welsh nationalist movement, narrowed his eyes to underline that Griffith's political affiliations, however worthy, did little to balance his listed deficiencies. He folded his arms and bumped them twice on the bulge of his prominent stomach as if to consolidate this last unspoken view. 'And you don't believe he died of natural causes, boss? From his asthma?'

'Asthma doesn't account for the state of his fingers, the bruising to the head and body, why he hadn't used the inhaler, why he'd walked twenty yards in the rain carrying his coat, and, if he did die say before eleven last night, where he was at the time, and how his body got to Aberkidy, because it couldn't have got there on a bus,' Parry rattled off his reasons. 'All that's got to be explained. Maybe it will be by the postmortem. Or some of it.' But he didn't sound confident.

'Funny about the inhaler,' said Lloyd. 'He might have used it, of course. Dr Maltravers said it could have been a brand-new one. Will it show in Mr Griffith's lungs if he used it, I wonder? When they open him up?'

'Shouldn't think so.'

'The pathologist said the makers can tell how often an inhaler's been used. It gives a known number of measured doses.' The sergeant wiggled his tongue between his cheeks. 'The doctor used one dose demonstrating to us. He'll report that, I expect.'

Parry moved his hands along the steering wheel, then back to where they had been before. 'But if Griffith had been *in extremis*, he'd have had the inhaler out, in his hand,' he said, 'not in his overcoat pocket.'

'Unless this was his spare, and he had another one?'

'Maltravers said it was unlikely he'd have had two inhalers. They're refillable. He might just have used up a refill, and chucked it away, of course. Only there wasn't one on the scene, or near it.'

'In the bus? He could have dropped it in the bus.'

'Possible. So that's something else that needs following up pronto, Gomer.'

'Right you are.' Lloyd made heavy going over reaching into his pocket for notebook and pencil. 'You know, if his wife said he got depressed, having his novels turned down and that –'

'Stressed, she said.'

71

'Yes, stressed. Same effect, though, I should think, wouldn't you?'

'No. Similar, perhaps,' Parry reflected.

'Right. And he had all those pills for his allergies. Could he have topped himself with an overdose?'

'There was no outside evidence of that.'

'No empty pill bottle, no. But he could have taken the pills much earlier.'

'And left the bottle on the bus too, I suppose?'

'Or on the train,' Lloyd offered, undeterred by the other's evident scepticism.

'Always supposing the pills were lethal in large doses.'

'Most chemicals are, boss.' Lloyd's wife favoured homeopathic remedies. 'Anyway, not using his inhaler during a bad asthma attack could have the same result.'

Parry was looking doubtful again. 'Well the PM will certainly show if he poisoned himself.' He accepted, though, that if Griffith had killed himself by refusing to use an inhaler, no postmortem was going to prove it. Yet he somehow couldn't credit the man with having the will power necessary for a terminal act of self-denial. There was also another reason why he couldn't believe Griffith had taken his own life. 'If suicide had been an option for him at any other time, would it have been with a baby on the way?' he questioned aloud. 'A baby he wanted more than his wife did even? Or so she says. Then there's –'

'Ah, but it doesn't always work that way with depressives, does it, boss?' Lloyd interrupted. 'Or people under stress,' he corrected quickly. 'If he had this sense of failure, perhaps the thought of being a proper family man was making the strain worse. The idea of the baby growing up with a washout for a dad? That plus the extra expenses involved? After all, he was out of work on top of the other.' Lloyd reckoned he was on sure ground when it came to assessing the cost of parenthood.

'Except he'd just inherited a very large fortune from his mother.'

'Ah.' Even a father of five had to accept the ameliorating effect of great riches.

They were approaching the outskirts of Tawrbach. 'Anyway, until we get something definite out of the PM, we'll treat it as a highly suspicious death,' said the chief inspector firmly.

'Meaning we –'

'Meaning, amongst other things, we need to account for all his movements yesterday. That's up to and including the time he reached Aberkidy.'

'Which should have been twelve-fourteen, when the bus was due. We're checking it was on time.'

'We also need to check he was on it.'

Lloyd glanced across at his chief. 'You mean you think the ticket in his pocket wasn't his?'

'I mean it doesn't have to be. There was a bin full of used tickets at the bus stop. What if he came along later and picked up someone else's ticket? Or someone else did it for him? And what if he caught the train he was supposed to catch?' Parry wasn't yet satisfied that Griffith would have switched trains without calling his wife at some point, even if he was absent-minded.

'He'd have got to Aberkidy later, boss. By some other means. The last bus leaves Cardiff at eleven-forty, before the train got in. Mark you, Mr Prothero said he wasn't on it.'

'Mr Prothero could have missed seeing him. And Griffith wouldn't have been looking out for him. Remember he was expecting his wife to meet him.'

'Right then.' Lloyd was writing again in his notebook. 'We should know soon if Mr Griffith got off the bus at that stop last night. And if anyone else got off at the same time. Depends on the driver's memory, of course. He's being interviewed about now. If he's not sure, we'll be talking to all the regular passengers using the service tonight. There's bound to be some.' He looked up as they drove over the little river bridge and began ascending the incline, with St Curig's Church on the right. 'Home ground for you, boss, Tawrbach?'

Parry nodded. 'Except I left more than a year ago now.'

'Is it that long already? Well, I never. But that's why you knew Mr Griffith, you said? And Mr Prothero? What's he like?'

'He's all right. Bit pompous,' Parry replied, a trifle absently. His mind had been on Perdita Jones, whom he had left in Tawrbach nine or so hours back. He knew she was a friend of Alison Griffith, though he didn't know how close. Perhaps he should have told her already about Griffith's death. She might have been the best person to comfort Alison. It was definitely a reason for him to call her soon. 'So, let's see what Mr Prothero has to say,' he went on, his tone sharper than before. 'Seems he spent the small hours of this morning cooling his heels on Cardiff Central Station. That couldn't have endeared poor Elwyn Griffith to him much.'

They had reached the top of Church Lane, and he turned the car right on to the High Street. Although the rain had stopped, it was still too early for the bulk of morning shoppers. He found a parking spot just short of the phony Georgian, bow-fronted offices of Prothero & Company, Solicitors, at the east end of the street.

'Dear, dear, dear,' Huw Prothero uttered a few minutes later after Parry had told him of Griffith's unexplained death. 'Dear, dear, dear. This is the most awful shock, Mr Parry.'

Although the lawyer's outward demeanour reflected the earnestness of his words, his immediate inward reaction was one mixed with more than a slight measure of relief. Having the police inform him of Griffith's demise lifted something of a weight from his mind.

'But what could he have died of so suddenly?' he asked. His wing chair was pulled tight into the kneehole of a partners' desk, the edges of which were supporting dauntingly high, uneven stacks of documents – symbolic ramparts against assault on their possessor's valuable time.

The room was on the ground floor, at the back, with a southern outlook over a paved courtyard, a narrow lane, and, beyond that, a well-kept public garden. The two visitors were seated on the other side of the paper defences. 'Was it a heart attack, perhaps?' Prothero went on, all solicitude. 'He was very young for that, though. Dear, dear, dear.' His mystified gaze left the faces of the others and searched the comfortable office – opulent by the standards of his nondeductible home. It was as though he was expecting the glazed mahogany bookcase, the inlaid conference table, the recently re-covered leather chairs, or the handsomely framed portrait of his late father somehow to provide the answer to his question.

'As I said, sir, the cause of death is still unknown,' offered Parry. 'He did suffer badly from asthma.'

'Terrible asthma he had, I remember. Could he have died of that?'

'Difficult to tell at this stage, sir. There's to be a post-mortem.'

'Of course. His wife Alison, is she all right?'

'Taking it very well, sir. It was a shock, naturally.'

'Naturally.' Prothero cleared his throat and bounced all ten fingers lightly on the leading edge of the desk. 'And you're making inquiries, Mr Parry, because of police suspicions. Is that it?'

'You could say that, sir, yes.'

'Well you're welcome to any help I can give.' He brought his hands together now, over the top button of his waistcoat. 'Even so I don't quite see . . .'

Lloyd leaned forward. 'Mrs Griffith told us you'd arranged to meet her husband off the train last night, sir. Off the twelve-eight,' he said, his gaze returning to his open notebook.

'That's right. But he wasn't on it.'

'Nor on the next one, sir? The last one. Gets in at two-fourteen. You met that too?'

'Yes.'

Parry smiled. 'That was a long wait, sir.'

'What else could I do? I assumed he'd missed the first train and would be on the next. His wife was intending to meet him. I'd said I'd do it, so it was my responsibility. I couldn't very well leave him in the lurch. There's no transport at that time of night.' He shrugged. 'Well, a taxi possibly. If you're lucky.'

'And he might not have been,' said Lloyd. 'An act of true friendship that was, if I may say so, sir.' Prothero's stoic look indicated he might indeed say so, and with justification, as

75

the sergeant continued: 'Mrs Griffith explained you didn't ring to say he'd missed the trains last night, but you did this morning.'

'No point in waking her up last night. It was so late. This morning she said he'd most probably stayed in London. It appears he did that sometimes.' Prothero frowned and fingered the silk handkerchief protruding from the top pocket of his suit jacket. 'When she told me, I wished I'd known as much last night. Might not have waited if I had.'

'Even so, he hadn't stayed over,' said Parry. 'And you didn't go home between trains did you, sir?'

'No. I debated about that, but decided it wasn't worth it. And er . . . I ran into a . . . someone who was also meeting a passenger who'd missed the earlier train. Quite a coincidence in a way. We had coffee together. To kill the time.' He had a growing presentiment that it was best to indicate he had a witness to his movements during the period.

Lloyd looked up. 'Is there any possibility you could have missed Mr Griffith, sir?' he asked.

The lawyer made a judicial kind of pause before replying: 'It's possible, of course, but highly unlikely, Mr Lloyd. More people got off both trains than I expected. But not as many as all that. Not so you'd miss seeing someone you knew. I was on the concourse, close to the tunnel exit, on both occasions.'

'You weren't by any chance waiting at the station when the previous train got in, sir?' the sergeant countered. 'That was officially at one minute to eleven, but it was six minutes late.'

'Certainly not. At that time I was still having dinner at the Angel. There was no reason for me to meet an earlier train.'

It was Parry who explained: 'It's just that it now seems possible that's the one he caught, sir.'

'Indeed? Well if he'd rung Alison to say so, I'm sure she'd have got word to me at the dinner. She knew where I was.'

'He didn't ring her, sir.' Parry smiled as he continued: 'By the way, Mrs Griffith did mention you were anxious to see him. On legal business. That that was the reason why you offered –'

'To meet him? Yes, it was. There were several things pressing. To do with the winding-up of his mother's estate. He and I were her joint executors.' He sighed. 'At least Madam Rhonwen was spared having to endure the death of her only child in her own lifetime.'

'Quite so.' Parry paused briefly to denote proper sympathetic agreement. 'Tell me, sir, would you normally have dealt with legal affairs in that way? Informally, after a late dinner? I mean, as opposed to seeing the client here in the office or at his home? In normal hours?'

From the altered look on Prothero's face as he straightened in his chair, the chief inspector had the feeling that he was about to be told to mind his own business. Instead though, the expression softened indulgently before the lawyer said: 'I'm afraid the clearest answer to that question lies before us on this desk, Mr Parry.' He waved his hand over the nearest stack of documents. 'I'm simply snowed under with work at the moment. I'd been trying to get hold of Elwyn for more than two weeks, for decisions I needed before we can go to final probate. He was simply never available.'

'Not even after the memorial service.' Parry was affirming not questioning.

'Precisely. He disappeared shortly before the end of the reception.' The lawyer shook his head. 'That's how these things can drag on and on, and the papers hang about.' He waved the same hand over two rampart stacks on his other side. 'I rang Elwyn yesterday morning to press him to drop in, but he'd already left for London. Meeting him off the train on his way back was a gift in a way.'

'Even if it meant waiting till two in the morning, sir?' Parry put in quietly.

'Yes,' Prothero replied promptly, with solid conviction.

'So he'd have been a captive audience on the drive to Aberkidy,' said Parry, surprised to meet a lawyer who professed to be as keen to get rid of documentation as he was to create it. 'Would it be possible for you to tell us which bits of legal business had been holding things up, sir?'

'Why d'you want to know?' The question was still kindly put because, in the circumstances, Prothero had decided it was in his interests to be cooperative – but without being obsequious.

'Because it might have relevance to further inquiries we may have to make about Mr Griffith's death, sir. Understand, we're very much in the dark. Mrs Griffith did say you'd mentioned yesterday something about Madam Rhonwen's literary estate.'

'A figure of speech, that was, Mr Parry. An overstatement in fact. It's hardly a literary estate. Madam Rhonwen was a prolific writer, of letters, notations of one sort or another on her musical productions, diary material you might say.' Prothero was pleased with the way he had covered the issue. 'In the event a biographer ever wanted to use it, it's important there should be clear and legal understanding about who owns the copyright. But it was really one of the lesser points for decision.'

'You think someone might want to do a biography of Madam Rhonwen, sir?'

The lawyer pouted. 'It's always possible. She was a distinguished and celebrated lady, with a life full of incident.' He looked up at Parry under arched eyebrows. 'Even though it lacked the scandalous element that seems to be essential in so many latter-day biographies. More's the pity.' He wondered if he had overdone the point. He had, because Parry's mind turned immediately to the late Reggie Singh and his takeaway restaurant in Ystrad Mawr. 'As to the more important matters I needed to discuss with Elwyn,' Prothero went on, 'there were several revaluations received from the Revenue, which I needed him to approve.'

'Had you approved them yourself, sir?'

'Yes. In their present state. After conducting a lengthy correspondence with the Estate Duty Office. I'd appealed over two of them before final sums were provisionally agreed.'

'So was it likely Mr Griffith would have disagreed with them?'

'Almost certainly not, but that's hardly the point is it? As joint executors we had to make joint decisions.'

'I understand, sir.' Parry looked from Prothero to Lloyd,

and then back again. 'Well, I think that's all for the moment, sir. You've been very helpful.'

'Not at all, Mr Parry.' Prothero stood up and walked around the desk. 'Anything more I can do, don't hesitate to ask. Poor Elwyn. Let's trust there was a natural reason for his death, sad as it was in any case.'

'We hope so, sir.'

The lawyer shook hands gravely with his two visitors and punctiliously saw them to the door of his office. As soon as they had gone he picked up the telephone and, looking even graver, dialled Abel Davies's number.

8

'This is bloody terrible news, Merlin. Sally rang me as soon as she heard, of course. A policewoman had been on to her. Told her what'd happened. Asked if she'd cope by herself with the shop this morning. Well, of course she will. And I gather you don't know what Elwyn died of? Poor Alison must be distracted.' Tony Lovelaw, the garrulous husband of Alison Griffith's partner Sally, shook his head, and searched in the side pockets of his black, waxed shooting jacket for his pipe and tobacco pouch.

The tweed-capped, rubber-booted South Wales Area Manager for Pitcher's Animal Feeds had been crossing the wet yard of the company's depot when Parry had driven in through the open steel gates. Lovelaw had been on his way from the small, single-storey office building on the left to the large, steel and concrete warehouse in the centre. A laden articulated lorry had been backing up to the loading platform that fronted the warehouse.

A farmhouse had once stood on the site, but had long since been demolished to make way for the depot. An open-sided barn had survived on the right of the yard, and was used now for extra storage. Next to this, but standing on its own, was an even older, low, slate-roofed outbuilding that had been turned into a double garage. A grey Land Rover was parked on one side of this with the sliding door left partly open.

The depot was strategically placed in open country below the major road junction at Coedar Down, a few miles to the east of Tawrbach, and well served by fast roads in all main directions. The chief inspector had driven over in ten minutes from Prothero's office. 'Sally told the WPC you'd been here since six-thirty,' he said. 'You're an early starter.'

'Can't avoid it when there's a big delivery. Except this artic driver was late this morning. Anyway, there aren't that many deliveries, and I'm cheaper than getting my storeman in early. I'd have to pay him overtime. Affect my unit profit that would. And my management bonus.' He pulled the pipe apart and blew sharply through the stem. 'He's here now though. On the forklift.' Lovelaw indicated that they should move towards the lorry.

'How many people do you employ, Tony?'

The other man smirked. 'Just two. Me and the storeman. And he's part retired. Only does a three-day week now. There used to be four here, but head office cut back in the recession. We don't deliver stuff ourselves any more, either. Cheaper to use outside carters, or give customers a discount to collect themselves. Excuse me a sec while I recheck something on this driver's documents.'

Parry watched as Lovelaw spoke with the driver, took some papers from him, and called up instructions to the man on the forklift truck who had just brought his vehicle on to the platform through the opened, roll-up door of the warehouse.

'Right, they'll be happy on their own for a bit,' said Lovelaw when he returned to Parry's side. He nodded again to the lorry driver as they moved off to one side. 'That poor sod's been on the road all night from Carlisle,' he said. 'Better him than me. So, what can I tell you about Elwyn?'

'We're trying to establish his movements through yesterday. I gather you picked him up first thing in the morning?'

'That's right. He was getting the five to seven London train. Typical of old Elwyn not to be taking the all-Pullman half an hour later. Faster and comfier that is, and they do you a bloody good breakfast, too, not just coffee and a toasted sandwich. Elwyn wouldn't spend the extra, see? I remember kidding him about it. Said life was too short for piddling economies. That you couldn't take your money with you.'

He made a tutting noise. 'Never gave better advice, did I? Money's no use to him now, and that's for certain.'

'Wasn't it out of your way to pick him up? And so early?' The Lovelaws lived on the outskirts of Tawrbach.

'Not really.' The two men stopped while Lovelaw lit his pipe. 'Bit of a detour at the start, that's all. Meant going into Cardiff and out again instead of round it. There's not much traffic at that time. Favour to Alison more than Elwyn. She'd have driven him otherwise. God knows why Elwyn never learned to drive.'

'So you weren't coming here afterwards?'

'No, no. I'd promised to see a farmer the other side of Caerphilly. Sorry.' Lovelaw was waving the air in front of him to stop smoke from billowing over his companion. 'Have to make your bread early in the day in this business, Merlin. And often late as well. Nearly midnight when I got home last night. Sally will tell you. Used to farmers' ways all my life, of course.' Lovelaw was a Brecon sheep farmer's son. He had been sent to a boarding school in England, but that hadn't altered his strong Welsh accent which was more pronounced even than Parry's − added to which Lovelaw was a lot more talkative. 'Not like being in the police force, eh, boyo? All office hours that is, or so I'm told,' he ended with a chuckle.

'But not by a policeman,' Parry countered drily. 'So, you dropped Elwyn at Cardiff Central at what time yesterday?'

'Oh, must have been twenty to seven. He was still worried about having enough time to buy his ticket. I told him he had time for that, and to get a cuppa and a jam butty on the station if he wanted. To save spending money on the train.' Lovelaw shook his head. '*Duw, Duw*, the silly things that come back to you after a tragedy.'

'Did he happen to tell you who he was seeing in London?' They were pacing slowly again to the right, along the drying concrete.

'Er . . . publishers, I think. Yes, that was it.'

'He didn't say which ones?'

'No. Wouldn't have meant anything to me if he had. Not my scene. Long time since I read a book.'

'And what sort of mental state was he in, would you say?'

'The usual bloody hopeless one.' Lovelaw halted, pressing down the smouldering tobacco in his pipe with the end of his lighter. 'Nothing ever seemed to get Elwyn out of that, did it? We all know he'd been made redundant, and couldn't sell his books. But he never seemed to find a bright side to anything. Never. Of course, the asthma got him down as well. Nasty thing, that. But with a lovely wife like Alison, and pots of money now, from his mother, you'd have thought he'd have cheered up lately. But not a bit of it.'

'Yes, but I imagine he'd only get satisfaction from success in his job,' said Parry. 'From either one of his jobs. Inherited money wouldn't count for as much. Not in that way, would it?' He had stopped short of mentioning the new consolation of Alison Griffith's baby.

'Huh, catch me bothering with animal feeds if I came into a bundle,' the other replied. 'If my dad had left me a fortune, instead of going bankrupt, I can tell you I wouldn't have been here at six-thirty this morning ready to hump sacks. Or any other bloody morning, come to that.'

'You're exaggerating, Tony. You'd hate not working.' They were halfway along the side of the open barn. Parry noticed a burst paper sack, one of the lower ones stacked on a laden wooden palette. It had been shedding white granules on to the ground. 'Losing a bit of stock there,' he added. 'Rats, is it?'

'Rats, mice, squirrels, rabbits, you name it. Everything gets at my stock before the paying customers have a look in,' Lovelaw responded hotly. 'Costs a fortune in what's called modern pest controls to keep a site like this vermin free.' He waved an arm at the well-grounded mesh fencing surrounding the whole complex.

'Keeps human prowlers out too though, Tony,' said Parry, regarding the fence with professional approval. He might have added something about some older methods of pest control except Lovelaw, crouched down trying to cover the hole in the sack, had missed his first remark. 'Did Elwyn say he might be staying in London for the night?' the policeman asked after Lovelaw had got up again with agility.

'No. He told me he'd be back on the train that gets in just after midnight. Alison was meeting him. So what happened about that? If she met him –'

'She didn't. Huw Prothero was supposed to meet him instead, but Elwyn didn't show. And he wasn't on the next train either.'

'So what train did he catch?'

'There's a possibility he was on the one that gets in around eleven. But there was no one to meet him.'

'And you found the body when?'

'Just after seven this morning.'

'So how long had he been dead then?'

'We don't know yet.' Parry hesitated. 'Eight hours. Possibly more.'

'Is that as close as you can get? I thought they gave you the time of death within minutes these days.'

'Most people think that. But it's not like the telly, Tony. It really isn't.'

'Well, they do better than that in an abattoir. Much better. I expect because there's a bloody EC regulation about it,' Lovelaw observed bitterly as Parry stopped them in front of the half-open garage and looked in.

'Bit of a dog's dinner in there, isn't it?' said Parry.

'You can say that again. Should have been cleaned out years ago.' Apart from the Land Rover, the space inside the garage was occupied, floor to ceiling, with assorted used farm gear. 'All that stuff was shoved in there when we took over the site. Thought some of it might have been useful at the time.'

'Looks like the attic in my father's old house,' the policeman offered, turning away. 'Another question about Elwyn,' he said as they began pacing again. 'How was he dressed when you last saw him?'

'Oh, that's easy. Grey herringbone overcoat and that bloody great dark fedora. Fancied himself no end in that hat, he did. Thought it made him look like the great author. More like a B-feature American gangster, I always thought. And he had a hairy sort of sports coat underneath, I think. Can't remember the colour. Is that important?'

'No.'

'And grey flannels.'

'He was wearing the coat and hat, not carrying them?'

'That's right. It was cold yesterday morning. And he had his briefcase, of course.'

'You didn't go into the station with him, by any chance?'

'To see he got his ticket, all right?' Lovelaw grinned. 'No, I didn't do that, but I did nip in after him to get a paper. Ours hadn't been delivered when I left the house. I had to be quick because you're not allowed to leave a car long in that setting-down area. I did see Elwyn go to the ticket office. Is there any doubt about him catching the train?'

'Probably not.' Parry looked at the time. 'Thanks, Tony, you've been very helpful.'

'Not helpful enough, probably. Since you've so little to go on.' He sucked hard on his pipe and the light blue eyes looked steadily at his companion. 'You're considering it might have been suicide, are you?'

'It's one of the possibilities, yes.'

'Except I was forgetting, you're only involved in crime. Serious crime at that. It's none of my business, I know, but if Elwyn had a bad day in London, had his books turned down again, that kind of thing, I wouldn't put it past him to have done himself in. Thinking about it, that really was the sort of mood he was in when he was with me.' He frowned. 'Wouldn't mention it to Alison, of course.'

'I'll make a note of that, Tony.'

Lovelaw seemed to relax, as though he was glad to be done with an awkward task. 'Cup of coffee in my office, then?' he asked.

'Thanks, but I'd better be moving off.'

'And if it wasn't suicide?' Lovelaw asked slowly. 'You obviously don't believe it was natural causes or you wouldn't be involved. So what's left?' He put a hand on Parry's shoulder and moved off with him towards the Porsche. 'Oh, don't tell me,' he completed amiably. 'It's too early for you to say, isn't it?'

Although, twenty-five years ago, the shopkeepers of Tawrbach had opposed the building of the bypass around their town, they, or their successors, had long since come to count it as a blessing.

What the bypass cost the town in 'passing trade' had been replaced many times over by affluent new residents and regular shoppers from outside, all attracted to Tawrbach by its rediscovered old world quaintness, the high and ever improving quality of its shops and restaurants, the richness of its cultural life, the unbroken tradition (and wholesome odour) of its centuries-old weekly cattle market, the excellence of its schools, and the altogether superior ambience that made its main street a place to see as well as to be seen in.

All this had been secured by an alert town council and dynamic chamber of commerce working in concert. Once awakened to the idea that prosperity could be the rich reward of conservation, they preserved what was left of the town's attractive old buildings, and then created many more of them by the judicious refacing of what was nondescript or plain ugly, whilst at the same time standing out against urban modernization – garish shop fronts, 'far out' street furniture, sodium lighting, and too many estate agent offices. In short, from being unremarkable, Tawrbach became picturesque – and famous for it.

Huw Prothero and Abel Davies had been more responsible than most others for the success of Tawrbach. Aspects of their common interest in the town had been the usual cause for their often frequent business meetings in the past. Their coming together in the lawyer's office today, on a now dry and nearly sunny morning, had a more sombre and personal reason though.

'That's what I thought myself, at first,' said Prothero, in answer to a comment from Davies. He was stirring a cup of coffee fiercely, as though it might jellify if he stopped. 'When Parry gave me the news I thought we were saved. Not that I wished Elwyn dead for trying to blackmail us, mark you. But it is a sort of . . .' He paused, looking in the swirling coffee for the right words.

'Divine retribution,' Davies provided firmly and without hesitation.

'You might say that, I suppose.' Except Prothero had used a lawyer's instinct not to have said it himself. 'Only since then I've come to the conclusion we could both be put under suspicion. Quite unjustly, of course.'

'And Evan Cromwell-Evans as well?'

'And Evan, yes. All three of us. Individually or collectively.'

'If the police see a copy of Elwyn's memo, you mean? And if they think he was murdered,' said Davies. He was standing in front of the long window at the end of the room, peering outwards. Staring from windows was his favourite thinking posture at home and outside it – appearing to concentrate on the view through his thick spectacles but without taking it in.

It was ten-twenty. Davies hadn't received Prothero's urgent message until fifteen minutes before this. When the lawyer had first called him, he had been a dozen miles away, showing an important prospective buyer over an empty house. He had left his mobile telephone in the car outside.

Prothero wrinkled his nose which, in turn, agitated his moustache. It always irritated him to be addressing the back of Davies's neck. 'They already think he was murdered. I could tell. Doesn't mean to say he was, mind you. But the South Wales police don't waste expensive senior man-hours on remote possibilities. Very cost conscious, they are. And quite right too,' he ended portentously, in the reflex way of someone who was at once a qualified court official as well as a substantial community tax payer – but hardly someone who recognized he could be implicated in a heinous crime.

'So is Merlin Parry on the case because he used to live in Tawrbach? Because he knows all of us?'

'The body was found in Aberkidy not here.' Prothero sipped his coffee, and noted that Davies's cup was getting cold on the desk.

'I know that. But all the people involved –'

'Parry was on duty so he was told to deal with the matter, that's all.'

'And you haven't spoken to Evan yet?'

'Evan has gone riding,' said the lawyer in a manner that suggested going riding at a time like this was pretty incomprehensible, not to say irresponsible. 'Don't know when he ever gets any work done. He rang me early, like you. Woke me up as a matter of fact. All I could tell him then was what I told you later. Elwyn hadn't been on the train last night.'

'So Evan is in for a shock.' Davies went on squinting through the window. Prothero made no audible reply to the comment. His expression still showed a lingering dissatisfaction over Cromwell-Evans's hedonistic lifestyle as Davies continued: 'Did Parry say anything about the diaries? Elwyn must have had them with him.'

'There's no must about it. He *may* have had them with him, of course, but they weren't in his briefcase when the police opened it.'

'Oh God. Someone else took them. His murderer probably.'

Prothero gave out an exaggerated, exasperated sigh, even though he had imagined something of the kind himself. 'The diaries may have been taken from the briefcase. But it's more likely he left them with a publisher in London –'

'But that's worse.'

'Or he could have left them at home,' the lawyer went on, ignoring the interjection. 'And I wish you'd come and sit down over here.'

'Sorry, Huw.' Davies came across from the window and dropped into a chair. 'And did Parry ask you to account for the time when you were supposed to be waiting between trains?'

Prothero sat up straighter. 'Yes, and there's no supposed about it.'

'Sorry, Huw,' he apologized again quickly.

'That's all right. You want a fresh cup of coffee?'

'No, no. This is fine.' He still made no move to drink it.

'So where were you between eleven last night and two this morning?' Prothero demanded.

'I was home by half past twelve. I'd had dinner with that chap Isaacs in Merthyr. The one who's buying the factory site. I had a flat tyre on the way back.' His brow furrowed. 'Why eleven?'

'Because Elwyn may have got an earlier train.'

'Well, I couldn't have known that.'

'Neither could I.'

'He might have called you from London in the day.'

'Why should he?'

'Because you'd been leaving all those messages on his answering machine. If he was coming back early he might have been arranging to see you.'

The lawyer scowled. If Abel Davies thought this, so could the police. 'Well he didn't. For that matter you've been chivying him about selling Woodstock Grange. So he's just as likely to have called you as me. He didn't, did he?'

'Of course not. I'd have said.'

There was a moment of silence as each considered the other's denial. Both wished there could be as good a reason for Elwyn Griffith to have called Cromwell-Evans – without either of them yet knowing that there had been.

Davies shifted uncomfortably in his seat. 'Could we ask Alison if she knows where the diaries are?' he said, changing the subject.

'I intend to, yes. It's still possible she knows nothing about them.'

'And if she knows all about them, she'll think . . . Oh God.' Davies stretched a hand out to his coffee. 'I suppose I could er . . . have a look round the cottage. When she's out?'

'Break into the place?'

'I've still got a key. There's no burglar alarm.'

The immediate look of conventional outrage on the lawyer's face slowly faded into something closer to cool calculation. In the silence that followed the sudden ringing of the telephone on the desk startled both men. It was a shrill invasion of guilty consciences, which is why both imagined it might be the police. In the event, it was Cromwell-Evans calling after his ride.

9

'Come in, Gomer.' Parry, in shirtsleeves, beckoned to the sergeant as he put down the telephone, then loosened his tie below the unbuttoned collar.

It was late afternoon. The detective chief inspector was in his office on the first floor of the still newish, mansard-roofed Rumney Police Station on the brow of a hill on the busy Newport Road. Lloyd, still wearing his raincoat, took a seat on the other side of the desk. The small room was a strictly functional, nearly square box – walls painted cream, the one with the door on to the general office glazed from waist level, the others covered in pin boards and maps. There were strip lights on the ceiling, and a long, steel-framed window facing west with a view of the car park. The desk was grey with an extension side table and a desk computer on it. There were two filing cabinets also grey, and a set of three wall shelves holding box files, directories, a dictionary, an atlas, a cookbook, some computer manuals, and a small radio on the top shelf gathering dust. The radio had been there for a month waiting for a new battery.

'Sorry it took me so long, boss,' Lloyd apologized, still catching his breath after climbing the stairs two at a time. He had just come back from his second trip to Aberkidy.

'I've only just got here myself. From the infirmary,' said Parry.

'You watched the postmortem, boss?' Lloyd made a face: he didn't care for postmortems personally.

'Most of it. Griffith died in *status asthmaticus*.'

'Like Dr Maltravers said?'

Parry nodded, pulling a notepad from his pocket. 'Atopic asthma.'

'So will it be natural causes, boss?'

'Not in the private opinion of our respected pathology professor. He thinks the injuries indicate stress played a part in the death.'

'Meaning the asthma was aggravated, boss?'

'He didn't say that, but I think he will in his report, and in what he says at the inquest. Or something like it. He can't understand why the attack went untreated.'

'That makes three of us, boss. Or four with Doc Maltravers.'

'When the professor spoke to Mrs Griffith, that was after she'd identified the body, she told him her husband used to take phenobarbital for sleep.'

'That's right, boss. I heard her.'

'Did she say how much?'

'Yes. A hundred milligrammes most nights. I made a note. His doctor says the same.' Lloyd flicked back the pages of his book to check.

'Good. That's what the professor thought. We didn't want to go back to her on it unless we had to. I said you were seeing Griffith's doctor. The thing is, the prof's found higher traces of phenobarb than that in the body.'

'Not a lethal dose though?'

'No. And he said it might not be particularly relevant, not to the death, but it's something that'll need explaining at the inquest.'

'Mr Griffith was young to be hooked on sleeping pills in any case,' Lloyd observed, a touch puritanically. 'Is there anything on where he died, boss?'

'Plenty. It wasn't where we found him. Gravity had settled blood at the back of the head.'

'And he was lying on his face?' Lloyd completed. 'What about the bruising and the cuts?'

'The bruise on the back of the head was more than superficial, but not much more. Caused by a single blow from something blunt and flat. Probably metal. Could have dazed him, or possibly made him unconscious for a second or two. And he was certainly conscious later. The other bruises were very possibly self-inflicted. Maybe the result of his trying to push or heave something open. The worst bruises were on the heels. Of course, we didn't see those.'

'We saw the lacerations to his finger ends, though, boss.'

'Yes. Caused by contact with something sharp and metallic. The prof agrees he could have been trying to break open a metal fastening of some kind. But that's not official, just off the record, intelligent speculation.' Parry looked up from his notes. 'I asked whether all the injuries could be consistent with his trying to escape from a room with a metal door, or maybe from a big metal container. The prof said it was possible.'

'Or a deepfreeze, boss? One of the chest type?'

'Right. Or a big car boot, or something bigger still like . . . like the inside of a van, or . . . or a lift cage. Oh, and there are minute particles of what is probably industrial paint under the fingernails.'

'Do we have the colour of the paint, boss?'

'Not yet. The particles are being analysed now.'

'And the time of death?'

'Not much better than we had before. Anything between noon yesterday and midnight.'

'So it's narrowed a bit?'

'That's right. His stomach contents show his last meal was white fish in batter, peas, fried potatoes, and apple tart or apple crumble.'

'Marvellous what they can tell,' said Lloyd, but his face showed he would rather be spared further details. 'Sounds like his lunch or supper, that does.'

'Not breakfast, anyway.'

'Which brings down the time of death to say two in the afternoon to midnight?'

'Possibly,' but Parry sounded less certain. 'Incidentally, so far the phenobarb is the only chemical medicament found in the body.'

'Would the stuff in the inhaler have shown if he'd used it?' He checked his notes. 'The salbutamol?'

'Yes. But there were no traces of it in the blood. And there would have been if he'd used an inhaler within four hours of death. The professor said it's inexplicable a known asthmatic wasn't taking anything. That he didn't use an inhaler he had handy during a serious attack.'

'Ah, well, that's where Mr Griffith's doctor comes into the picture, boss,' said Lloyd who had got up, taken off his raincoat, then sat down again and reopened his notebook. 'That's Dr Jago, late getting back from his rounds this afternoon, and by then his receptionist had gone home. Took him ages finding the patient notes on Mr Griffith.' The sergeant, a meticulously ordered person when it came to his work if not his appearance, scowled at the inefficiencies of others. 'Apart from the phenobarb tablets, one at night as necessary for sleep, the patient had been on ten milligrammes of a . . . a cortico-steroid for the last nine months. One tablet after breakfast every day. He never missed either.'

'Mrs Griffith had told the professor about that too. We had cortico-steroids in a case last year, didn't we?'

'That's right, boss. And they're difficult to trace because they don't show up in the blood.'

'The professor's arranged a special test on that one, but he doesn't believe it's going to be positive, for subjective reasons, he said.' Parry shrugged. 'What else, Gomer?'

'Just the salbutamol by inhaler. Two puffs, three times a day. More if needed in emergency.' Lloyd looked up. 'It's strong stuff. The doc said Mr Griffith's asthma was bad, but pretty well under control, so long as he kept to the treatment.'

'Except it's unlikely he took his pill after breakfast yesterday. Unless he forgot it in the rush to get ready early. Because he was being picked up.'

'Or if he didn't have breakfast, chief? His wife will know.'

'Even though anyone really dependent on medication wouldn't forget.' Parry rubbed his cheeks with the fingertips of both hands. 'Did Dr Jago say exactly what Griffith was allergic to, Gomer?'

'Like Mrs Griffith told you, it was a lot of things. Except they reckoned they'd already eliminated some of the ones she mentioned. The doc said Mr Griffith's biggest problem was cats. He couldn't be in the same room as a cat without breaking out in hives. Something in the dust of cat fur, I think. The professor didn't say anything about cats?'

'No, but sections of nose and lung tissue are still being analysed. To see what was being inhaled at the time of death.'

'We've arranged to have the clothes picked up from the infirmary and taken to Chepstow with the rest, boss. That includes the inhaler.' The South Wales Constabulary Forensic Science Laboratory is in Chepstow, twenty miles east of Cardiff, near the English border.

Parry leaned back in his chair. 'It'll be up to a coroner's jury to decide, but I definitely don't see how it can be natural causes. We still need to know why it happened the way it did. Especially how the body came to be where it was. Even if it was an accident of some kind, if he forgot to take his pill and forgot he had an inhaler with him, it doesn't explain the rest. Have we finished the house-to-house calls in Aberkidy?'

'Pretty well, boss. There'll have to be a few call backs. People at work, like. So far, nobody saw Mr Griffith last night.'

'Did anyone see him yesterday morning? In the Land Rover with Mr Lovelaw?'

'No, nobody. Mind you, it must have been pretty dark still, when they left. We had more luck with the driver of that bus. Interviewed him at home. Older bloke. Cooperative too. He's sure a man got on at the terminus, at Cardiff Central, wearing dark glasses, and a dark hat with a very wide brim. He was pretty certain about the overcoat too, but he didn't recognize Mr Griffith from the photo we're showing. Says he doesn't look at faces.' Lloyd leaned forward. 'No question about the hat though. Unusual, see? And the man bought a ticket to Aberkidy.'

'And this was on the eleven-ten bus, Gomer?'

'That's it, yes. It's the last bus but one at night. Gets more passengers than the last one though, on a week night that is. People coming out of the pictures and the pubs. The driver can't remember if anyone got off at the stop before the village. But he's pretty certain no one got on.'

'Pretty certain, but not sure?'

'That's right, boss. So they're checking it at the bus company accounts office for us. With the ticket machine print-out. Except it won't show anyone who got on using a bus pass. A lot have passes these days, of course.' Lloyd looked up suddenly. 'By the way, the actual bus we're talking about hadn't been cleaned since last night. Or used again. It went in for service at the depot first thing this morning. We had a team there by eleven. They cleaned it out themselves and bagged up what they got. You never know. The bags have gone to Chepstow as well.'

'No empty inhaler refill, I suppose?'

'Afraid not, boss. And no empty pill bottle either. There were two used plastic pill strips, one for Coldrex, the other for Nurofen. Nothing Mr Griffith was taking. Not so far as we know.'

Parry pinched the end of his nose. 'So the driver remembers nothing about that bus stop last night?'

'Yes, he remembers stopping there all right. He was early, and he waited there three minutes to make up. They have to do that.'

'What about regular passengers on the route?'

'There are four the driver can think of. Only one gets on at Cardiff Central, though. And one of the others gets off in the centre of Aberkidy, the next stop to the one we're interested in. We'll have someone on the bus tonight to question them, and all the other passengers.' He turned back a page in his notebook. 'Now then, we've talked to the ticket clerks at the station. There were two on duty between six and seven yesterday morning. One of them definitely remembers selling a return ticket to Paddington to a man wearing dark glasses and a wide-brimmed hat. He thinks he remembers the overcoat too, but he couldn't describe the face, or say if it was Mr Griffith from the photo.' He looked up. 'We'll question regular passengers on the platform tomorrow morning. That hat's a dead ringer on identification, so far as it goes,' he said, then looked down again. 'Next, London publishers. We've called every London company listed in Mr Griffith's address book. Not all of them were publishers, of course.'

'Some would have been literary agents, his wife said,' put in Parry.

'Yes, and other things. But it doesn't look as if he went to see any of them. A few we've got to ring back because they had different people on reception or the switchboard today. Doesn't look hopeful. Oh, and he rang his mate in Maida Vale late on Tuesday afternoon. Name of Ron Gilbert. Told him he'd be in London next day. Half arranged to see him for supper. Said he'd be at his flat between six and seven, but if he wasn't there by then, not to expect him because it meant he was tied up with a publisher. He never saw him.'

'He didn't ring Gilbert to explain why?'

'No, boss. Mr Gilbert wasn't surprised either. Said he was used to Mr Griffith being vague about things. And forgetful too.'

'Hm. Alison Griffith said the same.' Parry pouted and folded his arms. 'So there's not a lot to go on so far, Gomer?'

'Afraid not, boss, but it's early yet. Oh, about the incident room? I don't think we need that social hall. So far we've been controlling everything from here –'

'Yes. Keep it here,' Parry interrupted. 'There won't be any point having people camped in Aberkidy after tonight.'

'It was good of Sheila Cromwell-Evans to bring me over,' said Alison Griffith.

'I'd have come for you, if I'd realized,' replied Perdita Jones.

'Oh, I could have driven myself. It was just that Sheila dropped in. To see if there was anything I wanted. Very practical she is. Actually, she invited me to supper at their house. I was glad I'd already arranged to come to you.'

'Yes, Evan can be a bit overpowering. Especially at a . . . at a time like this. How many potatoes can you eat?'

'Any number of little new ones like those. Well five or six anyway. I don't suppose a grief-stricken widow ought to be hungry.'

'A pregnant one could though.'

'Bit early for that, isn't it? Anyway, I can't help it. Let me clean the carrots.' She was neatly dressed in a white blouse and dark skirt. Her black hair was well brushed and her face lightly made-up as usual. Only her eyes were slightly puffed.

It was nearly seven, and the two women were in the kitchen of Perdita's bungalow which was in a short avenue of newer detached houses at the extreme west side of Tawrbach. Perdita kept the place on after her husband left her. She had her physiotherapy consulting room here for the private practice she maintained in addition to her contract work at two of the local hospitals.

'If you'd rather go home for the night later, I'll take you,' she said, leaving the carrot cleaning to her guest while she prepared a small chicken for the oven.

'I shan't. I'd much rather stay here. And thanks again for inviting me. You're a darling. I'll look in at the shop in the morning. I'd rather work than not. Sally said she'll take me home when I want.' She moved her head sharply, then pushed some hair from her eyes with the back of her hand. 'I don't think I could have coped with any more sympathetic phone calls. Of course, everybody means well. Although you have the feeling they expect you to be in tears. Permanently. I'm not that sort, you see? Or I seem to have done the weeping bit. For the moment, anyway. Does that seem heartless to you?'

'No, quite natural. What d'you like with chicken? A white Australian Chardonnay or a red Napa Valley Sauvignon? They're both cheap and cheerful.' Perdita held out the bottle of each wine she had taken from the wall rack beside the refrigerator. The rack was made of oak like the rest of the kitchen fitments.

'The red, please. I should have brought some wine. I never thought.' Alison filled a saucepan with water for the carrots.

'Nonsense. You're excused all social niceties for the duration. Now then, the chicken will be ready in an hour and a bit. I'll put the vegetables on later. So how about a gin and tonic?' Perdita led her guest through the door into the sitting room. 'Listen. You're doing very well,' she went on, as she poured the drinks. 'You've had a hell of a shock but you're standing up to it marvellously. Don't be bothered about how people expect you to behave. Live normally. Or as normally as you can. The next few days are bound to be tough.'

'Till the funeral's over. And the inquest, of course,' Alison put in quietly from where she had seated herself on the sofa, in front of a crackling log fire. 'Anyway, thanks for the advice. It sounded professional.'

'It is. No charge though, and we'll all help meantime. You know that.' She brought the drinks over and sat beside Alison.

'The Lovelaws have been wonderful already. Like you.' Alison squeezed her friend's hand. 'Tony's going to make all the funeral arrangements. Mr Prothero offered, but I'd rather Tony handled it. And my mother's offered to come down. I've told her not to. Not till the funeral, with my father. I love her, but she fusses.' She took a sip of her drink. 'We can't fix a funeral date yet. Not till after the inquest. You know that's on Monday?'

'Merlin Parry mentioned it when he dropped in early this afternoon.'

'It's because –'

'Because it was an unexpected death. That's the law, I'm afraid.'

'This morning the police said they thought it might be a . . . a suspicious death. The ends of Elwyn's fingers were torn. I saw them. And there was bruising. And they don't know if he –' She took a deep breath. '– if he died where they found him, or somewhere else. The nice policewoman was back this afternoon. She said they still didn't know for certain what he died of. Really, I don't understand –'

'I expect they have to account for everything. To the coroner. For the injuries. They're very thorough.'

'But if it wasn't just an asthma attack, what are they saying? That it was suicide or . . . or something else? And where else could he have died? I mean –'

'Why don't you leave it to them to tell you when they're ready? Knowing how he died –'

'Won't bring him back. I know that,' Alison interrupted.

'I was going to say, it's something the authorities are paid to find out for your satisfaction, more even than the coroner's when you think about it.'

Alison nodded slowly, then sat up straighter and looked

about her alertly. 'This is such a pretty room.' She smoothed the arm of the sofa.

'All your doing.'

'Sorry, I wasn't fishing for compliments.'

'But I meant it. You're such a clever designer. This room's much nicer than before. When it was a dining room, I mean. Anyway, since I needed the other room for consulting there wasn't much option was there? I've got used to eating in the kitchen.'

'Where else? It's a lovely kitchen, and I remember telling you it'd be quite big enough for entertaining.' A year before, after Perdita's divorce, it was Alison who had reorganized the interior of the bungalow. The kitchen in particular had been completely done over to make more use of the available space. It had all cost a lot less than Perdita had expected – because Alison was a keen buyer and had taken only half her usual profit on the job.

'Anyway, single people don't have much use for dining rooms,' said Perdita.

'Yes. I expect I'll get used to that again.'

'Oh darling, I didn't mean that. I'm so sorry.' Perdita squeezed the other woman's arm.

'No need to be. Be normal, you said.' She shrugged. 'Anyway, I've decided already I shan't stay in Aberkidy.'

'Pity. You've made that cottage so nice.'

'I've never regarded it as a permanent home. Not really. Rhonwen chose it, of course. Because she was paying for it.'

'I didn't know that.'

'Nobody did. Not officially. People may have guessed. Elwyn wanted it kept a secret. It's why I never told my friends. We always said she'd loaned us the money. It was Elwyn's pride, I suppose. His mother chose Aberkidy, she said, so Elwyn could have peace and quiet for his writing. Really I think it was to make sure she wouldn't have to meet me too often. Not if we lived eight miles away.'

'Different if you'd been here in Tawrbach?'

'That's right.'

'But she didn't stop you setting up in business here?'

'She couldn't very well, could she? That wasn't done with

just her money, even though she'd have liked people to think it was. My part of the capital included money my father lent me, plus a bank loan. And Sally and Tony put in more than me.'

Perdita had got up to freshen the drinks. She and Alison were not the closest of friends, and it was becoming clear she knew even less about the other's private life than she had imagined before this evening. 'So you and Madam Rhonwen really didn't get on?'

'That's an understatement. I thought you knew. I thought everybody knew.' Her eyes followed her hostess as she returned to the sofa. 'Thanks.' She took the glass in her hand. 'Rhonwen never believed I was a good enough wife for her only child. Perhaps I wasn't.' She smiled wanly at the fire.

'Nonsense. Elwyn was very lucky to get you.'

'I wonder. Too late now to do anything about it.' She turned her head towards Perdita. 'Merlin Parry's a lovely man. Steel hand in a velvet glove type. Is that right?'

'Pretty well.'

'I never really knew him till today. We were introduced on Tuesday, at Rhonwen's wake, but we didn't talk then. I'd met his wife, of course. Through you, wasn't it?'

'Rosemary? Yes. We were very close for a long time,' said Perdita quietly.

'They must have been living here well before we moved into White Cross Cottage. Anyway, Elwyn never wanted anything to do with the Tawrbach establishment, with the Operatic Society, and the rest of his mother's domain. Or with other couples really. Was Merlin a friend of Gavin's?' Gavin Jones was Perdita's ex-husband.

'Not really. It was playing music brought us together mostly. The four of us, I mean. Playing it pretty badly too. Merlin never really took to Gavin. Couldn't blame him either,' Perdita completed testily.

'He said such nice things about you today. Very nice things.' Although Perdita made as if she was about to reply her guest continued quickly. 'I gathered there might be something going between the two of you. Is that right?'

It was Perdita's turn to study the flames in the fire. 'There might have been,' she answered slowly. 'If . . . if I hadn't been Rosemary's friend.'

'How come?'

Perdita's gaze lowered to study the contents of her glass. 'Because Merlin and I nearly had an affair after Gavin left me.'

'Nearly had an affair?'

'Would have had probably, and more. At least I imagine so. That's if they hadn't discovered Rosemary had a brain tumour. That was a year and a half ago. She had the scan the day after a party in the barn at Woodstock Grange. I'll never forget that party.' She paused, then went on slowly. 'Merlin and I were both a bit pissed. I was still crazy mad at Gavin and the bitch he'd left me for three months before. I wanted a man again fast. To prove something. Everything. A better man than Gavin. Merlin fitted nicely, of course. Good-looking, forceful, upwardly mobile. His being my best friend's husband didn't seem to come into it. Not at the time. I was that bloody selfish and sorry for myself.' She ran her tongue across her upper lip. 'He and I had left the party and gone over to the house. You'd just done over some bedrooms for Rhonwen. She'd been telling people about them. That was our excuse. Pretending we were going to see the rooms. We'd started to make love on the bed in one of them when Rosemary walked in, with Rhonwen.'

'Oh God, how awful. Were you actually . . . ?'

'No, not quite. But it was all pretty sordid.' Perdita drained her glass. 'Rosemary never spoke to me again. She died six months later.'

There was silence for several seconds before Alison said: 'But by this time surely you –'

'By this time nothing. Merlin would like it otherwise. I'm still in shock, I suppose.' She turned her face to Alison. 'And d'you know, you're the only person in the world I've ever told? Strange. And today of all days for you. I'm sorry, I just don't know why I unburdened like that, but if it's any consolation it's made me feel better. So now let's talk about something else.'

Alison looked embarrassed. 'Oh dear, I was going to ask if

Merlin had told you anything this afternoon he hadn't told me. About Elwyn's death. But if you'd rather not.'

'No, I'd tell you if there was anything. But I don't really think there was.' Her brow creased as her finger traced the rim of her glass. 'And he was only here a minute or two. Called on the off chance, he said. On his way back from somewhere.'

'But just as you got home from the hospital you said. Nice timing. He's obviously really gone on you.'

Perdita looked up with a modest smile. 'He did ask me out again tonight.'

'But you had me coming. Oh, you should have put me off.'

'Nonsense. And I'm sure he didn't think I'd accept. He was just . . . just testing.'

'To see how far your relationship had improved because of last evening.'

'Something like that. I did ask about Elwyn. If they knew how he'd died.' She hesitated. 'He said exactly what the policewoman told you, that it was too early to say.'

'He didn't say they thought he could have been murdered? You can say if he did. I can take it.'

'Well, perhaps he implied that,' Perdita answered carefully. 'But only in a very roundabout sort of way.'

10

'It's addressed to you, boss, and marked personal. Wedged under the front door at Tawrbach Police Station, it was. In the night. Duty sergeant there rang me at home first thing. Caught me as I was leaving. At ten to seven.' Gomer Lloyd never missed the chance to advertise that he was an early starter: it stopped people assuming he was as sluggish as he looked.

'Don't they have a letter box still at Tawrbach nick?' asked Parry, putting down a mug of coffee on his desk and taking the proffered buff envelope from Lloyd.

'Sealed up last year, boss. Terrorist precaution, that was. The duty sergeant told me they've had two anonymous letters left that way lately.'

'Cheaper than the post, I expect.'

'Quicker, more like. They think it's because there's no one to see who's leaving things, not since the station's been closed at night. Economy measure that was, of course.'

'It wasn't just an economy measure. It was to free more coppers for the beat . . .' Parry's voice trailed off as he read the single folded sheet he had hooked from the envelope with the end of a chrome-plated letter opener, and which he was now holding open with the same implement and a steel ruler.

Lloyd had his own ideas on how to improve available manpower, but they involved reducing paperwork, not closing police stations. He wiped the back of his hand across his mouth and moustache. 'Something important is it, boss?'

It was ten past eight on Friday morning. The detective

chief inspector had been about to go upstairs for an updating session in the incident room when Lloyd had appeared in the doorway to his office. The sergeant lived on the other side of Tawrbach and had picked up the envelope on his way in.

'Read it yourself, Gomer. And let's have it checked for prints. I'd say the envelope was done on a word processor, and it doesn't match the type on the enclosure. It'd be nice to know the name of the sender.' But Parry didn't sound hopeful. He assumed the envelope would be useless for fingerprint purposes since it had passed through at least four pairs of hands. For the rest, people who send anonymous notes to the police are usually informed enough to wear gloves.

What Parry had received was a copy of the memo about the Rhonwen Spencer Griffith diaries that the lady's son had posted to Evan Cromwell-Evans, Abel Davies, and Huw Prothero earlier in the week.

'It's dated March 16th. That was Tuesday, the day of Madam Rhonwen's memorial service,' said Lloyd, still reading. 'But whoever delivered this copy last night, it wasn't Mr Griffith, and that's for sure. Informer then? *Duw, Duw,* puts a new light on things, and no mistake.'

'The bit about the newspapers is useful,' Parry commented. 'Have someone check with the Literary Editors of the *Sunday Times* and the *Observer* will you, Gomer? Straightaway this morning. If either paper was interested in these diaries, Griffith could easily have spent all day Wednesday with one of them.'

'Right, boss.'

'If there's no luck with either, try all the other Sundays. Looks like we'll need to call every book publisher in London, too. Not just the ones in that address book.'

'Understood.' Lloyd rubbed the centre of his forehead with a clenched fist, wrinkling his nose at the same time: both actions signifying perplexity. 'Funny though,' he said, 'if Mr Griffith was offering the manuscript to the three gents listed here, for three hundred thousand pounds, why should he go to London and try and sell it to a newspaper?'

'Perhaps the three gents had already turned him down.'

'Ah. Well to do that they must have got the memo some-time on Tuesday, boss. The day it's dated for. Meaning it was delivered by hand not post. Mr Griffith was on the train to London before the post was delivered anywhere on Wednesday.'

'Unless the copies were shoved under doors in the night like mine.' Parry had settled with folded arms on the front edge of his desk. 'I suppose it's possible he gave them out at the wake, after the service. They were all three there. I spoke to them.'

'Did they mention the diaries?'

'No. They were all pretty relaxed, and at that point I can't believe any of them knew the diaries existed.'

'Not if they were as important as Mr Griffith says.' Lloyd looked down at the memo again and read aloud: ' "An unin-hibited commentary on social and cultural life in an impor-tant part of Wales, by the dynamic personality who did more than anyone else to guide it through the period." Strong stuff that is. But was he overstating things, like?'

'You mean, was Madam Rhonwen really that important, Gomer?' Parry paused and gave a sniff. 'No. Strictly speaking, I don't believe she was.'

'So would London newspapers and book publishers be that interested, boss? In her diaries?'

'In her explicit and frank diaries, it says, doesn't it? The diaries her son is ready to offer uncensored to all comers. I think it depends on how explicit and frank they were. And who gets the uninhibited mentions.'

Lloyd looked grave, and earnestly scratched his left but-tock. 'It's a lot of money for diaries, isn't it? Three hundred thousand?'

'Not if it's the price of protecting an important reputation.'

'Three important reputations.' Lloyd drew breath in through his teeth, making a hissing, censorious sort of noise. 'You think the memo is a blackmail attempt, boss?'

'It's what Huw Prothero and the others may have thought. Assuming they got their copies.'

'Mr Prothero never mentioned it, of course.' Lloyd's eyes opened wider.

'No. We must ask him about that.' Parry looked at the time.

'D'you want to do that now, boss?'

Parry nodded, and moved towards the door. 'After we've been through the situation report upstairs. And we'll need to see all three memo recipients, not just Prothero. Have somebody find out if Cromwell-Evans is in his Cardiff office. He told me once he's always there early on Fridays. If he's there now, we'll see him first.'

'Your name's the first one listed at the top of the memorandum, sir,' Parry was pointing out to Evan Cromwell-Evans, half an hour later.

'That's only because they seem to be in alphabetical order, Merlin,' the other man responded with unaccustomed modesty, and a friendliness that matched his familiar use of the policeman's first name. In contrast he had hardly yet acknowledged Lloyd's presence.

Cromwell-Evans's last comment made as little impression on his two visitors as Huw Prothero's reference to the same fact had done at the meeting on Wednesday morning – except that the short, heavily built speaker on this occasion affected to be too engaged to look round and gauge the reaction. He was sprinkling food over the surface of the long, illuminated tank of miniature marine fish set against one wall of his office at his company's headquarters. The look he was giving the colourful specimens seemed less benign than calculating – as if the food might be intended to force their growth into something more meal sized.

Shevan Electric Markets Limited occupied the fifth floor of an air-conditioned, six-storey building in Tyndall Street, the upper floors offering exceptional views of redeveloped Cardiff Bay. Cromwell-Evans's corner room was a meld of expensive fittings and state-of-the-art electronic gadgetry with floor carpet so thick and acoustic ceiling tiles so absorbent that in combination they would have reduced the sound of a loud slap to that of a muffled thud. The secretary's office guarding this inner sanctum had relatively less furniture in it but even more electronic gear.

The size of Shevan headquarters staff was modest. Besides the chairman, who was also managing director, there was a chief accountant, two head buyers, and three secretaries, all of whom, both policemen would have noted without Cromwell-Evans pointing it out, had been at their desks well before nine. He had not troubled to add that none of their glass-fronted offices approached the opulence of his own closed-in suite.

Lloyd had also noted that all three secretaries would easily have won the top places in a local beauty contest.

'You did get a copy of Mr Griffith's memo, sir?' the sergeant questioned now from the oval meeting table where he was seated, on the same side as his boss.

This time Cromwell-Evans turned about, but it was a moment before he replied, fish food dispenser still held high in his hand as if he was about to advance and sprinkle some of its contents on his visitors, like a priest with holy water. He looked tolerantly from Parry to Lloyd, and then back again, as though to emphasize the fact that he chose to treat with a chief inspector and not a sergeant. 'You going to tell me how you got hold of the memo, Merlin?' he asked.

Parry matched the confident gaze that had accompanied the question. 'In a moment, sir, yes. Perhaps you would answer the question first.'

The other's expression didn't alter, only the heavy jaw tightened. 'Yes, I got a copy of the memo,' he said briskly.

'Could you tell us exactly when you got it, sir?' This was Lloyd again.

'Why? Is it important?' He put the dispenser down and came over to the table.

'Quite important, sir, yes.'

Cromwell-Evans shrugged. 'So far as I remember, it was in the post Wednesday morning.'

'You didn't get it Tuesday, sir?'

'No, sergeant, I just said, it was Wednesday.' He switched an irritated glance to Parry.

'You said so far as you remembered, sir.'

'Well I'm telling you now it was Wednesday, definite. First post.'

'Addressed to you here or –'

'At home, sergeant, like the others,' Cromwell-Evans interrupted.

'Meaning Mr Prothero and Mr Davies got theirs at the same time in the same way?'

'Haven't you asked them?'

'Not yet, sir. We've come to you first because –'

'I was first on the list. Yes, yes. And the others got theirs in the post Wednesday as well.' Cromwell-Evans sat himself down at the table opposite Parry. 'You still haven't told me how you got a copy, Merlin.'

'It was delivered to the Tawrbach Police Station this morning, addressed to me,' Parry replied. 'Any special reason for asking, sir?'

'Just curious, that's all.'

'You didn't leave it there yourself, sir?'

'Of course I didn't. Why should I do that?'

'In an effort to help the police in their inquiries, sir.'

'What inquiries?'

'Into the death of Mr Griffith.'

'But I understood he'd died of asthma.'

'It may not have been as simple as that, sir. We're trying to trace his movements since early Wednesday morning.'

'I see. Well I hadn't seen him since Tuesday.'

'Did you discuss the memo with Mr Davies and Mr Prothero, sir?' Parry asked.

'We discussed it, yes. The matter was important to Elwyn obviously. He knew nothing about business, of course. Well that's clear from what he wrote in the memo. Needed our help, he did. That's why he wrote to us. As members of the Operatic Committee.' Cromwell-Evans lightly smoothed the thick hairs on the back of his left hand with the palm of his right. 'We talked it over on Wednesday morning. In Abel Davies's office.'

'And you decided on a course of action?'

'We decided Huw Prothero should contact Elwyn, that's all.'

'Did you intend he should offer to buy the diaries from Mr Griffith, sir?'

'Good God, no. It was early days for that.' Cromwell-Evans leaned back expansively in the leather chair and fixed Parry with a tolerant smile. 'We intended reading the diaries and then offering poor Elwyn the best advice we could on the way ahead.' He made a throwaway gesture with his right hand. 'I suppose we might have ended up with a joint financial venture, if that seemed the right thing.'

'You mean a joint publishing venture?'

'Possibly. To publish the diaries privately if they were good enough. But it was far too early to say.'

'But Mr Prothero wasn't able to contact Mr Griffith?'

'That's right. By the time Huw rang, Elwyn had left for London.'

Lloyd cleared his throat. 'You were all three at the memorial service for Mrs Spencer Griffith on Tuesday, sir?'

'Yes. Mr Parry knows that.'

'Did Mr Griffith mention the diaries to any of you then?'

'Not to me, he didn't, and not to either of the others, or they'd have told me then or later.'

'Did you find that strange, sir?'

'No stranger than usual for Elwyn. He was a strange bloke altogether. Well, you knew that, Merlin.' Again the speaker directed his words to the chief inspector. 'Possibly he had some idea that telling us about the diaries first off in writing would be the businesslike way of doing things.'

'And on a day when he'd have gone to London by the time you got the information, sir?' asked Parry.

Cromwell-Evans shrugged. 'Who knows? Probably he thought we'd like a day to consider things. Again, I can't imagine why since we'd got nothing to consider except the memo, and there's little enough in that.'

'But didn't it occur to you on Wednesday that he'd gone to London to talk to the two Sunday newspapers he mentioned? To sell one of them the diaries, sir?'

'Oh no, Merlin. Not at all.' The speaker leaned forward, forearms parallel on the table. 'He went to London to get someone to publish his own novels. No doubt about that.

None at all. Lost cause that was, by all accounts, but he kept trying, poor bugger. No, he wouldn't have been offering the diaries. Not before he'd discussed them with us. That was the whole point of writing, wasn't it?'

'Did you think his price was high, sir?'

The chairman of Shevan Electric Markets gave a bewildered frown. 'Price?' He paused. 'Ah, you mean the three hundred grand? Well, there you are again, see? No idea of the price of anything, old Elwyn. You'd think his mother had been Margaret Thatcher. Someone really important. Don't misunderstand me. We all loved Madam Rhonwen. Respected her. But the idea her old diaries would be worth six figures to anybody was a bit bloody hopeful wasn't it? We all three thought that.'

'You don't think Mr Griffith believed they'd be worth it to someone? Not to a publisher, perhaps, but someone who stood to be exposed by them, sir?' asked Lloyd.

At first Cromwell-Evans looked even more bewildered than before, then the heavy eyebrows lifted as his expression changed to one of seemingly profound interest. 'You mean the diaries might really have had something . . . something scandalous in them?' He appeared to give the proposition serious consideration for several moments. 'Oh no. I can't believe that. Can you, Merlin?' He invited Parry's agreement while shaking his huge head several times. 'Madam Rhonwen lived life to the full, but there was nothing wrong or . . . or improper about her. Oh no. That's out of the question.' He leaned back and folded his arms tightly across his chest, still looking for confirmation from Parry, though none was offered.

'Mr Griffith implies in the memo –'

'That the diaries were – what's the word? – uninhibited,' Cromwell-Evans interrupted Lloyd dismissively. 'We decided that was just Elwyn's arty-farty way of saying she was no respecter of the musical establishment. Nothing more was meant.'

'Have you seen the diaries yet, sir?' asked Lloyd after making a note.

'No. Nobody has. Not so far as I know. They'll be at Woodstock Grange somewhere, I expect.' The tone of voice suggested that the unearthing of anything so trivial was a matter of little urgency – without the speaker having to admit that Huw Prothero had spent a good part of the previous afternoon searching the place to no purpose.

'Or at Mr Griffith's cottage in Aberkidy, sir?'

'Well you'll have to ask Alison about that. No rush is there?' And no hope either, he thought bitterly, since Abel Davies must have searched there by now and would have reported if he'd found anything.

'Probably not, sir. And you weren't in touch with Mr Griffith at all during Wednesday?'

'In touch? No. He was in London, wasn't he? How could I have been in touch with him when I didn't know where he was?'

'He didn't telephone you during the day, sir?'

'No.' The sharp monosyllabic answer had been decidedly testy.

'So he didn't respond to the message you had broadcast at Paddington Station at two minutes past nine Wednesday morning, sir?' Parry put in. 'It asked him to go to the station manager's office where they were to tell him to phone your number straightaway. About a sudden illness in his family?'

There was stony silence for a moment, then Cromwell-Evans cleared his throat. 'No, he didn't . . . didn't respond to that,' he answered grudgingly.

'You sure of that, sir?'

'Of course I'm bloody sure. I've told you he never rang me.'

'But if he did contact the station manager's office, sir, and they gave him the message?'

'He didn't act on it.'

'And there was no illness in his family?'

'Of course there wasn't.' He had taken a gold ballpoint pen from his pocket and was pressing the ratchet plunger at the top of it up and down with a nervous frequency.

'So didn't you think it was overdoing it to say there was, sir?'

'Probably.' The speaker's scowl showed no regret over the

point as he went on: 'The people at Paddington weren't cooperative. Not at the start. Wanted reasons why they should broadcast. They were obstructive. So I laid things on a bit. I wanted action. Thought that was the right way to get it.' He stared at Parry belligerently.

'You thought, sir? Mr Prothero and Mr Davies weren't involved?'

'Not at the time, no. I er . . . I'm sure I mentioned it to them later. It was an idea I had in the car on the way here, after I left them.' He was still playing with the ball pen.

'And if he had phoned you, would you have tried to stop him from seeing publishers, or arranged to meet him, or what, sir?'

'I've no idea. It was a spur of the moment thing. I er . . . I wanted to tell him that Huw Prothero would be meeting him in the evening.'

'That's all, sir?'

'That's all, yes.' He put the pen away suddenly and shifted in his seat.

'To shop him showing the diaries to the newspapers?'

'No. I've told you, I didn't think he was going to do that. I just wanted him to know we were ready to help him.'

'I see, sir. And do you know if Mr Griffith phoned Mr Prothero or Mr Davies during the day, sir?'

'No, I don't think he did.'

'And so far as you know, sir, there couldn't be anything in the diaries likely to compromise you or either of the other two gentlemen?'

'Of course not. Good God, Merlin –'

'I'm sorry, sir,' Parry interrupted. 'I'm sure you understand in the circumstances we have to ask these questions.'

'What circumstances?'

'I mean the implications in Mr Griffith's memo. As you suggested, he was inclined to use . . . artistic licence.'

'Yes, artistic licence. That sums it up all right.'

Parry nodded at Lloyd who then asked: 'Could you let us have your copy of the memo, sir? We'll give you a receipt, and you'll get it back in due course, I expect.'

At first Cromwell-Evans seemed undecided, then he

shrugged. 'Have it if you want.' He got up and walked rapidly to his desk. Parry had wondered whether he would then pick up a phone and give his secretary an order, but wasn't surprised when he didn't. Instead, he unlocked a drawer of the desk and withdrew the slip of blue paper from there. 'I don't need it back,' he uttered abruptly as he returned to the table, handing the sheet to Parry.

'Thank you, sir. Sergeant Lloyd will give you a receipt all the same. And now, I wonder would you mind telling us where you were on Wednesday evening?'

Cromwell-Evans was still standing between his seat and the table. 'I might do, yes. Why d'you want to know?'

'Just routine, sir. We have to account for the movements of everyone involved in a case —'

'So I'm involved in a case now? Suspected of something, am I? All because of a piddling bloody memo?' His face had turned nearly puce with welling anger. A raised vein on the left side of his forehead was pulsing fiercely. 'Well let me tell you, Mr Chief Inspector, where I was on Wednesday night is my business, and had nothing to do with Elwyn Griffith or his death. Nothing whatsoever.' Planting clenched fists on the table top he leaned over towards Parry. 'When and if required by law, I'll account for all my movements from New Year's Day to now, if need be. Until then, like every honest citizen, I'm entitled to my privacy. That's right, isn't it?'

11

'Sorry if I kept you waiting, Mr Parry. Early meeting across at the Council Offices,' said Prothero as he hurried in through the front door of his own building. 'Cesspools,' he added in such a sharp and disparaging tone that the policeman wondered if it had been intended as an expletive and not an explanation. 'Chairman of the Drains Committee needed some legal advice,' the lawyer completed, resolving the point. 'If I'd known you were coming —'

'I haven't been here long, sir,' Parry put in, getting up from his seat in the reception area. It was less than twenty minutes since he and Lloyd had left Cromwell-Evans and driven to Tawrbach. 'Your receptionist just got me this cup of coffee.'

'Good. Bring it with you into my office, won't you?'

'Excuse me, Mr Prothero, there was an urgent message from Mr Cromwell-Evans,' his secretary offered as the two men passed her desk. She was a mature, married woman of austere appearance who knew her business priorities. Paying clients, even impatient and often rude ones like Cromwell-Evans, normally rated precedence over casual callers like policemen. 'He asked, could you ring him straightaway? He's been on twice. I tried to leave a message at the Council Offices, but they weren't sure who you were with.'

Prothero's nose twitched, and his moustache in sympathy with it. 'I don't recall receiving any message. They're not as conscientious over there as you are, Mrs Harris. I'll speak to Mr Cromwell-Evans when I've finished seeing the chief inspector.'

'Don't mind me, sir, if you want to make a call. Privately,' Parry volunteered, hesitating on the threshold of Prothero's office.

'No, no. Later will do well enough. Sit down, won't you?'

'As a matter of fact, I've just come from seeing Mr Cromwell-Evans.'

'Indeed?' Prothero was satisfied with the way he had handled the exchange about not recalling any message. He had recalled it well enough – and could admit as much later, if necessary, without seriously impugning his veracity. One couldn't be expected to remember everything. He had also acted on the message, using a payphone in the hall of the Council Offices. So he had been forewarned by Cromwell-Evans of the reason for Parry's no doubt imminent visit. Even so he felt it was more prudent to seem innocently unaware of the appearance of Parry's copy memo. Otherwise it might look as if he was involved in some kind of conspiracy. 'Now, what can I do for you, Mr Parry?'

'I've received a photoprint copy of this memo, sir. It was sent to me anonymously.' Parry passed the single sheet across the desk, then took a sip of his coffee while watching Prothero's face register interest as much as surprise. 'I understand from Mr Cromwell-Evans that you and he and Mr Davies got an original signed copy each in the post on Wednesday morning.'

'I got my copy in the first post on Wednesday, yes.'

'Might I see it, sir?'

'Certainly. I think it's in here somewhere.' Prothero got out his key ring, unlocked the centre drawer of his desk, and removed a transparent folder from it. 'Ah yes, here it is.' He lifted the blue sheet of paper from the folder and passed it across. There was nothing else in the folder.

Parry began comparing the copy with his own – after noting that Prothero also kept what Cromwell-Evans had coolly implied was an innocuous document under private lock and key. 'The signature on yours looks identical to the one on the Cromwell-Evans copy, sir,' he said.

'Is that surprising? Presumably Elwyn Griffith signed both of them?'

Parry shook his head. 'A marginal difference might have shown whether my copy was a photoprint of either of them.'

'But you say there is no difference? Well, it's a very simple signature, isn't it? Childish, almost. There's still Mr Davies's copy, I suppose?'

'That's right. Sergeant Lloyd is with Mr Davies now. Has your copy been photoprinted do you know, sir?'

'No, it hasn't.' The answer was unexpectedly adamant, and it came swiftly.

Parry's head inclined a little to the left. 'You didn't mention the memo when we met here this time yesterday, sir.'

'Should I have done? It skipped my memory, I expect, or it didn't seem especially relevant, Mr Parry.'

The policeman hesitated, his lips shaping as though he was about to start whistling before he asked: 'Except it was why you offered to meet Mr Griffith off the train Wednesday night, wasn't it, sir?'

'Mr Cromwell-Evans said that, did he?'

'Is it true, sir?'

'No, it isn't. It was one of the reasons, certainly. But as I've told you already, there were many reasons why I needed to see Elwyn Griffith. Why I'd been trying to get hold of him for weeks. The memo invented another reason, but still not as pressing as some of the others had become.'

'But pressing enough if he was going to see a Sunday newspaper with the diaries when he was in London?'

'That would have been highly unlikely. As he says in the memo, he was er . . . offering the diaries to the Operatic Committee. Very proper too, in a way. He could hardly have sold them to a newspaper as well. That's always assuming they were saleable at all. My view –'

'You don't think his offer to you was . . . was actually an attempt at blackmail, sir?' Parry interrupted, breaking the sentence into two and accelerating his delivery at the end. 'That's in view of what he calls the uninhibited nature of the diaries?'

The lawyer gave a solemn frown, as though he was considering such a possibility for the first time: this was more or less the performance the policeman had expected. It matched

Cromwell-Evans's affected reaction to a similar question.

'I've thought about it. Oh yes. But really I don't believe that can be the case.' Prothero was speaking with deliberation, as though they were debating aesthetics not criminal intent. He opened his fingers and brought the tips together lightly over his pinstripe waistcoat. 'We all three came to the conclusion that he meant the word "uninhibited" to mean honest – or forthright, perhaps. To indicate, d'you see, that the diaries pulled no punches in describing Madam Rhonwen's involvements in . . . in the public arena? To illustrate, Mr Parry, you should know that her dealings with what she liked to call the Welsh musical Tafia were frequently acrimonious. Oh yes. She often disagreed with BBC Wales, with the leaders of many of the well-known Welsh choirs, the eminent organist at Llandaff Cathedral, and many other powerful elements in the musical and artistic establishment.'

'And you think Mr Griffith used the words "explicit" and "frank" in the same way, sir?'

'Yes, I do. I suspect in an effort to er . . . to dress up the merchandise he was offering. I'm sure he didn't really believe a London publisher would be interested in the diaries of a lady of . . . of only local celebrity, and as morally exemplary as his mother. And that would surely apply to a national newspaper as well.' The speaker shrugged. 'More's the pity, but there it is. I'm afraid Madam Rhonwen was too good, in all senses, for her journal to appeal to common people. No, no. Plainly Elwyn was hoping that Mr Davies, Mr Cromwell-Evans and I would have the diaries published privately, as a memorial to his dear mother. He used loaded words to stimulate our interest. Quite unnecessary, of course.'

'Except he expected you to pay three hundred thousand for the privilege of having your interest stimulated, sir?'

The fingertips flew apart about a foot and froze there a moment, while the chin lifted. 'I don't believe for one minute that was really so. As I said before, he was window dressing, wasn't he? Giving the merchandise an excitement greater than it rated. That's in the purely commercial sense, of course. No doubt he'd have backed down over price. Given us the diaries for nothing probably, provided we agreed to have them published.' He leaned forward and sucked in his cheeks. 'That's the crux of it, Mr Parry. I have to say that I'm afraid Elwyn was a mean man by nature.' Coming from one of the reputedly meanest men in the district, Parry found the last remark comical. 'Of course,' Prothero continued, 'you can hardly blame him for that. His mother never exactly spoiled him with money. And he never earned much. Recently, nothing at all.'

'He's come into money now though, hasn't he?'

'Ah, but old habits die hard. Once he realized it might become someone's public duty to publish the diaries, he was no doubt anxious to prevent that duty from devolving on himself. Shifting the onus on to the Operatic Committee probably seemed an obvious solution.'

It was a point of view.

Parry reached for his coffee cup. 'So you and the other two gentlemen didn't feel the memo was in any way a threat to your reputations, sir?'

'Good gracious me, no. A threat to our chequebooks perhaps.'

'If you agreed to pay for the publishing? Nothing more than that?'

'That's right. The chequebook of Mr Cromwell-Evans more than Mr Davies and myself, because he's reputed to be so well off.' The lawyer's tone became conspiratorial. 'It was he Elwyn was targeting, no doubt.'

'Thank you, sir. That's a very interesting hypothesis.' Parry smoothed his right cheek twice with the flat of his left hand. 'And you're sure you had no contact at all with Mr Griffith at any time on Wednesday, sir?'

'None. I thought I'd told you that?'

'You had, sir, but things sometimes slip one's mind and . . . and come back later.' The policeman beamed encouragingly.

Prothero swallowed and shook his head. Fleetingly he even thought of saying he now recalled getting the message at the Council Offices after all, but then decided against it.

'Were you surprised when Mr Cromwell-Evans told you he'd had Mr Griffith broadcast for at Paddington Station?

That's after he'd left you and Mr Davies on Wednesday morning. After you'd met to er . . . to discuss the memo.'

Prothero had been surprised all right when Cromwell-Evans had told him as much for the very first time on the telephone in the Council Offices not ten minutes before this. 'I thought it a sensible initiative, Mr Parry,' he answered guardedly. 'There was no response, of course.' He was taking Cromwell-Evans's word for that, except a doubt now suddenly arose in his mind. What if . . . ?

'Quite so, sir.' Parry looked down at the small notebook in his hand. 'I wonder could we now just fill in the details of what you did while you were waiting to meet that last train on Wednesday night?'

The lawyer wiggled his shoulders and straightened his tie. 'If you think it's relevant to your investigations, Mr Parry.'

'It helps if we can know where everyone was at any given time that evening, sir.'

'I er . . . I understand.' Though from the hesitancy in the voice, the understanding was tinged with caution and apprehension – like the kind of understanding people glean from reading a video tape recorder handbook.

'You mentioned having coffee with a friend. Could you let me have his or her name and address? Oh, and could you tell me where you had the coffee, sir?' He'd had it checked. It would have to have been at one of the hotels, everywhere else around the station was shut by midnight.

Prothero seemed to brighten a little. 'Actually it er . . . it was in a caravan, Mr Parry. Or a mobile home, as I think they're called nowadays. This one was very comfortable. It was parked near the station.'

'I see, sir. And the name of the friend?' Parry's voice had lifted noticeably at the end of the question.

The lawyer made a noise that was somewhere between a short giggle and a dry gargle. 'It wasn't exactly a friend. More a brief acquaintance. Ships that pass in the night, you might say. It was a lady – charming person – who made herself known to me. Let me see, her name was er . . .' He made the noise again, only louder. 'It was er . . . Desirée. Yes, that was it. I don't believe she told me her surname. She's an exhibition organizer.'

'He was with a bird he picked up called Desirée? In a caravan? At the station? Was she a Tom then, boss?' asked Detective Sergeant Lloyd, ten minutes later.

Parry and Lloyd were seated at a window table upstairs in The Slice of Cake. This was Tawrbach's least fashionable but also least expensive coffee shop and patisserie. The place had started life as *Y Teisen Llaeth*, which means The Milk Cake, but not too many of the customers had known how to pronounce that, and fewer still had known what it meant. It was still too early for the regular mid-morning clientele, and the policemen had what the proprietor termed the upper coffee lounge to themselves. There was no lower coffee lounge — only some tables set outside on the pavement in the summer.

'She couldn't have been a prostitute. Otherwise he wouldn't have admitted meeting her, or going back to her caravan,' said Parry, breaking a piece off the rock cake he had chosen, and sorry now that he hadn't had a peach tartlet like Lloyd — who had actually had a peach tartlet and a rum baba, and eaten the rum baba before his boss had arrived. 'Though he was quite adamant it was she picked him up, not the other way round,' the chief inspector continued. 'Seemed to think it was some kind of tribute to his personal magnetism.'

'Not if she was on the game, it wasn't. Not difficult to know what sort of exhibitions she puts on either. Let's hope Mr Prothero wasn't filmed in one of them without knowing.' Lloyd slurped up some of his coffee, to wash down a mouthful of tartlet.

'Prothero said she was meeting her daughter at the station,' said Parry, still only toying with his cake. He hadn't ordered anything to drink. 'They were going to tour Pembroke in the caravan.'

'Well, they shouldn't be hard to find this time of year, boss. That's if they exist at all. Not so many caravans on the road till Easter. Not much to go on though. The caravan was white, he said? Anyway, we'll get on to it.' The sergeant scribbled in the notebook he had open on the table, wedged awkwardly between his cup and his now empty plate. 'Could be kosher. I mean he wouldn't have invented a woman called —'

'Desirée,' Parry completed. 'No, not in the circumstances. I thought that. And he was so relaxed about it too, after being a bit uptight earlier.'

'That was because he'd lied probably about not talking to Mr Cromwell-Evans, boss.'

Parry nodded. 'I think that's right. Anyway, he doesn't seem to have twigged yet he's in line as a murder suspect. And you say Abel Davies was the same?'

'Definitely, boss.' The sergeant had already reported that the estate agent had dismissed the suggestion that Griffith had been threatening blackmail in his memo. 'According to Mr Davies, Mr Griffith just wanted the three of them to pay for publishing the diaries.'

'Without having to cough up any three hundred thousand. Well that's the party line all right. And it might be difficult to fault as well.'

'Except that's not the way the memo read to you and me, boss.'

Parry nodded slowly, and thought for a moment. 'And Davies denied Cromwell-Evans had called him after we left?' he said, frowning.

'Yes. I didn't ask him till near the end of the interview. It threw him, and I'll swear he was lying.'

'Well, we can find out easily enough if Cromwell-Evans called any of his numbers. Doesn't he realize that?'

'People don't, boss.' Lloyd blew his nose. 'You know,' he went on, putting away his handkerchief, 'not one of those three has a complete alibi for the two hours starting at eleven on Wednesday night. Mr Prothero was with a bird from midnight, except he hasn't proved she exists yet. Mr Davies told me he was on the road back from a business dinner in Merthyr around eleven-fifteen, got a flat tyre, changed it himself, doesn't know exactly when, or how long it took, and got home at half past twelve.'

'And Cromwell-Evans refuses to explain his whereabouts

altogether. Meaning he was almost certainly with a woman, I suppose,' said Parry.

'And doesn't trust us not to tell his wife, boss?'

'His father-in-law, more likely. That's Stanley Johns, the builder. He's the real money behind Shevan Electric Markets. Well, that was always the rumour round here.'

'Motive for the murder there then, chief?'

'Possibly. If the diaries proved Cromwell-Evans had been philandering, Mr Johns definitely wouldn't like it.'

'Old-fashioned, is he?'

'Again, that's what they say.' Parry sat up straighter. 'Well, we gave Cromwell-Evans the gypsy's warning. If he refuses information next time we'll charge him with obstruction. Let me see those memos.'

Lloyd opened the hard black document case on his lap, and produced two copies of the memo from it. One was a photoprint of the copy left at the Tawrbach Police Station, the other, now in a plastic folder, was the signed original delivered to Abel Davies which the sergeant had just acquired from the owner. 'That's the one yours was copied from. No doubt. The signature's identical. Look at that slip on the ''r'' of Griffith.'

Parry studied the two, nodded, then passed the folder back to Lloyd. 'Prothero was right when he said the signature was childish,' he remarked. 'If it was that copy, we still need to know whether it was made by Griffith after he'd signed it, or by Davies after he got it. You say Davies admits one copy was made from his original?'

'That's it, boss. But he swears no other copies have been made. Not from either of them.'

'So why did he make a copy in the first place?'

'He didn't, boss. His wife did.'

'On his orders?'

'Not exactly. It was she opened the envelope when it arrived on Wednesday. She made the copy then, straightaway.'

'Without his knowing?'

'Yes. Except he says she told him later. But he swears neither of the copies have been out of their sight since.'

'Except they won't have been taking them to bed.' Parry sniffed, and pushed his plate away from him. He had gone off rock cakes. 'Anyway, if we accept his word, meaning the thing was copied by Griffith after he signed it, we still want to know who delivered it to the police here twenty-four hours after his death.'

'Someone he told to take it there, addressed to you, boss? That's if anything happened to him?'

Parry screwed up his face. 'I thought of that. Bit melodramatic.'

'Not when you remember there's reputations at stake.'

'But for a start, he couldn't have known I'd be in charge of the case, assuming anything did happen to him.'

'Ah, but he knew you personally?'

'Only just.'

'Even so, he'd have known you were in the Major Crime Support Unit.'

'He might have done.'

'Well, at least he knew you were a copper. Had enough of that cake, have you, boss?' Lloyd added in the same breath. He never let food go to waste.

Parry pushed the plate further across the table. 'Did you get samples of the copying paper they use at Davies's office?'

'Yes, boss.' Lloyd was now chewing again. He tapped the document case. 'To the naked eye, it looks the same colour as the sort your memo was done on.'

'Hm, which means it's the same as the specimens we got from the other two offices. Well, Forensic can sort that out.' Parry pinched the end of his nose. 'So when are you seeing Mrs Davies?'

'I'll try again in a minute. At their house. I went there after I left her husband. She wasn't in though.' Lloyd looked at the time. 'I left a message with the gardener saying I'd be back about now.'

'And it was Davies who suggested you see her?'

'That's right, boss. To explain why she copied the memo. Said it'd be better coming from her. Oh, and that it wasn't his idea, her showing the copy to anyone else.'

'You asked him who she showed it to?'

'Yes, I—' Lloyd jumped when the portable phone in his pocket began bleeping. 'Flaming thing,' he said, after pulling it out and then pressing the wrong button. 'Sorry, boss. Hang on, will you?' he said into the machine, then looked up. 'Dead end for us, I'm afraid, that one. It was the rector she took it to. The Reverend Watkins.'

12

'The cottage wasn't being watched then, Mr Parry?' asked Sally Lovelaw, business partner to Alison, and wife of Tony, the animal feeds manager. There was nothing accusing about her tone, just a simple, uncomplicated inquiry from a simple, uncomplicated woman. She was fortyish, short, and dark, with a concerned look on her ruddy face which was devoid of any form of make-up. A bit plump, she was wearing a knee-length, fawn mac over a chunky skirt and sweater, all of which made her look even plumper. She had driven Alison to Aberkidy from their shop in Tawrbach as soon as they got the news of the burglary. They had arrived ten minutes ahead of Parry who had also come from Tawrbach. He had learned of the break-in some time after them. Sergeant Lloyd had meanwhile gone back to Rumney Police Station.

The call on Lloyd's mobile phone in the coffee shop had been from the incident room at Rumney to report that Alison Griffith's cottage had been turned over by an intruder. Alison's cleaning woman, a Mrs Tidmarsh, had found the back door of the cottage forced when she had arrived at ten o'clock. Mrs Tidmarsh had telephoned Alison, first at Perdita's bungalow, which Alison had already left, then at the shop. It was Sally Lovelaw who had eventually alerted the police.

'We haven't been watching the cottage permanently, no. But it's been on the patrol cars' regular beat since yesterday,' said Parry, conscious that his answer might sound less than satisfactory to the questioner. Although he knew her husband fairly well, he had only met Mrs Lovelaw on one or two previous occasions.

'And were the police in the patrol cars meant to check the premises when they went past?' she pressed.

'They weren't specifically instructed to do that, no. They would have done, if they'd seen anything unusual, of course.' Nor, he thought to himself, had there been any real reason to have a policeman permanently stationed outside Mrs Griffith's door either, particularly since she hadn't been at home since early last evening – a fact that unfortunately now put a different complexion on things. He turned to Alison. 'I'm very sorry, Mrs Griffith. I wish you could have been spared this, on top of everything else. Or spared seeing it till we'd got it tidied up a bit, at least.'

The three were in the living room of the cottage where it seemed every drawer had been pulled out, every picture unhooked, every cushion and chair overturned, and every rug dragged back. The disturbance had been even worse next door in Elwyn Griffith's study. There the disarranged furniture and floor were shrouded in sheets of typescript, like bits of giant confetti, with books, and folders and their contents scattered indiscriminately by a despoiler whose actions appeared to have been little short of demented. And the upper floor had been as savagely assaulted as the lower: an angry Alison had just come down from there.

A sergeant and constable in uniform, plus two detectives from Parry's team, were in the study looking for anything that might help to identify the intruder while, at the same time, trying to produce some order out of the chaos. Attempts had already been made to find fingerprints around the damaged back door but the civilian in charge of that part of the operation had decided the candidate area around the broken lock had evidently been wiped clean.

'But what did he want, for God's sake?' asked Alison, still seething. Abruptly she moved across to the CD player in the corner, knelt down and began retrieving the discs that had been scattered on the floor, making haphazard piles of them. 'This is wanton, isn't it? There's not even anything missing. Not that I can see, anyway. It's just gratuitous bloody destruction.' She turned sharply and knocked over one of the CD piles. There were tears in her eyes. 'Bugger him, whoever he is. Bastard,' she uttered, holding back a sob with difficulty and wiping her eyes with the back of one hand.

Parry knelt to help her with the discs. Sally Lovelaw took off her coat and went quietly to the fireplace at the far end of the room to begin a more methodical clear-up from there.

'I'm not so sure this was gratuitous,' said Parry, after a few moments. 'Whoever did it was probably after something specific. And he or she worked in a systematic way. In a hurry though, which accounts for the mess.'

'OK, so what was he or she looking for?' Alison demanded hotly, though not as hotly as before. She sat back on her heels.

'At a guess, a pure guess, I'd say Madam Rhonwen's diaries.'

'Her what?'

'Her diaries. Your husband had them. He was er . . . thinking of having them published. You didn't know anything about them?'

She frowned, stopped what she was doing entirely, and was suddenly much calmer. 'Don't think so. He may have mentioned them, I suppose. Honestly I don't remember. But why would anyone ransack my home for Rhonwen's diaries?' She got up, holding a pile of discs.

Parry did the same. 'This might explain,' he said. He put the discs down on a side table and took a copy of the memo from his pocket to hand to her.

She read the text through quickly, her brow creasing as she did so. Then her eyes went back to the top of the sheet. 'It's dated last Tuesday. The day of the service. The day before . . .' She swallowed without finishing the sentence, then began a new one: 'Did copies go to all three of these people?'

'Yes. In the post. They got them Wednesday morning. You've never seen the memo before?'

'No.' She picked up the cushions belonging to one of the armchairs, plumped them, put them back in the chair and sat in it. Then she read the memo again.

'I was sent a photocopy of what we think must have been Mr Davies's signed copy this morning. Anonymously. That's a copy of it. Does the signature look authentic to you?'

She studied the foot of the document carefully. 'Yes. That's Elwyn's signature all right.'

'I wonder would you mind if we take your husband's computer away for a day or two? I want to see if we can find the text of the memo in it, plus any letters he may have written about appointments for his London trip?'

Alison hesitated for a second. 'No . . . no, I don't mind. Take it. But I told you, he'd given up making appointments.'

'But he might have written to people he aimed to call on at some point?' She nodded, though her expression was still doubtful. Parry opened his document case and withdrew a piece of light blue A4 paper. 'All the top copies of the memo were on paper like this. I just picked this piece up off the floor in the study. There was quite a lot of it there. Did your husband normally use it for correspondence?'

'Not normally. Only if he wanted to impress. It's continuation paper really. Matches the letterhead they used at the poly when he was there. He nicked enough when he left to last for quite a bit. Envelopes too. They weren't overprinted. Elwyn was a great grafter.' She gave a nostalgic smile, then jerked her head up. 'And you've spoken to Mr Prothero and the others?'

'Yes.'

'Had any of them spoken to Elwyn after they got the memo?'

'There was no chance. If you remember, Mr Prothero called him here on Wednesday morning but he'd left already.'

'I remember. Is this why he offered to meet Elwyn that night instead of me?'

'He needed to see him about the memo, and other things, he says.' Parry pulled over an upright chair and sat on it close to Alison. 'Could you say what you think your husband had in mind when he wrote the memo?'

'How d'you mean? I imagine he meant what he said. Either

they bought the diaries or he sold them to a newspaper. Sounds as if they could be salacious, doesn't it?'

Parry glanced across at Sally Lovelaw who was still busy at the far end of the room. 'We don't know that for sure, of course. If they were, could he have been intending some kind of . . . of blackmail?' He had put the question in a much lowered voice.

There was another abrupt sideways and upward movement of the pretty head. 'No. Not in the way you mean. Elwyn wouldn't have wanted to blackmail Mr Prothero. Or the others. He didn't really need money either. Not any more.' She paused for a second. 'It would have been more . . . more getting his own back. On his mother. Her memory. Doing down her reputation as a paragon of all the virtues.' She ran a well-manicured, tapered finger ruminatively beneath her chin. 'I suppose he thought the three of them would pay to stop him doing that. And he'd have taken their money. To teach them a lesson for crawling to her for all those years. Still, I'm not sure he was right. About their paying up, I mean.'

'Unless it also meant protecting their own reputations, which brings it back to blackmail, I'm afraid.'

Now she was studying the flower pattern on the chair arm. 'Meaning they'd been involved in orgies or something? At Woodstock Grange?' She looked up and straight into Parry's eyes. 'It's possible, I suppose. Were they going to pay?'

'They intended asking to see the diaries before committing themselves to anything.'

'That was smart of them.' She arched her back and crossed her legs, dropping a hand to smooth down her skirt.

'Of course, the diaries may well be harmless in the moral sense,' Parry offered. 'In fact, it'd be fairly surprising if they weren't. Bear in mind Madam Rhonwen left them for your husband to find after her death.'

Her chin lifted. 'Except that's not what happened, is it? Rhonwen regarded herself as indestructible. She was never expecting to die. Elwyn must just have come across them.'

'I see what you mean.' Her denial of his supposition had

been quite spirited. 'Do you think he took the diaries to London?'

She looked about the still devastated room. 'Well, the burglar didn't think so. Not if you're right about the reason for the break-in.' She sniffed. 'Elwyn could have taken them with him on Wednesday, I suppose.'

'But you didn't see him put them in his briefcase?'

'No. But I didn't actually see him put anything else in it either. Like those manuscripts he took.'

'We've talked to the two newspapers. He didn't go to see either of them. Nor to any book publishers. Well, not so far as we've discovered. There are a lot of them we haven't checked with yet.'

'But if he was selling the diaries to Mr Prothero and the others, he wouldn't have been touting them around London anyway, would he?'

'Possibly not. So if he left them here, would he have locked them up for safety? And if so, where?'

'Depends on how big they were. In the centre drawer of his desk, probably. Except I think he'd lost the key to that.' She gave an excusing little sigh over this further example of her late husband's ineptitudes. 'There's a steel document box in the study,' she added. 'Belonged to Elwyn's father. He locked things in that sometimes. One of your policemen asked me about it before you came. They found it open and empty. The lock hasn't been forced, but Elwyn could have lost the key to that as well. Everything in the centre drawer of the desk was tipped on the floor. I didn't see anything that looked like diaries.' She thought for a moment. 'They could be at Woodstock Grange, couldn't they? There's a safe there.'

'They're not there. As Madam Rhonwen's executor, Mr Prothero has access to everything at the Grange, including a key to the safe —'

'So he's had a bloody good look,' she interrupted. 'I don't blame him either.' Then, suddenly, her gaze hardened. 'But I will if he's just done the same here.'

'Come in, Mr Parry. I was told to expect a Sergeant Lloyd, was it?' said Megan Davies. She had opened the front door to its full width with an almost military alacrity. Parry would not have been surprised if she had saluted him – though since he was hatless he would not have known how to respond. In contrast to the Guides outfit she'd had on the last time he had seen her, Mrs Davies was wearing a green WVS uniform jacket and skirt, with a matching cap. Under the jacket she had a starched white blouse and black bootlace tie. Her face was healthily flushed, as though she had just completed some difficult job with a will.

'My sergeant had to go back to Cardiff. I was quite close. Shan't keep you long. Hope we haven't inconvenienced you.'

'No, no. I've finished Meals on Wheels for today. I'm not due for my volunteer hospital driving till half past one.' She directed her visitor into the dining room, and, after indicating he should sit at the head of the table, seated herself to his right. 'It's easier in here than the sitting room. Since you'll want to make notes,' she completed, as though she had worked out the logistics of a police visit in advance.

It was twelve-forty. The oblong mahogany table wasn't laid for lunch. Parry wondered if she took her own meals on wheels. 'You're very busy with charity work, Mrs Davies.' He took out his notebook more so that she shouldn't be disappointed than because he actually needed it.

'This is quite a light day,' she replied, without appearing to be joking, although her visitor didn't feel certain of that because of the natural tight set of her lips.

'Your husband isn't here?'

'No.' She looked about her sharply as if to make sure, then stretched out her arms and adjusted both pairs of jacket and blouse cuffs in turn. 'He usually has lunch at the office. And today he's gone to Bridgend, about some houses. Don't think he'll be back in Tawrbach yet. I wasn't aware you wanted to see him too.'

'I don't. Sergeant Lloyd saw him earlier.'

'My husband told me, yes. So is this about my showing the Elwyn Griffith memo to the rector?' she continued, in a so-let's-have-done-with-it kind of tone.

'Yes. I gather you'd made a copy of the memo. Did you

show it to anyone else? I mean other than the rector?'

'No.' She pushed her intimidatingly heavy spectacles up the sharp bridge of her nose, and lifted her gaze to take in the moving figure of an elderly man in a padded jacket who was visible through the window. He was pushing a laden wheelbarrow along the lawn. Mrs Davies opened her mouth as if to say something, then closed it again as the man stopped. She continued to watch him, evidently waiting on his next movement – except for several seconds he stood stock-still, breathing out hot vapour. Mrs Davies's lips began to separate again, just before the elderly man grasped a shovel with unexpected vigour from on top of his load and thrust it deep into the barrow's contents. Then she gave a gratified nod, and returned her whole attention to the policeman. A wood-chipping mulch was about to be applied to the azaleas.

'And exactly when did you show the memo to the rector?' Parry asked, having been almost as interested as Mrs Davies in the silent tableau just enacted.

'Let me see, it was in the church vestry. After the ten o'clock communion service on Wednesday morning. I polish the communion vessels and the moveable brasses on Wednesday. There was no one else present.'

'Thank you.' He wondered idly if there was regulation ecclesiastical garb she put on for the job. 'And did Mr Davies know you'd shown the memo to the rector?'

'Certainly,' she replied with asperity, almost before the question was completed. 'He told your sergeant that, I'm sure.' The implication was that if her husband had failed to do so he'd better look out.

Parry moistened his lips: he'd been equally sure on the point, but witnesses are not always consistent. 'Could you say whether there was any special reason why –'

'I showed it to Caradog Watkins?' she interrupted, sitting up even straighter than before and pulling down the front of her jacket. 'Or course there was. I needed to involve a reliable third party.'

'Involve him in what exactly, Mrs Davies?'

She took a deep breath. 'In the fact that my husband and I have no secrets from each other. That there was no possible reason why he should fear the publication of the diaries because of something he'd done, or because I wouldn't approve of something he'd done.'

'So the rector was to be a sort of sleeping advance witness to that? To come forward and say so if required?'

'That's it.'

'In what circumstances, Mrs Davies?'

'Difficult to foresee, of course.' It was her first even mildly evasive answer.

There was silence for a moment. 'And your husband approved of your showing the memo to the rector?'

'Yes, he did.'

'Did you tell him you were going to? In advance, I mean.'

'No. I didn't tell him till yesterday. He saw the good sense of it, of course.'

'I see. Could I ask, what was the rector's reaction to the memo?'

'He was surprised to know Madam Rhonwen kept a diary.'

'Did he have a view on Elwyn Griffith's motives in writing the memo?'

'I think you'd better ask him that yourself.'

'I intended to do that this morning, but there's been no one in at the rectory.'

She looked at her watch. 'Should be. She may have been out, but he's usually there after mid-morning on Fridays.'

'I'll try again after I leave you. Did you suggest to the rector that he should keep the contents of the memo to himself?'

'That was quite unnecessary, I assure you. It was he who cautioned me to do the same. What passed between us was a sacred exchange, Mr Parry. Like in the confessional. Not that we're high church.'

'Quite. And the rector didn't make a copy of the memo?'

'Certainly not.'

'Or have the opportunity to make a copy without your knowing?'

The frown on her face prepared him to be admonished for suggesting such a thing, but her reply when it came was a simple negative.

'Incidentally,' Parry continued, 'Mr Davies told Sergeant

Lloyd you're both against his being a party to buying the diaries?'

'Yes. And to stopping them from being published. Matter of indifference to my husband, that is. To both of us, in fact.'

'But you feel that other people might want the diaries suppressed?'

'That's up to them, isn't it?'

'True. But has it occurred to you that those same people might use unlawful means to get their way?'

'Violence you mean?' She hesitated. 'Elwyn Griffith died in suspicious circumstances, didn't he?' Her eyes narrowed to slits, and her chin receded even further into her neck.

'What makes you think that, Mrs Davies?'

'Well, for a start, you're here, aren't you? And you only see to very serious crimes, not things like car theft or burglary. Everybody knows that.'

'Burglary sometimes comes into my work.'

'Like the one last night at Alison Griffith's? But that's different, isn't it?'

'You know about that?'

'Meals on Wheels covers more than meat and two veg, Mr Parry. Somebody after the diaries, were they?'

'Difficult to say.' He smiled and put his hands on the wooden arms of the chair as if he was preparing to leave. 'Well, thank you very much, Mrs Davies. You've been very helpful. And frank.'

'No reason for not being, is there? And all said and done, it's very sad about Elwyn's death. Especially for his wife.'

Parry waited before getting up. 'One last question,' he said. 'It's really your opinion the memo didn't pose a threat to your husband?'

'I don't think Elwyn was trying to blackmail Abel, if that's what you mean.' She squeezed the thin lips together slowly. 'Blackmail only works if the victim's afraid something's about to be exposed. Something unsavoury. Well there couldn't be anything like that about Abel, not in Rhonwen's diaries. I'd know,' she ended with stolid conviction.

'I see. So you think the purpose of the memo —'

'Was to get the three of them to have the diaries printed

at their own expense,' she cut in. 'Because no one else would. No question of that, Mr Parry.'

'What about the money he asked for?'

'That was bluff. He didn't expect to get a penny. Or need to.' The party line certainly seemed solid enough. 'Anyway, Elwyn was too vulnerable himself to risk threatening others,' she added with a nod, lips closing tighter than ever.

'Vulnerable? In what way, Mrs Davies?'

'Nothing I'd want to repeat, Mr Parry. Not about someone just dead.'

13

'It'll have to be instant coffee. I'm out of the real till I go shopping tomorrow. Is that all right?' asked Perdita Jones, reaching into one of the high cupboards in her kitchen. She was in her professional outfit – a crisp white blouse with short sleeves and a knee-length skirt, except that the skirt rode up higher when she stretched for the coffee.

'Never have anything but instant at the flat,' Parry answered, unpacking the things he had brought and, at the same time, admiring the backs of her knees.

'That's because there's no one there to look after you.'

'You know the post is vacant whenever you want it?'

But Perdita refused to be drawn further on the subject, staying poker faced as she spooned the Nescafé grains into the cups. 'Sweet of you to bring the sandwiches,' she said. 'Smoked salmon too. From the deli, are they? And strawberries. There's a treat. They'll be lovely.'

'I got some cream too. The non-fattening kind. Since you wouldn't come out to lunch, I didn't have an option really.' He had called her on his portable phone from Church Lane when he had left Megan Davies, and after again failing to find the rector at home.

'I did offer you an egg. This is much grander. Anyway, I really couldn't have gone out to lunch today. I've got a string of patients coming, starting in half an hour. Except I bet the first one's late.' Friday was one of her private practice days.

'Perhaps I should come for treatment. I've got this terrible ache in my –'

'No,' she interrupted flatly, but this time having to try

harder to avoid showing her amusement. 'If you'd given me a bit of notice,' she added, 'I might have been able to rearrange things today. Here, I'll do those in the colander.'

He had taken the strawberries to top and wash at the sink. 'Well anyway, this suits me fine,' he said. 'I'll have one more go at the rectory when we've eaten, then I have to be back at the station.'

Their hands touched accidentally as he tumbled the fruit into the colander, and she hadn't drawn hers away. Earlier he had been half expecting her to make an excuse not to see him. In the circumstances she could have done so with justification. But she hadn't. Instead, as she said, she had pleaded pressure of work, but still offered him an egg and a cup of coffee in her kitchen. When she made the offer it had sounded to him more enthusiastic than just polite, or perhaps that was wishful thinking on his part. Whenever they were together it was clear there was still an interval before she stopped being firmly on her guard – but he was persuading himself that the interval was getting shorter.

'Was Alison very cut up about the burglary?' she asked later when they were settled at the table.

'Very. In fact more than . . . well, yes, very upset.'

'You were going to say more than by Elwyn's death, weren't you?'

'Was I? This was a different sort of upset. And coming on top of the other, you can understand her letting go the way she did.'

'She's not as cool as you might think about losing Elwyn. Only outwardly. She's good at controlling her emotions, that's all. Though maybe not so much over the burglary. She put a lot into making that cottage nice. Really nice. Some yobo wrecking it must have made her crazy mad.'

'It did, yes.' He wiped a crumb from his chin. 'How was she when she was here last night?'

Perdita opened her eyes wider. 'Is this a professional visit after all?'

'No. I'm just interested. As a friend.'

'She was very loose. Keen to work at the shop today. To take her mind off things. We had a good evening. Lots of girl talk. I gather she told you she's pregnant.' He nodded in response. Perdita hesitated. 'She wanted to know if you'd told me anything more about Elwyn's death,' she went on. 'When you came yesterday.'

'That was understandable. Anyway, she's up to date on everything since I saw her this morning.'

'Was it murder?'

He made a quizzical face. 'Officially that'll be up to a coroner's jury. But . . . yes, I think it was murder.'

'But the burglary wasn't connected, was it?'

'Might have been.' He opened his hands. 'We're in the dark still about that.' And a lot of other things, he reminded himself.

'I felt awful when I heard. Sally rang me. I mean if Alison had been at home last night instead of here, the cottage wouldn't have been empty, so a burglar wouldn't have –'

'Broken in? I wouldn't be too sure,' Parry interrupted. It was a concern that was still very much on his mind. 'He seems to have been very . . . determined.'

'You mean she could have been attacked?'

'Let's just say I'm glad she was safe here with you.' Because if she had been at home without police protection, he thought, there might have been more than a burglary added to what he had to contend with today.

'And nothing was taken?'

'Not so far as we can tell. Whoever broke in, it's probable he was looking for something specific.'

'And he didn't find it?'

Parry smiled ruefully. 'There's really no way of telling one way or the other. If we're right about what he was after, we don't know if it was in the cottage in the first place.'

'So what was it?'

'Possibly some diaries of Madam Rhonwen's. Why are you looking like that?'

Perdita was grinning. 'Intimate diaries, were they?'

'Again, possibly. Elwyn Griffith was aiming to have them published.'

'The sordid story of his mother's torrid sex life. That fits. Alison always said Elwyn wanted to spoil her image.'

'Would her sex life have been that sordid? Or torrid?'

'I don't know. I'm guessing too. The lesser *cognoscenti* used to imagine there were sometimes some pretty lively parties at Woodstock Grange.'

'Big parties?'

'No. Intimate small ones. Just enough to fill that king-size Jacuzzi she had installed. Well, that was asking for gossip in a way, wasn't it?' Perdita wiped her mouth with her napkin, then picked up her coffee cup. 'The parties would have included Reggie Singh. There was quite a lot of talk about him and Madam Rhonwen, of course. He invited me once to one of the parties. Last October. During a rehearsal for the show. He asked if I'd like to join them up at the house after. For drinks and a swim in the indoor pool. I said I didn't have a costume with me, and he laughed and said "join the group".' She drank some coffee before going on: 'He cancelled the invite later because Rhonwen had a sore throat. Another time, he said. But there never was another time. I got the impression Rhonwen might have regarded me as too much competition.'

'For Reggie Singh?'

'Yes.'

'She was right too, though I don't imagine –'

'I could have gone for Reggie? No, I couldn't,' she broke in. 'It was either that or Rhonwen thought I was too square for that sort of party. Or too close to Alison, perhaps?' she added thoughtfully. 'Rhonwen liked being in a group though. So long as she was the centre of it.'

'Including group sex?'

She shrugged. 'Honestly, I don't know. It's all scuttlebutt. But a lot thought she was still very active sexually. Despite her age. Well, she wasn't that old in any case, and she'd certainly kept her figure. And as for her way with men, well that was legendary, wasn't it?'

'So who else would have been a regular at these parties?'

'Difficult to say since I never got in on the act. The members of Madam Rhonwen's Academy perhaps.'

'Who were they?'

'Don't you know?' As she spoke she helped them both to

strawberries from the glass serving dish. 'Surely you remember she often had two or three young actresses staying? For four or five weeks sometimes. Young actors too. For coaching in elocution and dance techniques?'

'I vaguely remember, yes. But weren't they mainly to add a bit of professionalism to the shows? They were always in them.'

'Sure. That was the price they paid if they were staying when the Operatic had a show on. That wasn't always the case, though. And either way they didn't have to pay Rhonwen anything. Not for bed and board or the tuition. I had one of them here once for treatment, and she told me. And the tuition was good. No doubt about that. Rhonwen was a real pro. Only I wondered if adding glitter to the shows was all those girls had to do to earn their keep. Jealousy that was, I expect.' She gave a little chuckle. 'Hey, I forgot the cream on your strawberries.' She pushed the open carton towards him.

'Thanks. But you mean the girls were also available as . . .'

'Party fodder? Yes.'

'Or for more than that?'

'For sex, you mean?' She shrugged. 'Who can say? Probably a case of every girl choosing for herself. I'm sure they'd all have enjoyed the partying. As part of living at the big house. None of them ever seemed to be exactly star material. And most of them were dead common with it. That's where the elocution lessons came in. And meeting some of Rhonwen's influential men friends could have been good for them in . . . in lots of ways.'

'Which influential men friends?'

'Now you're being too specific.' She thought for a moment. 'Rhonwen always had plenty of men around her. And usually without women in tow. Some were divorcés like Reggie Singh. Others just liked to give the impression of being unattached.'

'You met some of those?' The look in her eyes had indicated as much.

'One of them, yes. Last summer. At Rhonwen's July garden party. Very much on the make, he was. Not my style though. Even before I found out he was married.' Her gaze met his, then dropped to study her empty cup.

'I'm still interested in who else could have been at the small, private parties,' he said.

'Officially interested?'

'Yes. Would you include the other members of the Operatic Committee?'

'Rhonwen's three wise men? Possibly. Even probably, come to think. Is it slanderous to say that? They're all married and I never actually saw them at it.'

'But their wives have never been involved in the Operatic Society, have they?'

'No,' she answered slowly. 'But I don't imagine any of the husbands would risk conduct unbecoming a Tawrbach godfather.'

'Except possibly in circumstances where discretion was guaranteed?'

Again, she paused to consider before replying. 'One of them, perhaps.'

'Which one?'

'I'm not going to say. More coffee?'

'Please.' He watched her get up. He was not that concerned about which of the three men she might have nominated. He thought he could guess which one it would have been. Despite what Megan Davies had said, it was his view that if one of them had been involved in orgies at Woodstock Grange, they all had been. This fitted the scenario forming in his mind. 'So how well did Elwyn know Reggie Singh?' he asked.

'Very well. It was Elwyn who introduced Reggie to Rhonwen. It was after that they fell out. Elwyn and Reggie, I mean.'

'Any special reason?'

'The obvious one, yes. Elwyn got the idea Reggie was angling to marry his mother. Reggie was a suave sort of drifter. He put it around that he was ex-Indian diplomatic. I thought he might have been a clerk in the High Commission in London, or a waiter even. Never seemed to have any money, but he was always well turned out, and always getting people to back him. Like with the takeaway in Ystrad Mawr.'

'Which Rhonwen paid for?'

'That's right. And if he really had persuaded Rhonwen to marry him, Elwyn believed it would have done him out of his inheritance. Or a good part of it. That's what people were saying.'

'And Alison would have felt the same way?'

Perdita stretched her slim neck. 'I've never thought of it before, but yes, I suppose she would have. Sounds uncharitable, but since Elwyn wasn't much of a catch for anyone as attractive and . . . and resourceful as Alison, who could blame her if she thought of old Councillor Spencer Griffith's fortune as . . .'

'The icing on the bun?' he completed for her.

'And a pretty boring bun, at that,' she completed.

'Hello, it's Karen, isn't it? Hasn't my husband answered the door? I'm so sorry you've been kept waiting. I really am. I'm sure he's in, but he's getting a bit deaf, I'm afraid. Well we both are. It's age, d'you see? Down Elishama. Down Eliasaph. Naughty doggies.'

Mrs Esme Watkins, the slight, timid and self-effacing wife of the rector of Tawrbach, had just drawn up her battered Austin Mini in the middle of the rectory's gravelled forecourt. Or nearly in the middle of it. The awkward way the car was angled, and its inconvenient distance from both the house and the garage suggested its engine may have failed, and not that the driver had intended to end her journey at that particular spot. Attempts by the diminutive Mrs Watkins to emerge from the vehicle, clasping an overfull pillowcase to her flat bosom, had been hampered by the manic contortions of two boisterous red setters who had long since and easily succeeded where she was still failing. They had scrambled over her from the back seat and were already outside, cavorting around the young couple standing near the doorstep of the Gothic, stone-built rectory. The dogs had been oblivious to their mistress's admonitions, delivered, as these had been,

in a woefully unassertive voice – like a starving beggar plead-
ing for bread, but not very much bread.

'It's about the banns, Mrs Watkins. The rector said to be
here at half past one. This is Nigel Snoddy, my fiancé. He's
come down from Aberdare special.' Karen Graser, dark,
buxom and wearing too much eye shadow, was a young
woman born with few really noteworthy physical attributes,
excepting for her well-shaped legs. All but the top half-inch
of these were presently being exhibited in black designer
tights worn under a very short red duffle coat and an even
shorter black pleated skirt. The searching muzzles of the setters were now jointly and persistently attempting to cancel
what modicum of modesty these garments were affording
around Miss Graser's nether regions, to the discomfort and
embarrassment of their wearer. 'Nige has to go back soon,'
she went on, bothered and bent double while she weaved
and retreated against further canine onslaughts on her
crotch.

'How d'you do, Nige . . . er Nigel?' said Mrs Watkins,
choosing to ignore her pets' performance, which was easier
than trying to control it. She was now standing upright in
the drive, and still clutching the bulging pillowcase, plus a
handbag and a very old green plastic carrier bag with Harrods
emblazoned on it in gold.

'Thank you,' said Nige, because he had to say something.
A bullet-headed garage mechanic with a sour face and a gold
ring in one ear, he was not given to lengthy discourse, or
discourse of any kind really. He had wanted to get married
in front of a registrar, not a parson, to save time and money
– like the kind of time and money being wasted today. It
had been a losing battle though. Karen's parents were
'church', and Karen herself wanted to be married in white
at St Curig's. Also, Karen's father had made it clear to Nige
that any money saved if they had a civil ceremony Karen's
father would be keeping for himself and not handing over
to the couple. So Nige had thought 'sod it', and stopped
arguing.

'I've been to Swansea, to my mother's. She's ninety in
November. This is her washing, see?' Mrs Watkins offered

as though these facts excused all shortcomings so far. She shifted the pillowcase upwards so that she could get at something else, only then she couldn't see anything else. Nige stepped forward and took the pillowcase, but only after an urgent nodded directive from Karen.

'Oh, thanks ever so much,' said Mrs Watkins who began searching for her key in a capacious leather handbag with a flap that could easily have done service as a chair seat. 'I take the dogs because they get under my husband's feet otherwise.' The still weaving Karen thought he should be grateful it was only his feet. 'Traffic was terrible,' the rector's wife continued, half of her head now actually inside the bag. 'Knew I wouldn't be back till now.' She looked up. 'I left him his lunch. Ah.' She had found the key in the bottom of the bag, and by feel only, since she hadn't actually been looking at the time of discovery. 'When you getting married then?' she asked, with her standard rector's wife beam of approval – warmer than sometimes, too, since there was no evident sign yet that Karen was pregnant.

'Not till May the fifteenth. But Mr Watkins said to come today. For the banns and . . . pre-marital instruction.' The sudden flush to Karen's cheeks that followed the last words were matched by a deepening in Nige's glower. He'd argued already that since he and Karen had been sleeping together for two years they didn't need sex instruction from any parson, and if it wasn't sex instruction on offer he didn't want to hear it anyway, because he wasn't interested in anything else, definite.

'Well he's usually very good about time,' said Mrs Watkins opening the front door – an immediate signal for the dogs to barge through to the hall with such thrust that she was left standing with the key held in her hand at lock level because they had involuntarily separated it and her from the door. 'Now then, come in, won't you? My husband will be in his study. That's on the left.' She dropped the lonely key back into her bag, ready to be searched for the next time it was needed: it was not attached to anything as practical as a ring. Then she pushed up the sleeves of the serviceable Guernsey fisherman's sweater she was wearing. She had got

144

the sweater for a song at the Oxfam shop last year. It was still too big for her, but it was the warmth that mattered. 'Except he's not there, is he?' she completed.

'No,' said Karen disconsolately, standing in the doorway beside her.

Nige was still too far away to see. He was looking for somewhere in the hall to drop Mrs Watkins's mother's laundry.

The door to the study was open, but the room, overfurnished with heavy, dark Victorian pieces, was certainly empty of any human presence, a fact established by the dogs who had been in and out without pause before the rest of the party had reached the hall. A massive black cat, evidently disturbed in its slumbers by the dogs, was stretching itself on the seat of a very worn armchair.

'He's upstairs, having a lie-down after lunch, I expect, and overslept,' was Mrs Watkins's final adjudication as she glanced at the cluttered surface of the immense wooden desk before the window. 'He's been writing letters. That always tires him.' There were two unsealed envelopes on the desk blotter. 'I'll just pop up and wake him. You stay in the study. Take a seat. He won't be a second, I'm sure.'

Mrs Watkins made for the dark oak staircase. The cat followed, stiff legged at first, but loosening up, and eyes alert in the expectation of food. The staircase was at the rear of the square hall: it was uncarpeted so that the woman's hurried upward steps clattered through the house – like the sound of castanets played by someone entirely devoid of rhythmic sense – until she halted at the first floor landing and looked up. It was then that she let out the great curdling cry of despair that quickly brought the two visitors to her side and sent the black cat scuttling back the way it had come.

The red setters had meanwhile been chasing up and down the next flight of stairs in an unstoppable frenzy – barking, jumping, and bumping into each other, bared claws slipping on the polished wood, paws now up on the bannisters, muzzles now trying to force the spaces between balustrades as they fought to find a way to reach their master or have him reach them.

But the Reverend Mr Caradog Watkins was beyond

making contact in any animate sense with man or beast. His cassocked body was suspended in space in the stairwell, hanging by the neck from the black rope girdle that had earlier encircled his ample waist but which was now knotted around the stairway newel post. He was swaying slightly, probably from the disturbance of air from the still open front door. In a curious way the movement appropriately suggested an ascension more than the opposite. This was lost though upon his wife who had collapsed, weeping, on the cold boards to be comforted by a shaking Karen.

It was the normally taciturn Nige who sealed the tragic event with a dramatic phrase more apposite probably than he knew or intended. 'Jesus wept,' he uttered quietly.

14

'Right, boss. Two Cardiff passengers on the six fifty-five this morning remember someone answering Mr Griffith's description. They say he was waiting for the same train Wednesday,' said DS Lloyd, seated across the desk from Parry with a file of reports in front of him. Both men were in shirtsleeves.

Lloyd had come down from the incident room when he got word of Parry's return. The detective chief inspector had been talking on the telephone when he had come in a moment before. Neither man yet knew about Caradog Watkins's death. 'DC Innes was on Platform 2 by six-thirty. He was wearing Mr Griffith's hat, dark glasses and overcoat, and carrying his briefcase,' Lloyd continued. 'WPC Susan Flowers was with him, from uniform. They spoke to people catching the train, then travelled with it as far as Reading. Went through every carriage.'

'Neither of the two witnesses knew Griffith personally, Gomer?'

'No, no. And it was the hat again that clinched it. One of the two passengers was a daily commuter. To London. Can you believe?' Lloyd's eyebrows rose and his mouth stayed opened for a second after his question.

'Takes all sorts,' said Parry.

'And he lives in Cowbridge,' Lloyd added, his incredulity increased. It's a good fifteen-minute car journey from Cowbridge to Cardiff's main railway station, even in the early morning. 'Anyway, he spotted the man he thinks was Mr Griffith again after they arrived at Paddington – at the barrier, talking to one of the ticket collectors. Then the witness saw him heading in the direction of the tube station.'

'Not for the station manager's office?'

'Ah, same direction, that was. And it's now been reported he did go to the office.'

'But they told us yesterday they weren't sure?'

'That's right. Well they're sure now. The clerk he spoke to yesterday wasn't in when we talked to them from here. The Met sent someone to Paddington for us this morning. He talked to the bloke who was on duty Wednesday. He confirmed Mr Griffith came in, and was given the number to ring.'

'Cromwell-Evans's office number?'

'Yes. Except he didn't ring it.'

'Not according to Cromwell-Evans.'

'We can try to confirm that with BT and Mercury. But since it would have been an incoming call, probably from a phone box, it may be difficult.'

'What about that ticket collector?'

'The officer from the Met spoke to him too, boss. Mr Griffith had heard the broadcast and was asking him where the station manager's office was.'

'Information usually included in that sort of broadcast.'

'Well, if it was he must have missed it.'

'Hm.' Parry removed a sliver of strawberry from between two of his teeth. 'Any other London sightings?'

'Yes. The best one yet.' Lloyd was beaming at the top sheet in the file as though it was a full-house card at a Bingo session. 'We've had a call from that literary agency in Baker Street. Name of . . . let's see, ah yes, Butler and Robinson. They were in Mr Griffith's address book. The office manager rang just before lunch. When we talked to her yesterday she said they hadn't heard from Mr Griffith in six months. Today, she said she'd made a mistake.'

'Conscientious citizen.'

'Ah,' Lloyd uttered without enthusiasm, implying the first mistake would have been better avoided than excused later. 'Seems Mr Griffith arrived at their office about twenty past nine. That was before they were open. Except there was a secretary waiting outside. Not a regular secretary. A temp, she was, on her first day, who thought she had to be there at nine.'

'That place is full of conscientious citizens,' said Parry.

'Yes, but forgetful with it in this case,' Lloyd responded. 'Mr Griffith told the girl he thought they opened at nine, as well, and he couldn't wait because he had an appointment in Wapping. He gave her his name, and asked her to tell one of the partners he'd be back later. Except the girl forgot. At least till this morning.'

'But Griffith didn't come back?'

'The office manager said he didn't, boss.' Lloyd's voice sounded as though he'd like to have had further corroboration.

'The Wapping date was probably with a newspaper,' said Parry.

'That's what we reckoned, except we've been on to the papers there already. We're ringing them again.' Lloyd was now fingering a different report selected from the bunch under his hand. 'DC Innes and WPC Flowers were at Central Station last night as well. Meeting all the London trains from the nine-one arrival onwards. On Platform 3 that was.'

'Those two have clocked up a lot of overtime, Gomer.'

'Yes, they have. Earned it though. Lady, regular traveller, who got off the ten fifty-nine arrival, she remembers someone fitting Mr Griffith's description leaving the platform just in front of her on Wednesday night.'

'That would be off the er ... nine o'clock from Paddington?'

'That's right. Only this lady catches it at Newport.'

'But nobody saw him getting on at Paddington, or during the journey?'

'Not so far. But now we know which train to check we can have a bigger team join it at Newport tonight, with time to work through all the carriages.' Newport is east of Cardiff, eleven miles back along the line to London.

Parry looked dubious. 'Anything else?'

'Yes. Bloke who was the first to board that eleven-ten bus at Central Station on Wednesday night, he remembers someone fitting Mr Griffith's description. Says he got on just

149

before it left. Witness says subject went to the upper deck and must have been the only passenger up there. He remembers he was carrying a canvas holdall as well as a briefcase.'

'He's very observant, this witness.'

'Ah, except he said the man he thinks was Mr Griffith dropped the holdall and the briefcase climbing the stairs. You'd remember that, wouldn't you? He thought Mr Griffith might have been drunk, but then decided he was just cack-handed.'

'The holdall must have been something he bought in London. So what happened to it? It wasn't found with the body.'

'Nicked by the murderer, boss? Or someone else?'

'Or he could have left it on the bus.'

'That's right. Except it wasn't found there. Unless another passenger nicked it before the terminus.'

'Did this witness see Griffith get off at Aberkidy?'

'No. But he thinks he was asleep by then. Nobody else saw Mr Griffith get off either. That includes the regulars. Dead loss they are.'

'Was the bus crowded, do we know?'

Lloyd consulted the report. 'There were hardly any passengers at the start, but it was packed out at the next stop in Mary Street. Always is apparently. People coming out of the pictures and the pubs.'

'No other witnesses?'

'Only the bus driver who —'

'Told us he also thinks he saw Griffith.' Parry frowned and leaned forward, elbows on the desk, closed fists supporting his chin. 'So, we know now he got to London. We don't know what he did there, not after the Baker Street call. We have a witness who thinks she saw him get off a train in Cardiff in the evening, but earlier than the one he said he'd catch. Then he may have been seen on the last but one bus to Aberkidy.'

'The one the time and date of the ticket in his pocket says he caught, boss.'

Parry nodded. 'It's progress, Gomer.'

'And you've seen the forensic report on the particles under

Mr Griffith's nails. Oh, and the cat hairs in his clothing?'

'In the clothes he had on, not his overcoat. The particles were red paint and primer. Both probably British manufacture.'

'And probably off a car, which narrows the makes and models, but not so it makes it practical to identify either.' Lloyd was now reading from his own copy of the report. 'Fragments of paint with no rust or weathering, but the paint was applied more than ten years ago.' He looked up. 'So most likely interior paintwork. On an older car. Fits the car-boot theory, anyway. We're checking on vehicle ownership. So far, no one in the frame owns or uses a red car or van.'

'The one Griffith seems to have been locked up in with a cat. That was pathology on the phone when you came in. The professor's secretary. He'd promised to let me have the results of the lung tissue report, unofficially. It shows Griffith's whole breathing mechanism had been gradually silted up with cat dust.' He glanced at the notepad in front of him. 'Airborne feline emanations, the report says. And they'd built up over a period of at least four hours. The cat hairs on his clothes had already shown he was exposed to cats in some way.'

'Poor bugger. It's what he couldn't have stood at any price, isn't it?' Lloyd sounded genuinely grieved. 'My brother-in-law's an asthmatic,' he added. 'But Mr Griffith wasn't scratched by a cat or anything?'

'No. If he had been I think it would have come out at the postmortem, when I was there. Anyway, they don't allow loose cats on buses to Aberkidy, do they?' He rubbed his upper arm. 'Doesn't add up, Gomer.'

'Not unless he was kidnapped after getting off the bus, boss.'

'And left for hours to die locked up in a car boot with a cat? Except he'd been dead for at least eight hours when he was found.' Parry shook his head. 'So anything on those alibis?'

Lloyd was delving again for reports. 'Yes. First on Mr Prothero's caravan. Four taxi drivers all confirm they saw a white caravan towed by a blue Volvo Estate on Wednesday night. It was parked on the approach to the station multi-storey car park, from some time before midnight. It was last seen there by one of the drivers at half one in the morning.'

'It was there all that time?'

'Longer, if the lady stayed to meet the last train like Mr Prothero said.'

'So still no sightings reported by uniform patrols? We shouldn't be operating on casual info picked up from cab drivers,' Parry observed testily.

'Ah, but we got this through uniform branch inquiries, boss,' Lloyd put in quickly, which didn't answer the criticism but was aimed at stopping it being repeated as a grumble higher up the line. Lloyd tried not to create waves for colleagues in other branches, apart from which the report on the caravan had come in a little while back and should have been processed earlier. 'The caravan was in a spot usually covered by traffic wardens, but not at that time of night,' he went on. 'Anyway, it fits the description, so far as it goes. And it shouldn't be long before the West Wales Police pick up Desirée and her daughter.'

'So Prothero's movements between twelve and two should be accounted for. Not that there could have been very much doubt.'

'And effectively for the hour before that, boss. He left his friends at the Angel Hotel just after eleven-thirty. He wouldn't have had time to get to Aberkidy and back between then and eleven-fifty, the time he got to the station. That's been confirmed too. By someone who saw him. I've got that somewhere.' He shuffled through some more reports.

'Taxi driver, I expect,' said Parry caustically.

'I think it was, boss. Oh, and on the second alibi,' Lloyd went on, pulling out another report, and taking it as read that further corroboration of Prothero's movements could wait. 'The AA confirm Mr Abel Davies rang them at eleven forty-two. He wanted help changing a flat tyre two miles south of Mountain Ash on the A4059.'

'Didn't he tell you this morning he changed it himself?'

'Yes. Before the AA got to him. Seems their patrols were very busy Wednesday night. Usually are in my experience.

I packed up my membership because of that,' he added with a frown, although the real reason had been the size of his increased subscription. 'Anyhow, Mr Davies rang them to cancel the request for help. That was at twelve-four according to the AA telephone log. And he must have been where he told them he was in between. Wouldn't have risked them turning up pronto otherwise. Finding he wasn't there, like. Not if he was setting up an alibi.' Even so, Lloyd's tone didn't suggest total conviction.

'When you saw Davies this morning, he hadn't been sure of the time of his breakdown had he?'

'That's right. But the chap he spent the evening with, a Mr Isaacs, he's confirmed Mr Davies left his house outside Aber-nant just on ten past eleven.'

'The time we're assuming Griffith was boarding the bus.' Parry paused for a second before adding: 'But if Davies had had an uninterrupted run, he could easily have been in Aber-kidy before the bus.'

Lloyd looked up at the ceiling while he did a mental calculation. 'Driving fast on a clear road, yes, with no breakdown.'

Parry pulled his bottom lip between forefinger and thumb. 'Except he's got the AA on his side to prove otherwise,' he said.

'Sort of,' Lloyd half agreed.

'Which only leaves Cromwell-Evans wholly unaccounted for,' Parry observed. He was thinking of Perdita's refusal to name which of the three Tawrbach godfathers she thought was most likely to behave indiscreetly enough to build future trouble for himself. 'Anything on the burglary?'

'Not so far. You still think that was done to get the diaries?'

'I'm positive it was.'

'Meaning the burglar and Mr Griffith's murderer are likely the same person?'

'Or different people with the same interest.'

'The interest being the diaries Mr Griffith didn't have on him?'

Parry got up, stretched both arms above his head and turned to look out of the window behind his desk. 'In the end, there were no keys found on the body, were there?' he asked.

'No. Mrs Griffith said her husband didn't carry keys.'

'Except sometimes a latchkey to the back door.'

'Oh, that's right.' Lloyd sucked the end of his pencil. 'So if the killer was also the burglar, he might not have needed to break the back-door lock.'

Parry turned around. 'But if he didn't take a key from the body, he hadn't found the diaries with it either. Otherwise he wouldn't have gone looking for them in the cottage.'

'Either way, he still wouldn't have known whether Mr Griffith left the diaries with someone in London, boss. Not unless Mr Griffith said so before he died. Under duress, perhaps?'

'It's possible. But Griffith was no hero. If it had been a question of the diaries or his life, or even the diaries and his not getting hurt too much, I'm pretty sure the diaries would have lost.' He moved to the wall shelves and began rearranging things there.

'He could have snuffed it unexpectedly though, boss. When someone was just roughing him up, like?'

'Someone who wasn't accepting Griffith's word over the whereabouts of the diaries?'

'Or what was written in them. Could have been someone who went on harassing him, without knowing what it could lead to. Like someone who didn't know his health problems were so . . . so acute. The asthma, I mean. Even people who knew him well might not have thought it could mean curtains for him in some circumstances.' Lloyd pushed the file away from him on the desk and delved in his trouser pockets for a tube of peppermints. 'You think it definitely has to be someone exposed in the diaries? Exposed for . . . for immoral activities?'

'Yes.' Parry returned to sit at his desk, bringing the portable radio with him. 'But that could mean all kinds of immorality. Sexual, legal, business —'

'Hasn't it got to be sexual, though?' Lloyd, a lapsed Methodist, interrupted, deep voiced and accusing. 'That's if it really is a murderer we're looking for. People don't usually kill for the other things do they?'

Parry opened the empty battery compartment of the radio. 'Except as you just said, Gomer, the murder might have been unintentional.'

'Ah.' For a moment the sergeant savoured his own prescience. 'Only you think the three who got Mr Griffith's memo are more likely to have been mixed up in some . . . some business scam with Madam Rhonwen, say, than in a sex orgy with her, and others?' Lloyd involuntarily smacked his lips at the last thought, gave the round white mint in his hand a careful examination, then slowly raised it to his mouth.

'No, I don't think that.' He was recalling again what Perdita had said at lunch. 'The sex angle has to be the likeliest.'

'As well as the one most worth killing for?'

'That's debatable if it was a premeditated killing. The fact still remains, they're all three involved in business together.'

'But the property dealings everybody knows about only involve Mr Davies and Mr Prothero together. Mr Cromwell-Evans isn't part of that. And Mr Prothero is only his personal lawyer. He doesn't do work for the company, so it couldn't be anything to do with Shevan Electric.'

Parry considered for a moment. 'I suppose not,' he said, lowering his head and scratching the top of his spine under the unbuttoned collar of his shirt. 'And whatever Griffith was threatening them with, if he was threatening, it almost has to be something that concerned them all.'

'I'm betting on sex, then. Middle-class people who go to orgies only do it with close cronies,' Lloyd pronounced, as if he were a well-versed, dedicated, middle-class roué. 'Then if there's a chance of being found out, they can rely on each other for cover. To swear they were somewhere else at the time, like.'

Parry leaned back in his chair. 'Like the way each of our three is dismissing the idea that Griffith could have been blackmailing them.' There was silence for a moment as they both considered just how apposite that could be, before the speaker went on: 'There's still the question, if Griffith was murdered because of the threat in his memo, was the crime carried out by those three men in collusion, or by two of them, or only one?'

Lloyd made a pained face. 'Trouble is, not one of them's a natural suspect for a serious crime. Not as serious as murder, anyway. They're just the handiest ones we've got. By the way, Mr Griffith might have made them into a foursome by including Reggie Singh in that memo. That's if Mr Singh had survived. There's an old report says he was on a charge in North Wales five years ago. For using an amusement arcade he owned for immoral purposes.'

'What kind of immoral purposes?'

'The usual. He'd been using drugs to entice teenagers of both sexes into prostitution. Mostly boys in this instance. Except the case was never allowed to come to court. Quashed over a technicality, it was. His smart-aleck lawyer proved part of the police evidence was inadmissible. The DPP wouldn't proceed after that. We've been on to the officer in charge of the case. He said amongst other things that Singh was gay.'

Parry showed surprise. 'Hm, now I wonder if that would have been news to Madam Rhonwen?' He paused, pinching the end of his nose. 'Anyway, as you say, Gomer, he certainly can't be in the frame now. And until we see those diaries, we can't know what other reputations they're likely to wreck.'

'Or which other pillars of the community they could turn into murderers. I tell you what, boss,' Lloyd continued, but with his powerful voice now in competition with the telephone that had started ringing on the desk, 'if it's going to be just one of those three, my money's on –'

'Parry,' said the chief inspector into the receiver. He listened, gave several acknowledging grunts, followed these with: 'The coroner's office know about it? . . . OK, we'll be right there. Thanks.' When he put the phone down, his expression was grim. 'That was the Tawrbach police. Caradog Watkins has hung himself. He left a note for his wife – and a confession for the coroner.'

15

'Straightforward suicide, Mr Parry. That's about all one can say. He made a neat enough job of it, though I'm surprised that girdle held him. Heavy man like that. If it hadn't, the fall would have killed him, I expect. Always sad, a suicide. More so with a clergyman. Body's gone to the morgue already.' The speaker was Dr Maltravers, the police surgeon. His bag thrust under his arm, not carried by its handle, he had been crossing to his car in the driveway of St Curig's rectory just as Parry and Lloyd were getting out of the Porsche.

'It was his wife who found him, doctor?' asked Lloyd.

'That's right. Nasty for her. Fortunately there was an engaged couple in the house too. Come about their banns. The young man had the presence of mind to cut him down sharpish. Tried resuscitation, but he must have been quite dead, I'm afraid.' The doctor lifted the wrinkled, narrow brim of the ancient tweed hat he was wearing in what might have been an involuntary gesture of respect to the deceased, though it could just as easily have been because he was making it more comfortable for his head. He looked older than he had in the yellow sou'wester he'd been wearing the day before, above the same fraying waxed jacket he had on now.

'Is Mrs Watkins inside?' asked Parry.

'No. She's gone to the home of one of the churchwardens. House is over the bridge, a few doors down, I think. He and his wife came up when they got the news. There was a woman constable here earlier too. She left with them. Mrs

Watkins was in a state still. Understandable, of course.' He paused, taking a deep, considering sort of breath through his nose. 'Watkins might have arranged to do the deed where his wife wouldn't have been the first to come on him. People don't think of these things, of course.' As he finished, the doctor seemed to be directing an admonishing gaze at Lloyd, as if he judged the sergeant to be a potentially inconsiderate suicide.

'I understand the rector left some letters?' Parry put in.

'That's right. To his wife and-and-and ... the coroner!' Maltravers's leathern face had suddenly contorted. He sneezed three times in quick succession into a red check handkerchief produced in the nick of time. It was clear that it had been the onset of this eruption and not Lloyd that had prompted his previous, apparently accusing look. 'Sorry.' He blew his nose loudly. 'They keep cats in there. Bloody creatures always affect me this way, as they did Elwyn Griffith, of course.' His eyebrows lifted. 'You knew he was exposed to an army of cats before he died?'

'Yes. I heard that an hour ago,' Parry answered.

'Rum business altogether, that one. No doubt you lot'll sort it out. Oh, about the letters. Geoff Beynon, the coroner's officer, he's taken charge of the one to the coroner. I saw the other one. Very short. Just asked for his wife's forgiveness, and says he had no alternative but to top himself, that's all.'

'In his own handwriting were they, doctor?' Lloyd inquired, overcasually.

Maltravers gave a wry smile. 'Yes, sergeant. No question but both letters are genuine.' He looked across at Parry. 'Beynon's inside with Inspector Edwards.' He glanced at the time. 'Well, I must be off. *Prynhawn da.*'

'Good afternoon, doctor.'

A moment later, Parry and Lloyd had joined the two uniformed men in the rector's study. Inspector Edwards, youngish, with a freckled face and an open expression, was the officer in charge at Tawrbach Police Station. Sergeant Beynon, approaching sixty, was shorter, larger and rubicund, with a shock of white hair, a voice as resonant as Lloyd's, and the air and exaggerated movements of a character actor of the old school. He had stayed on in his present post well after normal retirement age.

'Mr Watkins addressed the envelope to the coroner and to whoever else it may concern, sir,' said Beynon in answer to Parry's first question. 'He didn't seal it. The inspector here's read it. No reason why you shouldn't see it too, sir, off the record it'll have to be for the moment. That's if you tell me you feel it's relevant to current investigations.'

'Thank you.'

Parry took the single sheet which Beynon had presented with a flourish, as though it were an invitation to some grand function, and read what was written on it in a clear italic hand.

To the Coroner

I am ending my life because I cannot face the disgrace and humiliation of going on with it. I am not out of my mind, but distracted by shame and guilt, and terrified by what will soon be disclosed in Madam Rhonwen's diaries, coming on top of my vile, uncontrolled behaviour on Tuesday afternoon.

Remorse is not enough to excuse the sinfulness of what I have done. The thought of prison is unbearable. I should not have yielded to temptation, but I blame myself alone for everything that has happened. What will be detailed in the diaries was no way the fault of Madam Rhonwen or Reggie Singh.

I am no longer worthy of God's trust, and can only hope for His eventual forgiveness in the hereafter. Pray for me.

Caradog Watkins

PS. It was I who broke into Alison Griffith's cottage. I was looking for the diaries which I thought might be there. I never found them. I am sorry for the damage.

'If you're wondering about Tuesday afternoon, it happened in the gents near Roath Park Library, in Cardiff,' said Inspector Edwards flatly, after Parry had finished reading and passed the letter for Lloyd to see. 'He was reported for persistent importuning of juveniles, charged, then released on police bail. There's also a drink-driving charge. Imbibed too much at Madam Rhonwen's wake, I expect. All three boys he's alleged to have solicited were underage. Well underage. He was due to appear before magistrates in Cardiff this morning, but he didn't show. We had instructions after lunch to find out why.' He paused. 'I know you're looking for those diaries. That's why I called you.'

'Was his wife aware there were charges pending against him, do you know, sir?' asked Lloyd.

'No, I don't. Shouldn't think so. And his lawyer knew nothing about them either.'

'That would be Mr Prothero?' said Parry. It was more of a statement than a question.

'That's what we found out, yes. We've been on to him. Very shocked, he is. Can't understand why Mr Watkins didn't send for him when he was charged on Tuesday.'

'He was offered the chance to have his lawyer present at the time, of course?'

'Yes. It's in the report. All done by the book. Just as well too, in view of what's happened.'

'There's something else may be of interest to you as well, Mr Parry,' put in Beynon, clasping his hands across his stout, uniformed middle. 'Possibly relevant to your investigation into Mr Elwyn Griffith's death.' He paused, gave a slow nod to acknowledge the quickened interest on the faces of Parry and Lloyd, and then went on. 'I checked for messages on Mr Watkins's answering machine. That was with his widow's permission, of course. This coroner always wants to hear about last known contacts after a suicide.' The pointed, knowing glance that followed embraced all present. 'There's two messages from a Mr Waldo Niedlich. London number. Mr Edwards had the WPC who was here get on to him just now.'

'Yes. He's a theatrical agent. Office in Denmark Street. Shoestring outfit by the sound of it,' Edwards supplied in a more matter-of-fact tone, after allowing the coroner's officer to collect the kudos that worthy had obviously believed due to him for sparking an important initiative. 'Said Mr Watkins had been leaving messages on his own answering machine almost hourly since yesterday morning. Explained he'd been

160

at home in Golders Green since Tuesday with the flu. Got back to his office at noon today. Said he might know why Mr Watkins had been ringing him, but insisted it was a private matter. We didn't press him at this stage. No authority to really. His only contacts in Tawrbach had been the late Madam Rhonwen, and her son, but only recently with the son. He claimed he'd been Madam Rhonwen's agent for more than forty years. Said he'd been sorry to miss the memorial service. We took his office and home numbers if you want them. He'll be at the office till six today, and at nine-thirty again in the morning.'

'So not exactly the confession we'd expected, boss. Or hoped for, either. Not after the message we got,' said Lloyd, when the two policemen were outside again in the rectory drive.

Parry unlocked the doors of the Porsche and they both got into the car. 'But Watkins is the only one so far who's admitted being scared to death over what was in the diaries,' he said. 'And then proved the point with a vengeance, unfortunately.'

'So how could he have known what was in the diaries without seeing them?'

'Shows a guilty conscience and a vivid imagination is a bad combination, Gomer.'

'He had that, did he, boss? The rector? Vivid imagination?' The comment was dismissive not complimentary.

'Yes. Used to colour his sermons with rich analogies, I remember.'

'Well, there you are.' Lloyd produced a lone peppermint from his pocket, examined it suspiciously, then popped it into his mouth. 'And at least we know now who did the burglary. My money was on Mr Cromwell-Evans or Mr Davies.' He studied the gabled rectory porch with its Victorian wrought-iron traceries.

'Not Prothero?'

'Too ham-fisted for a lawyer. The way it was done.'

Parry wondered where a clergyman rated on that basis. 'Well it wouldn't have been Davies either,' he said. 'He almost certainly has a key to the place. Wouldn't have needed to break in. He arranged the sale to the Griffiths. Before that it was a holiday let for years. His firm were the managing agents.'

'You knew that from when you lived in Tawrbach, boss?'

'No, only since lunch time. Miss Jones happened to mention the cottage was in a bad state of repair when the Griffiths took it over, and why.'

'Ah.' Lloyd sniffed energetically. 'Do you want us to get on to this Niedlich bloke? Sounds as if he could shed fresh light if he wanted to.'

'No. I'm going to London to see him in the morning.'

'Reckon he's that important, then?'

'He was to Caradog Watkins, and what's happened here is the strongest indication yet that those diaries are dynamite.' Parry was increasingly conscious that the trail to Griffith's murderer had been cooling by the hour – or up to the present hour at least. Without something to stop the dust settling, the case threatened to extend itself into infinity, like too many other murder inquiries that weren't solved in the first few days.

'Right then. And in the meantime –'

'We're going back to the Rumney nick, calling on Alison Griffith on the way,' Parry interjected as he started the car engine. 'We've got to put more effort into finding that red car. Since it doesn't seem to belong to anyone connected with Griffith, let's see if it was hired locally.' His eyes narrowed. 'Or bought recently, and kept under wraps. If it was bought, it might have been by someone in the frame already.'

Lloyd was making notes. 'Could be a tall order, especially if the buyer didn't want it known he'd got it. Tracing an official hire should be easier.'

'Maybe. It's an older car. If it was hired, it won't have been from one of the big outfits. They don't keep vehicles for anything like ten years.'

'So we'll try all the little ones, boss. If it was bought on the quiet, it would have been a private sale for sure,' said Lloyd with conviction, and still writing as the car moved off. 'Of course, it could have been nicked for the occasion. We'll have the stolen vehicle list scanned.'

'And you've got that team lined up to get on the train at Newport tonight?'

'Yes. DC Innes in the hat, and seven other officers interviewing and handing out leaflets asking for information.'

'Good. I'd still like to know if anyone saw Griffith get on at Paddington, or anywhere else along the line. He seems to have been conspicuous enough at some times, but invisible at others.'

'And if he did have a holdall when he got off at Cardiff, like the witness said, we have to find out what happened to it,' said Lloyd.

Parry nodded. 'He definitely didn't have it with him when he left Wednesday morning. His wife would have said.'

The sergeant gave an amused grunt as he settled back in the seat. 'Our Detective Constable Innes won't be looking forward to wearing that fedora again.'

'Feels conspicuous in it, does he? But that's the whole point of –'

'No, it's not that. It's so big he has to keep it up with his ears. He reckons Mr Griffith must have had the biggest head in Glamorgan.'

'You've got things tidied up quickly, Mrs Griffith,' said Parry a quarter of an hour later. He was standing in the centre of the living room at White Cross Cottage. Lloyd had gone into the study where WPC Norris was replacing books on the shelves.

'Not as quickly as the time that swine must have taken to untidy it,' reflected Alison Griffith, stepping back from straightening a picture she had just rehung on the wall. 'Sorry I was so angry this morning. I never knew before how it would feel. Having your things . . . defiled by a stranger.' The pretty head jerked sharply as the shoulders gave a shudder of distaste.

The room was nearly back to normal.

A high-pitched female voice from beyond the kitchen door called: 'Cup of tea, Mr Pa-wee? For you and your friend? I was just making it when you arrived. I've got enough cups all ready.' The 'ready' had emerged as a crescendoing 'weddy'.

'No thanks, Mrs Cromwell-Evans, we aren't stopping.'

It had been the red-headed Sheila Cromwell-Evans who had let in the two policemen earlier. Now she was appearing again, from the kitchen, making mincingly short steps in high heels, and carrying a tray of tea things. She was heavily made up, and dressed in a tight-fitting white denim trouser suit. Under the jacket she had on a blue silk blouse. Both blouse and the low-cut jacket were pouting open to show off two heavy gold neck chains and an overgenerous amount of sunburnt cleavage. The chains matched a collection of rattling bracelets on both wrists, as well as gold ear hoops the size of bangles. It was a moment before Parry realized who it was she reminded him of, with her 'heart of gold' manner and her glaringly loud appearance: it was Madam Rhonwen of course. All three of the secretaries in Cromwell-Evans's office had looked to him to be subtly more alluring than Mrs Cromwell-Evans, or perhaps that was merely because they were all a good deal younger than she was. Something made him wonder, though, if her husband's preferences in women might now be closer to them than it was to her.

'Mary Norris could probably do with a cup of tea, Sheila. She's been such a help since she got here,' said Alison, the last remark directed at Parry. 'You know she doesn't have to stay, Mr Parry? I really don't need protecting.'

'That's not what my chief superintendent will say if you're burgled again,' he said, except it wasn't burglars that worried him: Madam Rhonwen's diaries appeared to have accounted for two lives already, and he wasn't prepared to risk another. 'Mary will stay here till six this evening,' he went on. 'Male constables will then be on patrol outside through the night.'

'That makes me feel like a drain on the public purse.'

'I've said you can come and stay with us, Alison,' put in Mrs Cromwell-Evans quickly, and looking up from pouring tea. She shook her expensively tousled hair without a strand of it budging from its carefully allotted 'random' place. The red-taloned finger ends of her free hand were doing intimate things to the chains inside her blouse.

'I'd rather stay here tonight, thanks,' said Alison with quiet determination.

'The reason we came over,' Parry began awkwardly, as Lloyd came back into the room and stood behind him, 'we thought you ought to know the Reverend Watkins has confessed to breaking in here last night.'

'Good God,' Alison exclaimed, her arms dropping limply to her sides.

'Has he gone waving mad?' demanded Mrs Cromwell-Evans shrilly.

'I can't answer that because he was found dead in the rectory early this afternoon,' said Parry.

The two women looked at each other. 'How did he die?' Mrs Cromwell-Evans asked, less piercingly this time. 'Natural causes, was it?'

'I'm afraid not,' the policeman answered. 'He hanged himself. We have reason to believe he was deeply concerned about the contents of Madam Rhonwen's diaries. That and other matters. And I have to say, Mrs Griffith, that if you have any idea where those diaries could be you ought to tell us, in your own interests.'

Alison sank into an armchair. 'You mean because you think someone may have murdered Elwyn to get them? And now Mr Watkins has . . . Oh dear, this is terrible.' Her two clenched fists had moved to cover her mouth. 'But I've told you already I don't know where they are. I've never even set eyes on them.'

'Have this tea, love,' said Mrs Cromwell-Evans. She passed a cup to the other woman, then turned to Parry. 'Alison's told me about the diaries, and the memo Elwyn wrote. He sent a copy to my husband, didn't he?'

'Yes, to him and some others.'

'Well, I'm sure he'll help you find them if he can. Have you asked him?' she continued ingenuously, and making it plainer still that she and her husband hadn't discussed the diaries, the memo, or his visit from the police.

Lloyd took a step forward. 'Ah, we were hoping he could tell us where he was on Wednesday evening. That would be a great help at the moment. To our general inquiry,' he

165

put in, with matching ingenuousness but a good deal less innocence.

The woman shook her head again, and then one of her wrists for good measure. The bracelets jangled and sparkled to order. 'I can't help you there, I'm af-waid. He wasn't home till late, I wemember that. After midnight it was. You'll have to ask him yourself. I tell you, though, wherever he'd been, he'd dwiven a long way. Looking at sites for new stores, I expect. That's his usual. Funny enough, I've been meaning to ask him. The Lexus did fu-wee hundred and fifty miles on Wednesday. Ga-weff, that's my son, he makes a note of the mileage every day. When Dai Sugden wuns him to school early, before my husband leaves. Ga-weff loves the Lexus. I wemember him saying about the big mileage on Thursday. When I picked him up in my car after school.' Her face clouded. 'No, it wasn't my car. My car was in for service Thursday. I bo-wode Dai's old banger. Ve-wee bu-wite Ga-weff is, for seven,' she ended, oblivious to more important topics, mouthing the commendation to her son with a riot of dropped Rs, and completing with: 'He wants to be a wacing du-wiver. Well they all do, don't they?'

'Mr Sugden's your gardener, is he, ma'am?' asked Lloyd.

'That's right. Gardener and ge-woom.'

'I see.' He glanced at Parry. 'Would you remember the make and colour of this banger of his?'

Mrs Cromwell-Evans's brow furrowed. 'I'm no good at makes. Not with little cars. I know the colour though.'

'The colour, yes, ma'am?' Lloyd pressed, then held his breath.

'It's gu-ween.'

Which only proved you couldn't win 'em all, thought Parry and Lloyd in perfect if silent unison.

16

'Rhonwen was a fine woman. Outstanding talent, yes. When she married it was a diabolical loss to the legitimate stage. Diabolical. But that was forty years ago. And now she's gone from us. May she rest in peace.' After delivering this pious valediction in a clipped unwavering tone, and an accent that owed as much to North London as it did to his German origins, the immense Waldo Niedlich blew a farewell blast into his handkerchief, so loud he might have been trying to frighten the pigeons half a mile away in Trafalgar Square. He carefully examined the results of this last endeavour, wiped an eye with one hand, while, with practised dexterity, the other broke off an end piece of the Danish pastry on the paper plate in front of him. 'Sure you won't partake, chief inspector?' he inquired. 'I got another pastry in the bag, and there's plenty more tea in the pot.'

'No thank you, sir. I've just had coffee and biscuits. In the snack bar opposite.' Parry had caught the same early train to London that Elwyn Griffith had taken on Wednesday. It was now only just after nine-thirty.

'That snack bar's OK. But, I tell you, chief inspector, if you're in there again, mention my name,' Niedlich offered expansively, with a nod implying that such a commendation would produce truly untold benefits of a size and nature not normally afforded to strangers and the unconnected. Using his elbows for leverage on the arms of his ancient desk chair, he shifted his huge torso slightly, held it partially suspended in the air for a moment, then, with evident relief, let everything subside again. Throughout this performance he had fixed Parry with a challenging expression, while continuing to chew the pastry slowly – which is what he had been doing when the policeman had arrived.

Niedlich was not simply a large man. Adipose flesh oozed through every end and gap in his clothing, with each done-up button on shirt and waistcoat threatening to burst open from the strain being exerted beneath it. The top of his head was bald except for four distinct and well separated black hairs which traversed the otherwise empty and blotchy pate. These prized strands originated in the narrow but still hairy fringe at the back of his neck, emerging from behind his left ear and ending in a roughly corresponding spot behind the right one. That their owner was attached to these threads, not just physically but emotionally as well, was clear from the way he lightly combed and caressed them with bent podgy fingers and with irritating frequency, as if to ensure both their perfect arrangement, and their continuing survival. He had scarcely any eyebrows or eyelashes, and no other facial hair, not even the unkempt protuberances from nose and ears common in men of his age, which Parry knew to be seventy-three. The heavy white forehead, the puffy cheeks, the bloodless lips, and the equally anaemic fleshy plinth where a chin should have been, gave the whole visage a death-mask paleness each time the layered lids closed like roller shutters over the bulging eyes. When the lids opened again, the contrast was as surprising as it was showy, for Parry noticed for the first time that Niedlich's right eye appeared to be bluey-black, while the left one was a wholly unnatural tortoiseshell.

'I understand you were Mrs Spencer Griffith's –'

'Madam Rhonwen to me always. Do me a favour, chief inspector, call her that please,' Niedlich interrupted in his baleful monotone.

Parry smiled indulgently. 'You were Madam Rhonwen's agent from the start of her career?'

'Got the child her first engagement at sixteen, didn't I? At the Hulme Hippodrome, Manchester. In *Puss in Boots*. Lovely little dancer she was. Strong soprano voice, too.'

'So that was in pantomime?'

'But such pantomime we had in those days,' Niedlich reminisced, while gently smoothing the top of his head.

'And her full-time stage career lasted how long, sir?'

'Five years. Five great years. Could have led to thirty greater ones. Thirty at least.' He waved his already uplifted hand towards the framed photographs covering the nearest wall.

The two men were in the larger of the two rooms that made up the second floor offices of Niedlich & Ross, Theatrical Agents, and which lay at the top of some dilapidated wooden stairs. Parry had observed the man he had taken to be Niedlich enter the three-storey building at the door between two shops in Denmark Street. He had followed him in a few minutes later. There was no sign of a Ross – or any accommodation for another partner. The outer office had been a windowless cubicle furnished for a secretary – except there was no sign of a secretary either.

So far, Niedlich had shown no surprise at being visited unexpectedly by a senior police officer. When Parry had first appeared the elderly man's demeanour had been one rather of tired resignation.

The photographs their owner was indicating now were all in black and white, and mostly of scantily clad young women in the hairstyles of the 1950s and '60s. 'There she is. Third from the right in the middle row of photos,' he said. 'She was nineteen then. Soon to play the third, no, I tell a lie, the second lead in *Bless the Bride*.'

The long-legged *ingénue* in the picture, leaning backwards, wearing a white satin top and shorts, and waving a white top hat, bore little resemblance to the Madam Rhonwen that Parry had known. He would scarcely have recognized her, but he took Niedlich's word that it was her. 'That show was before my time, I'm afraid, sir. It was very successful, I believe. In the London production, was she?' Parry was aware that the story of Madam Rhonwen's early stage career had very little bearing on why he was here, but he was interested to pursue the topic.

Niedlich hesitated, then half closed his eyes before replying carefully: 'Not exactly the London production. This was later.

It was a good road company. Toured Scotland and the er . . . the Middle East. Great notices it got.' Except it sounded as if the speaker didn't believe his own last comment.

'Did she ever play on the London stage?'

The eyes narrowed again. 'Sometimes.' He poured himself more tea from the dark brown pot.

'And after she married?'

'She made guest appearances. For charity. Came up specially from er . . . Wales.' He blinked slowly. 'Yes, Wales. Every time. Never spared herself. Not when it was for helping charity. Then she moved on to being an impresario, and teaching. Doing good for others.' Niedlich patted the part of his jacket beneath which Parry guessed his wallet might be lodged, in an involuntary gesture perhaps to indicate that the good had been shared in some measure by Madam Rhonwen's agent.

'We know about her stage productions in South Wales, sir. Did she back shows in other parts of the country? Was she an angel, as you call it in your business?'

Niedlich blew breath out loudly through his open mouth. 'An angel in every sense, she was. Across the world. Sent cabaret troupes everywhere.'

'Cabaret? She financed travelling cabarets?'

'That's right. I hired them, then booked them all over the place. Resort hotels, cruise liners, night clubs in European capitals, holiday camps.' Niedlich raised both hands to emphasize the breadth of the enterprise. 'All high-class establishments,' he went on. 'Always she took my judgement on the right little production companies to get behind. The ones that deserved backing. Made a bit of money for Rhonwen they did. And she deserved it.'

More money possibly than she had made in her brief and hardly remarkable career in what had just been described as the legitimate theatre, thought Parry, even though the pickings from the dance troupes didn't sound as if they could have been massive. 'And it was performers from these companies that she had down to her house for coaching?' he asked.

Niedlich looked from side to side, then at the door, as if

he might be planning some kind of an escape. 'A helping hand. To deserving, talented girls and boys.'

'And you picked those people too?'

'No. Rhonwen liked to do that herself. She'd come up to London to watch auditions with me. Usually chose the ones who hadn't been hired. The disappointed ones. Hope, she gave them.'

'But after they'd had tuition from her, these . . . girls and boys got the next jobs they auditioned for?'

'Very often.' Niedlich reached for his handkerchief again and began wiping his face and neck with it. It was a cold day, and although the office was scarcely heated, he had begun to sweat.

'And that would be with companies that Madam Rhonwen was backing financially?'

'It could have been, yes.' He wiped both his eyes.

'So she could influence who got hired?' He noticed that Niedlich's eyes were suddenly matching: they were now both bluey-black.

The theatrical agent made a rumbling noise in his throat as he examined something in the palm of his hand. 'Influenced to a degree. To a degree,' he repeated, then looked up. 'But all had talent. Madam Rhonwen developed it.'

'Did the cabarets feature nude acts?'

'Some. Always in good taste.' The answer had come without hesitation, as though the question had been expected.

'Were some of them principally nude shows?'

'To a degree. Nothing illegal. Wholesome. Like the *Folies Bergère*.' He now carefully placed what Parry could just see was one of a pair of tortoiseshell contact lenses beside the other in the small box he had taken from his pocket. He followed Parry's gaze. 'They take getting used to,' he volunteered. 'I wear one at a time. They were Madam Rhonwen's last treat to me. So kind of her. She was always so kind.'

'Since her death, what's happened to her cabaret business?' asked the policeman.

Niedlich blinked twice with effort. 'It's dried up. No seed money. I don't have her reserves to risk. I've never been a saver.'

'She was the only backer?'

'How d'you mean?'

'Do the names Prothero, Davies and Cromwell-Evans mean anything to you.'

Niedlich looked thoughtful and blinked once slowly. 'Close harmony act was it? I remember –'

'No. They were all friends of Madam Rhonwen.'

'Then I haven't heard of them.'

'None of them have been in touch with you since her death?'

The fleshy face showed strain. 'Not that I remember. No, definitely not.'

'How did Madam Rhonwen arrange for funds to be sent to you, and how did you send her the profits she made?'

'That was all done through her London accountants. Very legit, I'm telling you. All strictly according to the book with them.'

'Did you ever do business through her lawyer? He's in Tawrbach. Name's Huw Prothero, one of the three I mentioned just now.'

'Never.'

'If you don't mind my asking, Mr Niedlich, was Madam Rhonwen your biggest client?'

'Yes.'

'Your only . . . legitimate client, perhaps?'

'What do you mean legitimate? All my clients are –'

'Our information is the others are strippers you place around the clubs. And I gather you've had warnings recently. About not checking the ages of some of them?'

'Who said that?'

'Scotland Yard.' The information had been provided after he had contacted the Met for clearance to interview Niedlich in London. 'But I'm not interested in that,' Parry added. 'I only want information about some things that have happened on my patch since Madam Rhonwen died.'

Niedlich breathed in slowly. 'There's been one or two mix-ups over ages. Genuine.' He shook his head. 'So, I'm closing down this business. Retiring. Too hard to keep up with the red tape at my age. Employment regulations. Only it's hard when you have to end something like this.' He paused. 'My partner's dead. My dear wife's dead. My daughter's in Australia and doesn't want to know. I come here for the company, see? The memories.' He looked about the room, but not at the ancient small desk in front of him, its top crammed with office impedimenta, or the two shabby chairs, or the wardrobe in one corner with a broken door. His narrowed gaze was scanning the photographs that adorned all the walls, along with a few framed and yellowed playbills. 'The memories,' he repeated. 'Music hall was my speciality, see? I never got into telly and that. Madam Rhonwen saved me in the end. After being the best talent that ever went through my hands. Could have made it to the top. The very top. If she hadn't got married and gone to live in the sticks.' He looked at Parry. 'No offence meant.'

'You mean she gave you a second chance with the cabaret business?'

'That's right. But I should have packed it all in when she died. I'm too old. Maybe the money wasn't as big as I make it sound. But she gave me more than my rightful share. A lot more. It kept me going. What I'm doing now doesn't pay the rent here. Or for a part-time secretary. Makes problems as well.' Niedlich's gaze had lowered on the last sentence.

'Did you ever meet Elwyn Griffith?'

'Never. He phoned a few times.'

'When?'

'Three, four weeks ago. Wanted the names and addresses of the kids Rhonwen helped over the last five years.'

'Meaning the ones who'd been down to Woodstock Grange?'

'That's right.'

'Why did he want their names and addresses?'

'He was going to send them money. Little legacies out of what Madam Rhonwen left, he said. In her memory. Nice gesture, I thought. Don't know whether he did it. He said he'd got me down for something as well. That was nice, too.'

'She didn't leave you anything in her will?'

'No. But she didn't expect to die before me, did she? Otherwise I expect . . .' The voice trailed off, then returned with:

'Elwyn said what he was talking about would take time to come through. I haven't had anything yet, and now you say he's dead.' The heavy shoulders gave a low-energy shrug.

'But you sent Elwyn what he asked for?'

'Yes. Why not? Didn't have to send it though. Everything was done on the phone. He'd ring me. Didn't want me ringing or writing to him. I couldn't, anyway. He never gave me a number or address. Didn't want his wife knowing about the little legacies, he said. About him giving money away. I could understand. So how did he die? Accident was it?'

'A bad asthma attack probably. There's going to be an inquest.'

'Nasty. I'm sorry. He was a cheerful person. Just like his mother.'

'Cheerful?' It wasn't a characteristic that Parry would ever have applied to Elwyn Griffith, and he doubted anyone else had ever done so until now. 'Do you remember anything else about him?'

'He had a strong Welsh accent.' Niedlich's hand went to gentle the four hairs on the top of his head. 'He sounded older than I expected. How old was he? Thirty something? Yes, he sounded older than that. In this business, a person's age is something you get a knack for judging on the telephone. Saves time and aggravation later. Like it may be a forty-year-old trying to pass for twenty, know what I mean?'

Parry nodded. 'Can you let me have the names you gave Elwyn, with the addresses, sir?'

'Expect so.' Niedlich moved a hand to open the top right-hand drawer of the desk. 'I made a list. Got it here somewhere. I think I included everybody, but some of the addresses could be out of date. I told him that. Yes, here it is.' He passed two sheets across the desk.

Parry quickly scanned the list which wasn't long – around twenty entries on the two sheets, written in a heavy longhand. 'Thanks. I'll let you have this back,' he said. 'Now I'd like you to tell me about the Reverend Caradog Watkins.'

Niedlich sighed. 'Thought we'd come to him. It's him you're here about, is it? He's leaving messages. Since Thursday when I wasn't here. I called back yesterday but he was out, so I leave messages too. Well, you know about that. Otherwise there's nothing to tell. He's been here a couple of times. With Madam Rhonwen. He came up with her sometimes to auditions.'

'He came to this office?'

'Yes. But he never dressed like a reverend. Very colourful. Stagey. He didn't want me to know what he was, except Madam Rhonwen let on once by mistake.'

'When he attended the auditions, did he have anything to do with picking the people who came down to her house?'

'Yes. The boys, not the girls.' Niedlich's mouth gave a nervous twitch. 'Is he in trouble?'

'I'm afraid he's dead, sir.'

'Not murdered or anything?'

'Why do you think he might have been murdered?'

'Because you're in London asking about him.' He paused. 'And because he wasn't too particular about the company he kept.'

'He's committed suicide.'

'Happens, doesn't it? With reverends. If they get in trouble.'

'Had he ever phoned you before Thursday?'

'Yes. Plenty of times since Madam Rhonwen died. Always about the same thing. The address and phone number of a boy called Terence. Terence Krimbly-Daze. He's on that list.'

'Did you give Mr Watkins the address?'

'No. Terence said not to.'

'Was there any special reason?'

Niedlich shifted heavily in his chair. 'Mr Watkins had taken a fancy to him. It wasn't mutual, that's all.'

'Had Mr Watkins helped choose him for a visit to Woodstock Grange?'

'Yes. Last October. He was here at the end of September.'

'Did Terence know Mr Watkins had been involved?'

'I should think so. But Terence wasn't his sort.'

'Wasn't gay, you mean?'

Niedlich's head and eyes practised their escape-planning movement. 'Not for the Reverend Watkins, he wasn't. He got on all right with Reggie Singh though, Rhonwen's boyfriend.'

'Singh is dead.'

'I know that. There was some kind of a row.'

'Between Singh and Watkins?'

'Over Terence, yes. I don't know the details.'

'Was Singh gay?' As the North Wales police had mentioned yesterday.

'He was . . . ambidextrous, I think. Madam Rhonwen didn't mind that. She was adventurous herself in that way. But she didn't like people to quarrel around her. Terence left early, without finishing his training. Madam Rhonwen was very upset.'

No doubt upset enough to enter the whole episode in her diary, thought the policeman – and no doubt Caradog Watkins had thought so too.

17

'Trip worth the effort, was it, boss?' Gomer Lloyd inquired loudly as he fell into step beside Parry who had just emerged, with a continuous stream of others, from Cardiff Central Station.

It was just after two o'clock in the afternoon, and raining. The chief inspector had caught the noon train back to Cardiff. He had called Lloyd from Paddington, and the sergeant had arranged to meet him.

'Well worth the effort,' Parry answered. 'Where's your car?' He had walked to the station earlier.

'Over there, in the commuters' park. Too much of a scrum outside the station at the moment.' Lloyd nodded towards the open-air car park on their right. 'And that reminds me,' he went on. 'We've found Desirée. In Haverfordwest. Mrs Desirée Grindley she is. Very up-market, and straight-laced, according to the West Wales police. And she does organize exhibitions. Horticultural ones, like he said. They discussed roses and heather for two hours.'

'I never doubted it,' said Parry with a chuckle.

As the two men pushed through to the car park they had gradually separated from the happy, hurrying throng of rugby union supporters still pouring out of the station. The crowd was heading for Westgate Street and the match at the Arms Park. Cardiff was playing Newport, and the kick-off was at two-fifteen.

'Tell me first how you got on in Bristol?' Parry asked as Lloyd unlocked the unmarked police Ford.

While Parry had been in London, the sergeant had driven

177

over the Severn Bridge to Bristol to interview the proprietor of Fairbody's, exclusive West Country purveyors of high-class men's outerwear. It was Fairbody's who had supplied the fedora that DC Innes had been parading in for the delectation of travellers on trains to and from London over the last forty-eight hours.

The prematurely bald Elwyn Griffith had owned quite a large collection of hats, including the tweed cap, Barbour rain hat and brown trilby that had been hanging on the back door of White Cross Cottage. Lloyd had checked the sizes of all of them when he had been in the kitchen, ostensibly to inspect the new locks just fitted on the door and windows there. That had been just before he and Parry had left the cottage on the previous afternoon. The rain hat had been marked 'Small', and the cap and the Trilby had both been size 6¼, suggesting that Griffith should have had as much difficulty with the 7¼-size fedora as the detective constable had been experiencing.

'Fairbody's has only sold five of those hats since they put it back in their range eighteen months ago, boss.'

'Not a big mover then?'

'Not that one, no. They have a different kind of wide brimmer that's cheaper. Fifty-two pounds. It sells better. Well, that's not surprising, is it? Our one's very expensive. Ninety-six pounds a throw.' Lloyd, who didn't own a hat of any description, paused to allow for the mental digesting of what he considered a prodigious sum for such a dispensable item. 'Anyway, the owner, that's Mr Alfred Fairbody, he remembered selling one to Mr Griffith. It was just before Christmas the year before last. A present it was, from his mother, Madam Rhonwen. Well, at that price it's not likely he'd have bought it for himself, is it? Not with the state of his finances then. She was with him when he got it. Mr Fairbody described her.'

'He's got a good memory,' said Parry settling into the passenger seat.

'For rich customers, yes. It helped that with people buying expensive things Fairbody's makes an effort to get them on the mailing list. They ask for names and addresses, like. For sending invitations to preview days at sale times. That sort of thing. Mr Griffith gave his address care of his mother. He was still living in Bristol then, but probably about to move. The hat he got was a size 6¼. Fairbody's had all the details in a ledger. Very thorough and businesslike they are,' Lloyd completed with approval.

'So there's no doubt that was his regular size?'

'Or that the hat found by the body couldn't have been his, boss. Definite, that's got to be. Two of the other four hats they'd sold went to regular customers. Neither was a 7¼, but both the others were. One went in the June sale last year. The other, at the full price, three weeks ago today. It was bought by a red-headed woman as a surprise present for her husband, she said. She was aged probably between thirty and forty-five, and she may have been wearing an off-white Burberry trenchcoat.'

'But she didn't give her name?'

'Or address. Well, that'd be getting jam on it for us, wouldn't it?' said Lloyd, and wistfully enough for a police-man who might just have missed solving a murder investi-gation in one stroke. 'And she paid cash.'

'She didn't by any chance have a Welsh accent, a high-pitched voice, difficulty with her Rs, and a lot of jewellery?'

'It was an assistant who served her, boss, not Mr Fairbody. He couldn't remember much about her. The store was crowded. The lady was in a hurry and knew exactly what she wanted. The assistant got it for her and she left, pronto. He only thinks he remembers the Burberry because Fair-body's sells them. If I'd had a photo of Mrs Cromwell-Evans I could have shown it to him. It was something I wasn't expecting, see?' Lloyd offered, half in apology. Sitting behind the wheel, he undid the buttons of his short rainjacket and produced his notebook from an inside pocket. He hadn't yet put the car key in the ignition.

'None of this fits, does it, Gomer?' Parry shook his head. 'If the Cromwell-Evanses were conspiring to murder Griffith three weeks ago, they must have known about the diaries then.'

'But nobody did know about them till Wednesday

morning. Or nobody said they did.' Lloyd was turning the pages of the notebook. 'Of course, it could be coincidence. If it was Mrs Cromwell-Evans who bought the hat, it could really have been as a surprise for her husband.'

'And she went all the way to Bristol for it?'

'Ah, a lot of people would. Fairbody's is *known*, isn't it?' Lloyd argued. 'Although I expect you could get a wide-brimmed hat locally if you wanted. At Austin Reed in Capital Arcade probably. That's if you didn't need to have the Fairbody label in it.' He paused, frowning. 'And Mrs Cromwell-Evans did offer that information about her husband driving three hundred and fifty miles on Wednesday. I mean, she wouldn't have done that, would she? Not if she was meant to stay stum about what he was doing that day.'

'So what *was* he doing that day? Could he have been poncing around in a fedora, so people would think he was Elwyn Griffith?'

'Except he's a different height and age to Mr Griffith.'

'Not with that hat, the dark glasses and a heavy overcoat on. Not so different, anyway. His height would have been a problem, I suppose,' Parry agreed grudgingly. 'But so far, the only people who are supposed to have identified Griffith had never set eyes on him otherwise.'

'They've all been shown pictures though.'

'Except we don't have one where he's wearing the hat or the glasses. You said yesterday, everyone recognizes that bloody hat. It's like . . . like being able to identify the invisible man because he's the one with the bandages on. It could have been anyone those people saw. A woman even.' Through the rain-splattered windscreen, Parry studied a double-decker bus moving out of the terminus across from the railway station. 'But why would Cromwell-Evans have been impersonating Griffith, if that's what he really was doing?' He paused for a second. 'Taking the bus to Aberkidy so people would say Griffith was still alive after eleven on Wednesday night?' he went on, answering his own question.

'So would Mr Griffith have had to be dead by then, or still alive?' asked Lloyd.

'Dead most likely. Giving the impression he was alive could

have been part of someone's alibi. Cromwell-Evans himself, or possibly his wife.' The chief inspector shook his head. 'Or am I pinning too much on the hat being bought by a redhead.'

'Seems more than a coincidence though,' said Lloyd. 'And Mr Cromwell-Evans is still the only one who hasn't told us where he was Wednesday night. Of course, his wife was having supper with Mrs Griffith – '

'Who told me Mrs Cromwell-Evans left late,' Parry interrupted sharply, his brow knitting.

'Did she say how late, boss?'

'No, and at the time it didn't matter. I assumed she meant close to midnight, but if it'd been earlier – '

'Early enough for her to drive into Cardiff, and catch that bus herself, done up as Mr Griffith?' Lloyd put in.

Parry thought for a moment. 'OK, let's run that a bit further, Gomer. She could have driven here to the station, gone to Platform 3 with the hat, coat and whatever else she needed, shoes probably . . . all in that holdall. We'll assume she was wearing trousers already.'

'Like she was when we saw her yesterday.'

'I remember, yes. So she puts the other stuff on in the ladies' loo, shoves whatever she's taken off in the holdall, waits for the train to arrive, then slips back on to the platform behind the other passengers and . . . yes, then catches the bus herself, all in front of witnesses,' he elaborated. 'Have we got anyone yet who saw Griffith get on at Paddington?'

'No, no one. Nor anyone who saw him during the journey.' Lloyd smoothed the centre of his moustache. 'It'd take an extra large size hat to stuff all that red hair in, too,' he offered. 'With the brim down and the coat collar turned up, Mrs Cromwell-Evans might have got away with it, I suppose.'

'And according to the witness in the bus, the person we assume was Griffith went straight to the upper deck,' Parry continued, not wanting to abandon the hypothesis quite yet. 'The witness said there weren't many passengers at the start.'

'That's right, boss. None at all on the upper deck except Mr Griffith.'

'So if it was Mrs Cromwell-Evans impersonating him, she

could have sat at the back with no one up there to look at her too closely, not till the bus filled up, which it did at the first stop when people would be too busy scrambling for seats.' Parry had been studying the crowd hurrying to the rugby outside.

'But I don't understand, boss,' Lloyd questioned. 'Wouldn't she have wanted someone to notice her getting off the bus as well as on?'

'Not if she got off before Aberkidy. And that could be it, of course. After making sure the bus driver noticed her, and that other passenger –'

'By dropping the bags on the stairs,' said Lloyd helpfully.

'Right. Once she's on top, she becomes a woman again. Gets out whatever clothes she'd put in the holdall, stuffs the hat and overcoat back in to it, lets her hair down, and gets off the bus as soon as it's filled up, which is why no one sees Griffith get off.'

'But why not wait till the bus got to Aberkidy, boss? Make a performance of getting off, the same as getting on?'

'I don't know yet. Maybe they only needed to prove Griffith was alive at eleven-ten, when Cromwell-Evans will eventually prove he was with someone else.'

'So if that's his alibi, why hasn't he told us already?'

Parry's shoulders lifted and fell. 'I wish I knew. If it is an alibi, maybe it's gone wrong. Maybe whoever he was with isn't cooperating after all. Doesn't want to be involved in a murder investigation. But if there is a witness to where Cromwell-Evans was that night, he'd better be ready to tell us right now.' He glanced at his watch.

'Or go to jail.' Lloyd was fishing in his pocket for a peppermint. 'So you reckon he could have arranged Mr Griffith's death earlier than eleven? In London, say?'

'In London, or else he met him there, drove him back and then did it. That car mileage certainly fits.'

'And does that match with anything Mr Niedlich told you?'

'Indirectly, yes. Whatever Prothero and the other two say, those diaries are deadly damaging. Exactly as we thought Griffith was saying in the memo.'

'And nothing to do with trivialities? Like . . . like Madam

Rhonwen being frank about her relations with the Arts Council, sort of thing?'

'Exactly. It can only be the kind of frankness that drove Caradog Watkins to suicide. Exposing some gross immorality, probably. By the way, the young actors, not the actresses, who were brought here for coaching came because he chose them. He and sometimes Reggie Singh between them. There's one in particular called Terence Krimbly-Daze who Watkins must have expected would be featured in the diary. I don't know in what kind of way, but Watkins obviously thought it would have been unacceptably damaging to him. He'd been pestering Niedlich for the boy's address. Probably because he wanted to shut him up before the media got to him.'

'So it's *News of the World* material all right, boss?'

'Griffith suggested the up-market Sunday papers, but that's about it, yes. He'd asked Niedlich for the names and addresses of all the young performers Madam Rhonwen had down in the last five years. I've got the list. Some of them were probably underage when they came. Niedlich specializes in underage artistes.'

'But Mr Griffith couldn't have been aiming to blackmail them too?'

'No. They wouldn't have been worth it, anyway. Even if money was his object. He told Niedlich he wanted to give them all token legacies. Small sums, out of Madam Rhonwen's estate. Prothero hasn't mentioned anything like that to us, and he's the joint executor of her will. So I think it was invention. I'm pretty certain Griffith was after a source of more input on the goings-on at Woodstock Grange if needed. More than was in the diaries. Promising these people money would have been a way of getting them to talk.'

'And has he been in touch with them?'

'Not so far as Niedlich knew. But he only gave over the information recently.'

'So it's back to him blackmailing the three gents? For the price of the diaries?'

'I suppose so.' Parry made a strained face. 'You know, he wouldn't let Niedlich phone him at home, or write to him there? Said he didn't want his wife to know about the token legacies.' He paused. 'Does Alison Griffith seem the kind of woman who'd object to helping young people?'

'The opposite, I'd say,' Lloyd answered promptly.

'I think so too. Another thing, Niedlich has never met Griffith face to face, but he's talked to him a number of times on the phone. He described him to me as always cheerful. Well, I can tell you, if Elwyn Griffith was always anything, it was always morose. He was one of the most sullen men I've ever met.'

'Are you saying it wasn't him that Niedlich was talking to, then? Just someone impersonating him?'

Parry shook his head. 'Right now that's overstating it. Let's assume it may not have been him. Except if it wasn't, and if we knew the reason for the impersonation, we'd probably have the name of his murderer.'

'So we should find out if calls were really made from the Griffith phone to Mr Niedlich's number?'

'Yes. And from the home or office phones of everyone else connected with the case.' He reached for his seat belt, noting through the windscreen that there was now hardly a person visible on the street, and that the few in sight were running like mad. 'OK. Now the happy throng has dispersed, let's go and see if Cromwell-Evans is ready to unburden himself.'

'I'd rather be going to the match.' Lloyd started the car and moved it off out of the park, towards Westgate Street.

'No you wouldn't, Gomer. It'll be a mud bath if this keeps up. Incidentally, have we got that handwriting report yet?'

'Yes. Inconclusive though. The signatures on the memos were all by the same hand, and they compare with the specimens the bank sent. But Mr Griffith's writing was so immature, and his signature so short, they can't swear the ones on the memos were definitely his.' Lloyd cleared his throat before adding: 'But they're sixty-five per cent sure they were.'

'That's a big help. Wonder how they arrive at sixty-five per cent? Anything else new?'

'Two things. We're going through everything stored on the hard disk in Mr Griffith's desk computer. The memo's there, and the three envelopes for the copies he sent out, but not the envelope addressed to you, and nothing else that's relevant. I mean, no letters about London appointments. Nothing about the diaries. Not so far. But it's a long job. DC Mike Price is doing it. He likes working on computers. Keen too. He's taken Mr Griffith's computer home this weekend. Says Mr Griffith wasn't very professional about the way he used it. The books he's written are mixed up in the machine with correspondence and other stuff. No organization. That's why it's taking a lot of sorting. Oh, and I've just remembered, the memo and the envelopes were originated on February 24th. That's according to the automatic record in the machine.'

'Three weeks before they were sent out?' Parry questioned.

'Finally dated and sent out, boss. He decided to wait till after the memorial service, I expect.'

'Or for a day when he couldn't be reached after the post was delivered. Or ever again, worse luck for him,' he added grimly. 'What's the other thing? You've got something from Griffith's polytechnic, have you?'

'Yes. His old head of department's been away all week at a conference. Came back last night. Name of Blatton. He's coming up for retirement. Lives in Bath. Wife works at the old poly too. University now, of course. She's in admin. I went to see them on my way back this morning.'

'Anything useful?'

Lloyd nodded. 'Mr Blatton wasn't responsible for Mr Griffith's appointment in the first place, and he never liked him. Seems nobody did.'

'Any real enemies?'

'None that would have murdered him, Mr Blatton says. They were sort of academic enemies, if you see what I mean? People who didn't like his teaching methods, or some of his theories.'

'So they were glad when he was made redundant?'

'Except he wasn't.' Lloyd scowled and changed gear as they drew away from some traffic lights. 'That was a story put out to save face. He was fired. For dishonesty. Nothing huge. That's why they didn't prosecute. He'd been fiddling his expenses and indenting for books he'd never bought. And equipment. But he'd been doing it over a longish period.'

'And the Blattons told you this?'

'After I explained we were treating Mr Griffith's death as possibly suspicious.'

'And Griffith had admitted he was guilty?'

'On condition they didn't charge him officially, yes. He was beside himself not to be exposed as a thief, see? Made up what he'd stolen out of his redundancy payment.' Lloyd made a tutting noise to indicate he disapproved of people who were fired for dishonesty getting redundancy payments. 'Except it wasn't enough.' There were more tuts at this. 'He got his mother to find the rest, I expect. And he wrote a letter apologizing for making errors. It was as good as a confession Mrs Blatton says. Anyway, it's all on file in their registrar's office.'

'But nobody here knows about any of it?'

'I wouldn't say that, boss, because – Sorry!' Lloyd had suddenly rocked them both forward in their seats after stopping the car sharply at a pedestrian crossing.

'You mean his wife probably knew?'

'Not just her. Abel Davies's wife has known for a long time he was sacked. And she rang Mrs Blatton for more details Wednesday evening.'

'They know each other?'

'Better than that. They're sisters.'

'Hm. So now we know what Mrs Davies meant about Griffith being too vulnerable to risk making threats to other people.' Parry's eyes narrowed. 'Pity his murderer hadn't known it too. Might have saved his life.'

18

'Afternoon, Mr Pa-wee. And Mr Lloyd. Awful old day, isn't it?' called Sheila Cromwell-Evans in her sharp soprano. She had appeared, stepping briskly, from around the eastern corner of Ridings, and waved to the two policemen as they were approaching the front door on the north side of the house. It was still raining and the wind had increased. 'My husband isn't here,' she explained as she came closer.

'Out riding is he, ma'am?' asked Lloyd.

'No, no. On business. He said he'd be back in time to go out with the children though. In time for lunch too, but there's no sign of him yet. It's him you want, is it?' She was dressed over all in a billowing, yellow rain cape with a hood. The cape covered her whole body down to the tops of her green Wellington boots. Only one wet-gloved hand and jewelled wrist protruded through an armhole in the cape. The hand was grasping a shallow wicker basket loaded with daffodils and sprigs of yellow forsythia in full bloom. There was a large raindrop on the end of her nose that Gomer Lloyd considered quite fetching.

'We were hoping to catch both of you, really, Mrs Cromwell-Evans,' said Parry. 'Those flowers are nice.'

She looked down sharply at the basket, dislodging the raindrop. 'Yes. Well you wee-ly feel sp-wing's a-wived cutting blooms like these fu-wom your own garden. Come in this way, then. The front door's open. Sow-wee I'm in such a mess.'

Once inside the large main hall, with its floor of mammoth black and white square tiles, Mrs Cromwell-Evans threw the

187

glistening smock off over her head with all the abandonment of an enthusiastic stripper – except that underneath she was wearing a white halter-necked sweater and dark blue slacks, the slacks tucked into the boots. She pulled the boots off next with great energy and clever balance control, while standing and briefly hopping on alternate legs, making the gold chains around her neck jangle and glint.

Lloyd regretted that the boot removal would be the end of the show. Despite what his boss had called her tarty looks, he quietly admired Mrs Cromwell-Evans's appearance. Indeed, he was generally partial to buxom, mature women with pretty faces, which is why, he would have said, he was married to one, and very happily married too. He would also have openly admitted that his wife Hilda was no dazzler like Sheila Cromwell-Evans, whose hair and make-up were still at nearly bandbox standard, despite the weather and the things she'd been doing.

'Should have come in the back way, I suppose. I'll clear all that away later,' the lady offered next, referring to the flower basket and her outdoor clothing abandoned on or under the modern oak refectory table in the centre of the hall which it dominated. 'De-wop your coats there too, if you like,' she continued. 'Come through to the conserva-twee.' She led the way down the hall in her red stockinged feet, throwing open a wide glass door at the end. 'It's bu-witer out here on a dull day. Shall I make some tea?'

'That's very kind of you. But I don't suppose we'll be staying long,' said Parry, anxious to get on with interviewing her while her husband was out.

'Later, pe-waps. Sit down then,' she said, doing so herself in one of the unusually low, cushioned bamboo armchairs. 'We keep it warm in here for the te-wopical plants. Lovely, aren't they?' She looked about her with pride.

Both men smiled and nodded a tacit agreement while lowering themselves into chairs set only a slim distance across from Mrs Cromwell-Evans. The interior of the con-servatory, although high and wide, seemed to be in use more as a hothouse than simply as extra living space. The exotic plants displayed were certainly impressive, some huge leafed and tall, others with colourful, wax-like blooms, but they occupied too much of the space for comfort and made things darker not brighter. Parry felt as though he was sitting in a jungle clearing, and a confined one at that. Lloyd wished he had taken off his raincoat before sitting down, as the other man had done: it would have meant too much of a heave to get up again from the almost legless chair he was in.

'We're hoping, Mrs Cromwell-Evans, that you and your husband can give us some more help over our inquiries into the death of Mr Elwyn Griffith,' the sergeant said, opening his notebook and trying to twist himself into a position where he could write in it.

'I'm sure we'll help in any way we can, Mr Lloyd.'

'Thank you. Can you tell us what time you left White Cross Cottage on Wednesday night?'

'So far as I wee-member, it was close to half past twelve. I hadn't meant to stay so late, but we went on chatting.'

'It couldn't have been earlier than midnight?'

'Might have been, I suppose. But not much. Pe-waps Alison will know?'

'And you came straight back here, ma'am?'

'That's right.'

'So you got here at?'

'Well, it would have been quarter to one, wouldn't it? It usually takes about quarter of an hour. I never hu-wee at night. Not on na-wow woads.'

'Quite right. And did you see or speak to anyone here after you got back?'

She frowned, crossed her legs, and absently stroked the top of her thigh. 'Let me think. Claire and the children were all in bed. Claire's the au pair. Fe-wench, she is. Plain girl, but a beautiful nature. I wee-member the light was still on in her woom. I expect she heard me. But no, we never spoke. Is it important?'

'Not really, Mrs Cromwell-Evans.' Not if the au pair had been briefed to confirm the point, both policemen were thinking; and if she hadn't, in a twisted way it would be no less confirmation that Mrs Cromwell-Evans was probably telling the truth. 'And your husband got home later than that, did he?' Lloyd continued.

'Yes. And I know what time for certain. It was ten past one. I'd just de-wopped off, see? He woke me, and I wee-member looking at the time.'

'Thank you.' The sergeant glanced at Parry.

'Are you familiar with Fairbody's in Bristol, Mrs Cromwell-Evans?' asked the chief inspector.

'You mean the hat shop? Yes. Why?'

'Have you bought anything there recently.'

'Let me see.' An index finger attached itself to her closed lips, then sprang away again. 'Yes, wi-ding hats for the children. Last summer. When we were over one Saturday for a matinée. In August, it was. Don't know why we waited to buy them in Bu-wistol. There's plenty of good places for wi-ding hats here. It was for the Fairbody label, I expect. My children are awful snobs. Worse than my husband. Oh, and he bought a hat for himself at the same time.'

'What sort of hat?'

'A bowler with a curly bu-wim, it was.' Her head went up as she gave a disparaging huff. 'I ask you? Of all things. A bowler. For going to London, he said. I told him he'd never wear it. And he hasn't. Except the once. To a funeral here in Tawrbach. He thought it was ve-wee with it, dashing like, till the rector said it made him look like the fat one in Laurel and Hardy, only shorter.' The smile on her face died quickly. 'Poor Ca-wadog Watkins. He was always joking. And fancy taking his life like that? No need in this day and age, either. Whatever he'd done, people would have understood, wouldn't they? Understood and forgiven? It's te-wible for Esme, his wife.'

'Terrible,' Parry agreed solemnly, but wondering if people would have been as understanding as all that, or as tolerant towards a parson. 'And you didn't buy anything at Fairbody's in June last year? In its sale?' he asked, after a seemly pause.

She thought for a moment and began disentangling one gold neck chain from another. 'I don't think so.' She leaned forward while squinting down at the chains. Lloyd immediately opposite her could hardly prevent his gaze from following hers intently into the depths of the cleavage exposed by the sweater's sagging neck, as Mrs Cromwell-Evans added: 'No. Definitely not. We're on their mailing list. But no. I don't go to sales much.'

'I see. What about Saturday, February 27th this year? That's three weeks ago today.'

She shook her head. 'My parents were here. It's my mother's birthday. We stayed here all day. My mother likes to spend as much time as she can with the children. Well, it's understandable, isn't it? There are no other gu-wandchildren. But why d'you want to know about Fair-body's?' She looked up suddenly and before Lloyd could alter the direction of his fascinated gaze. She gave him a half admonishing, half appreciative look, while smoothing a hand backwards and forwards under her breasts.

'Just routine, Mrs Cromwell-Evans,' Parry replied. 'As a matter of interest, do you happen to know your husband's hat size?'

'Yes. He's a 7¼. Real big head.'

Parry nodded at Lloyd who made a note, then Parry continued: 'Thank you. In fact we're trying to find out when Elwyn Griffith bought that wide-brimmed hat of his.'

'His famous fedow-wa?' Leaning further forward, she clasped her hands around her knees. 'That was from Fair-body's, was it? Oh, Elwyn had that hat this long time. Never saw him out without it. Always wore hats, of course. Because he went bald so early, I expect. Alison told me you found the hat next to the body.'

'Yes. The one we found may have been bought for him quite recently. By a lady with hair the same colour as yours. She was wearing a white Burberry trenchcoat.'

'Is that wight? Well, it wasn't me. I don't have a white te-wenchcoat, and I don't usually buy pe-wesents for other people's husbands.' She smirked, and nodded knowingly at Lloyd. 'Pe-waps it was his mother? D'you know what age the lady was?'

'Not accurately, but it was bought since her death.'

'Ah. Anyway Won-wen was a lot older than me.'

'And Madam Rhonwen wasn't a redhead, was she, Mrs Cromwell-Evans?' asked Lloyd picking up the point.

'If the fancy took her, she was. She had wigs for all occasions. Lovely ones. Didn't you know that? Lot of people didn't, I suppose. Blonde and auburn they were mostly. Well, aw-wiginally she'd been a wed-dy blonde, of course. Or so she said. We didn't know her then.' She leaned back, and twice ran both hands fiercely through her own hair to demonstrate that it all belonged to her. 'Pa-wis-made, some of those wigs were. And Mayfair. Cost a mint. I hope Alison's looking after them. Anyway, as you said, it couldn't have been his mother who bought the hat for Elwyn. Not if she was dead all-wedy.'

'Dead, but not lying down,' said a gravelly male voice. All three looked around to see Evan Cromwell-Evans standing half behind what looked like a grossly oversized rhubarb bush. He was wearing a well-cut, blue pinstripe suit. There was a burning cigar held between two fingers of his left hand, while a twelve-bore shotgun was cradled in the crutch of his bent right elbow. 'Nice to see you again, Merlin. And you, sergeant.' He raised the cigar to his lips and drew on it heavily, with his gaze now locked on to Parry's.

Lloyd had already heaved himself out of his chair with surprising alacrity. Parry had come to his feet as well. Both men had eyed the gun. Lloyd was still doing so.

'Good afternoon, sir. After rabbits in the garden, are you?' Parry asked.

The newcomer opened his stance and gave a grunting chuckle that seemed to originate from well below his stomach. 'I'm always after vermin, yes. Little buggers even get in here if they can. Especially if you're not looking.' He switched his gaze to Lloyd.

'I wouldn't let that off in here, though, sir,' said the sergeant unblinkingly.

'Well of course I bloody won't. You don't think I'm that *twp*, do you? Whatever the provocation.' Cromwell-Evans completed the words in a studied, even tone. 'Anyway, it's not loaded.' Sharply, he broke open the gun to prove the point, then leaned it against a chair, the breach still open.

'It's been for a check-up. I just picked it up at the gunsmith in Penarth. Don't worry, sergeant, it's going back in the locked gun case in my study.'

'You're later than you said, Evan,' his wife remarked.

'Very important meeting that went on a bit, that's why. Where are the children?'

'Down at the wi-ding school. Claire went with them on their bikes after lunch. When you didn't show up. Or wing me.' The wife's side of this exchange had been noticeably cool.

'Right, I'll go down there later. Have our guests been offered refreshment?'

'Thank you, yes. But we're not stopping,' said Parry.

'But now you're here, you must come and see that new horse of mine before you go, Merlin.' Cromwell-Evans drew in hard on the cigar. 'So, to what do we owe the pleasure of this visit? Still working on Elwyn's death, are you? Oh, do sit down.' He moved to a chair himself beside his wife.

'We were just asking if Mrs Cromwell-Evans could help us over when Mr Griffith bought his fedora hat. In Bristol.'

Cromwell-Evans's gaze went to his wife then back to Parry. 'And has she?' He didn't appear to have found the question in any way unexpected.

'Not wee-ly, love,' she said. 'It came from Fairbody's. Where you got that silly bowler.'

'Is that so.' He looked at the two policemen as though daring them to make anything out of the last piece of information. 'Bit up-market for Elwyn I'd have thought, Fairbody's,' he added.

'They were saying it was bought for him by a wed-headed lady,' his wife added, it seemed almost too promptly, and just possibly as though she might be alerting him. 'I said it was more likely to have been his mother, if she was still alive at the time.'

'At Fairbody's prices, it would have to be her. Unless he had a rich fancy woman somewhere.' He blew cigar smoke in his wife's direction. 'No, not Elwyn. Didn't have the puff for a double life.'

'We were just about to explain the hat we found by his

body wasn't his size, sir,' said Lloyd. 'It was a 7¼. His size was a 6¼.'

'I've just said 7¼ is your size, Evan,' his wife volunteered, and again as if she were warning him.

'Perhaps it wasn't his bloody hat,' said Cromwell-Evans chuckling loudly, leaning back in the chair, and stretching his legs out straight in front of him. His appearance was altogether a study in unruffled confidence.

'Seven and a quarter is your size, sir?' asked Lloyd.

'Yes. And most probably the size of enough men in Cardiff to fill Roath Park twice over,' came the relaxed rejoinder.

'We realize that. It was just the coincidence, you see?' This was Parry. He looked at his watch. 'Well, thank you very much for your help, Mrs Cromwell-Evans. We'd better be going now. Perhaps I could have a look at that new horse of yours on the way out, sir?'

'Now you're talking.' Cromwell-Evans was already on his feet. 'You interested in horses too, sergeant?'

'Only slow ones, it seems, sir, and never by intention,' said Lloyd ruefully. 'I'll leave it to the chief inspector to see whether you've got a winner or not.' He turned to Parry. 'See you out front then, boss, in the car.'

A minute later Cromwell-Evans was leading Parry alone along the stone path that linked the west end of the house with the stable and garage yard. There was still a strong breeze, but the rain had stopped, and a watery sun was appearing fitfully behind fast moving clouds.

'I wonder if you've had a chance yet to remember where you were last Wednesday evening, sir?' said Parry.

'Oh, I didn't have to remember, Merlin. I never forgot.' The smile was expansive and the tone wholly tolerant, even genuinely amused, as the two rounded the side of the yard. 'It just wasn't possible or prudent to tell you or anyone else. Up to today, at least.'

'Well, I hope it's possible now, sir? It's important.' His tone had become perceptibly more official. 'I'm afraid if you're not ready to explain —'

'Is that why we're out here?' Cromwell-Evans interrupted, in time to stem what was evidently going to be some kind of warning. 'So I wouldn't have to own up to anything embarrassing in front of my wife?' They had reached the padlocked door to the first of the looseboxes.

'I thought it might possibly be easier this way, yes, sir.'

Cromwell-Evans put a hand on the other man's shoulder. 'Well that was very thoughtful of you, Merlin, boy. But I wasn't shacked up on Wednesday with a bird, if that's what you've been thinking.' He took a last puff on the cigar, dropped the end and put his foot on it. 'By rights, I should wait till tomorrow, but since we're old friends, and since it'll be in all the papers in the morning, I'll tell you the exciting facts now.' He turned to undo the padlock with a key he had just taken from his pocket. 'I drove to London Wednesday afternoon for a meeting in the City with the directors of a public company. And their bankers and lawyers. It went on till pretty late in the evening. After that, I had supper in a private suite at the Savoy Hotel with the chief executive and the finance director of the public company before driving back. Got here about one in the morning.' He opened the upper half of the door and clipped it back on a metal catch. 'How's that for a show stopper, then?'

The big horse inside had moved across, loudly rustling the straw on the floor. Now it was dipping its head and glistening neck after thrusting both through the opening.

'Lovely animal, sir,' said Parry, except he was contemplating a different sort of show stopper. It seemed that Cromwell-Evans might just be about to remove himself from the top of the suspect list for the murder of Elwyn Griffith.

'Oh, you're better than lovely, aren't you, Panther, my beauty?' crooned Cromwell-Evans, vigorously smoothing the horse's chest with the flat of his hand. 'And we're going out later, aren't we? Never mind what the weather does.' He turned to Parry, while the animal butted its owner's shoulder. 'Didn't have our regular outing this morning, d'you see? Had to be in more meetings, since first thing.'

'With the same people, sir?'

'Some of them, yes. In Cardiff this time, though, not London. Ended with what's called a formal completion an hour ago. You see, I've done a merger with the DTB Electric

Group. Marvellous deal. I'll be going on their main board, with special responsibility for new store development. They like my style, see?'

'Congratulations.'

'Thank you, Merlin. You understand why it all had to be hush hush? From everybody. Even my wife. No exceptions. If the deal hadn't gone through, I couldn't afford people thinking Shevan Electric Markets hadn't been good enough for DTB, could I now?'

'I suppose not, sir.' From what he knew of the matter, the 'people' referred to meant primarily Mrs Cromwell-Evans's father.

'And with great respect, I couldn't afford to have directors of DTB bothered by detectives checking my movements on Wednesday either. Especially when the detectives are work- ing on a serious crime. Little things can easily upset a merger deal.'

'I take the point, yes,' said Parry. 'Does it mean the Shevan stores will disappear now?'

'The opposite. The number will double at least. And we'll have all the money we need for expansion from now on. No grubbing about for pennies from here, there, and every- where. I'll have more financial independence than I've had for years. Great bunch of people DTB Electric. And it's a lot of money for me personally, I can tell you, Merlin. We'll be paying off the loan capital in Shevan. Getting rid of the min- ority shareholders too, at a fair profit for them, of course, so no grumbles.' The last phrases came like private thoughts spoken aloud, but with relish.

Again, Parry, like many others, had understood that there was only one person with a minority shareholding in the company, and that was Stanley Johns, the chairman's father- in-law, who was also reputed to be the provider of most of its substantial loan capital. He wondered if Cromwell-Evans's obvious delight at being rid of his dependence on Johns would have any effect on his relations with Johns's daughter.

'And it was the DTB directors you were with on Wednes- day, sir?'

'Right enough.' Cromwell-Evans had returned to pampering his horse.

'Did you see Mr Elwyn Griffith when you were in London?'

'No.'

'And he didn't call you from Paddington earlier?'

'No. I thought I'd told you that already, Merlin?'

'But that was when you had to keep your own trip to London secret, sir.'

'Well, I'm telling you again, he didn't call me.' Cromwell-Evans beamed benevolently at the policeman. 'So, now are you satisfied?'

'Just one or two other questions, sir. What time did you leave the people you had supper with?'

'On Wednesday night? Er . . . about ten. Just after. They'll tell you I'm sure, if you want.'

'And you had a fast drive back?'

'The Lexus went like the wind after we got out of sodding London. Who'd want to live there, eh? Bloody marvellous car the Lexus. Thoroughbred, like you, my beauty,' he added, turning back to the horse.

'So you reached Cardiff in what . . . two hours fifteen minutes?'

'Less. Two hours maximum. And don't tell the traffic cops, except I hadn't drunk any alcohol all day.'

It was almost inconceivable that a guilty man would have walked into so obvious a trap, but this man was so high on his own achievements it was just a possibility still. 'So can you account for your movements between midnight and one o'clock when you said you finally reached home, sir?'

'Sure. I dropped Nye Vincent at his house in Radyr, went in with him for a quick –'

'Who's Nye Vincent, sir?'

'Local director of our bank, in Cardiff. You don't know Nye?'

'No, sir.'

'Very able man. Shrewd and discreet with it. You can trust him totally.'

The policeman's polite expression implied that he would

keep the commendation in mind. 'And Mr Vincent had been with you on Wednesday?'

'Yes. Didn't I say? A lot of the time, yes. He had to be party to the deal, see? We're into the bank for a tidy sum at the moment. Our second biggest piece of loan capital. We're paying off the biggest one, that's from a private source. My father-in-law, as a matter of fact. Not the best sort of arrangement that. Too restrictive, if you follow me? Anyway, DTB want to keep the overdraft facility with the bank going. At the same rate as I've been getting.'

'But Mr Vincent wasn't with you all day, sir?'

'No, no. He went up by train in the morning. Had to square things with his own people in the City. Then he joined us for the afternoon meetings.'

'He had supper with you, sir?'

'No. Just coffee at the end. He's got a married daughter somewhere in St John's Wood. He popped up there to see her. Then he drove back with me. Didn't I say that either?'

'No, sir. And what time did you leave his house?'

'Oh, it was about ten to one. It's not far from here, of course.'

'Or course, sir.'

19

'What were the Rebecca Riots, Uncle Merlin?' asked the pert, seven-year-old Hannah Ellis. The 'uncle' was a courtesy title: the child was Perdita's niece not Parry's. She flicked one corn-coloured pigtail out from under the collar of her rain jacket. This briefly interrupted her close study of the guide-book to the unusual museum, but not her consuming of a second, still warm, and sugared Welsh cake held in her other hand.

'The Rebecca Riots started one night in er . . . May 1838,' Parry replied, with only momentary hesitation and an exact-ness that impressed Perdita Jones a good deal more than it did the child: Hannah's father was a Cardiff head teacher and she expected grown-ups to know everything. 'It was in Efailwen, Carmarthenshire,' the policeman went on. 'Around four hundred poor farmers dressed themselves up in women's clothes, blackened their faces, then marched on a new tollhouse and wrecked it.'

'Was it the same as the tollhouse over there, Uncle Merlin? There's a picture of it in here too.' She held up the guidebook for him to see, after pointing at the squat, whitewashed build-ing with its Gothic windows and flanking five-bar gate, set a short distance from where they were sitting, well wrapped up, in the open air. The day had been sunny, but the late-afternoon temperature had turned crisp.

'Very much like that one, I expect, although I think your guidebook says the one over there was built in 1771. So it had been around a long time before it was dismantled and brought here to the museum.'

'And why did they destroy the one at . . . er?'

'Efailwen? Because the farmers objected paying tolls for bad roads when they took their produce to market.'

'So why were they dressed up as women, Uncle Merlin?'

Perdita was glad he had joined them, but wondered if he felt the same. He had been dutifully answering the child's relentless questioning since their arrival at eleven in the morning. It was now nearly five.

Parry had called Perdita on Saturday night, asking her to have lunch with him next day. She had explained that she was looking after her wearing and intense young niece for the day, but that Parry was welcome to go with them to the outdoor Welsh Folk Museum at nearby St Fagans, on a trip promised to the child whether the weather was wet or fine. After this intentionally off-putting invitation – the weather forecast had indicated rain – Perdita had been mildly surprised, and quite flattered, when Parry had accepted with alacrity. She had also been surprised that the sky had stayed blue all day, something Parry privately ascribed to virtue getting its own reward.

Parry had used the occasion to prove to Perdita that he was good with children. Why this was suddenly so necessary he couldn't explain, but it was. He was only thankful that Hannah had turned out to be bright and interested, rather than wearing and intense. He had quickly and rightly concluded that the prior descriptions of her had only been offered to discourage him from coming.

'The farmers disguised themselves so they couldn't be identified afterwards,' he said now, in answer to Hannah's last question. He had cheated a bit with the Rebecca Riots. He had sensibly boned up on them, and a few other likely topics, before leaving his flat that morning.

'But that would've been why they blacked their faces, Uncle Merlin, not why they wore women's clothes,' the child responded with quiet but firm assurance. 'You could have told they were men by their beards and things. It's the same with women when they dress up as men. People always know. I always know.'

Parry suddenly had a mental picture of the ample Sheila

Cromwell-Evans dressed up to look like the spindly Elwyn Griffith. 'I think you're probably right, Hannah,' he replied, still unsettled by the image.

'So why were they called the Rebecca Riots, Uncle Merlin?'

'Because it said in the book of Genesis that the children of Rebecca would take over the gates of her enemies.'

'Did that mean the children would be getting all the enemy's money as well?'

'Er . . . yes. Chapel people relied on the Bible a lot in those days. They used scripture to justify their actions. To make them look right.'

'Especially when they were about to wreck a building,' put in Perdita, cynically.

'Well, if it made them feel better,' Parry said, a bit absently. The last exchange had set him thinking about who would be getting Madam Rhonwen's money. Although he had promised himself the day off, he was finding it impossible entirely to dismiss the Griffith case from his mind.

'So was the tollgate taken over, Uncle Merlin?' Hannah interrupted his musings again. Her deep blue eyes showed she was giving the subject solemn consideration. She curled one leg up under her on the seat and thoughtfully scratched the bent knee through the thick woollen, orange tights she had on under her pleated blue skirt.

'Not straightaway. The house and gate were repaired and used again by the people who owned it.'

'So the poor farmers lost?'

'No, they won in the end. Rebecca Riots went on all over Wales, and after ten years the government in London finally accepted there was a wrong that needed putting right.'

'Oh, good.' She looked from Parry to Perdita. 'Please may I have another Welsh cake from the bakery, Auntie Perdita?'

'No, I think we've had enough, darling. And Uncle Merlin bought us such a good lunch. Anyway, it's time we were going home. It'll soon be dark.'

'Then please can we see the farm machines again on the way out?'

'I expect so.'

The three got up from the long wooden seat outside the

century-old, brick bakehouse where they had bought the freshly made bakestone cakes. Like the tollhouse, the bakehouse had been removed from its original site and brought here to the fifty-acre museum, a few miles to the west of Cardiff. Over thirty carefully dismantled buildings from all over Wales had been re-erected on the lush green, and pleasingly undulating site to show how the people of Wales had lived, worked, farmed, shopped, worshipped and been educated from the sixteenth century onwards.

Although it had been Hannah's second visit, she had insisted on missing out nothing she had seen before, including the indoor galleries attached to the modernistic entrance building. They returned to these now.

'Is that the very first tractor ever used in Wales, Uncle Merlin?' she demanded as, for the second time that day, they moved through the little girl's unpredictably favourite Farm Vehicle Gallery.

'If it's not the first tractor, it looks as if it ought to be, doesn't it?' said Parry.

'Combine harvesters are much bigger than this one now, aren't they, Uncle Merlin?' Hannah pressed, a moment later, when they were standing in front of the next exhibit.

'Yes, many times bigger. This one only did part of the job the big machines do today. Its very basic, and probably kept breaking down, like the old motor cars.'

'What's that long black box on the back for, Uncle Merlin?'

He wondered too. 'It's a tool box, I should think. And a place for carrying spare parts, petrol cans, and anything else the driver might need on a long day in the fields.'

'Looks big enough for him to sleep in too if he wanted, don't you think, Uncle Merlin? Would he have needed somewhere to sleep in the fields as well?'

'I shouldn't think so.' Parry was trying to remember where he had seen something similar recently when Hannah took his hand and pulled him over to see a horse-drawn reaper. It was also the moment when the phone in his pocket started ringing.

'Lucky nobody wanted me till now, I suppose,' he remarked later as he caught up with the others near the main exit. 'I've been on call all day.'

'Something important, is it?' asked Perdita.

'Yes. Developments we weren't expecting till tomorrow at the earliest. Credit to my army of workers. Look, I'll drop you both in Tawrbach, then I'll need to head for my flat. I'm meeting Gomer Lloyd there.'

'Pity. We were hoping you'd have supper with us at home. Before Hannah's mummy picks her up, weren't we, Hannah?' said Perdita, sounding genuinely disappointed.

'Uncle Merlin could come back after, couldn't he, Auntie Perdita? Even if I've gone?'

'It might be rather late, I'm afraid,' he said.

'That wouldn't matter would it, Auntie Perdita? If it's very late he could stay the night at your house, couldn't he?' the child suggested, showing either a refreshing innocence, or a developed capacity for intrigue that should have been beyond her years.

'What a good idea,' the policeman agreed with enthusiasm.

Perdita tried unsuccessfully to stifle a smile.

'Are you in love with each other?' Hannah inquired in the same earnest way she had asked about tollgates and tractors.

'I'll tell you if your aunt will,' Parry answered, looking hard at Perdita as he opened the car door for her.

'Mind your own business, Miss Matchmaker,' said Perdita, her face reddening, and her hand tugging at one of Hannah's pigtails as she bundled her into the back seat. 'I thought you were supposed to be my best friend?'

'Shouldn't I have said that, then? Sorry, Auntie Perdita. Sorry, Uncle Merlin.' She looked first surprised, then suitably penitent before taking a very deep breath. 'Laura Jackson, she's not my best friend, just an ordinary friend, she says best friends can be the worst because they're always letting you down without meaning to.' She took another and even deeper breath. 'That's because best friends know *everything* about you. And they can take your things sometimes, and say they're theirs not yours, and try to keep them, because sometimes they think the things really are theirs. That's what Laura Jackson says, anyway.'

Perdita stared ahead not caring to look at the husband of the dear, dead Rosemary Parry, her closest friend over many years, and believing he was thinking exactly what she was thinking about the appropriating habits of best friends.

But Perdita was wrong about the close friendship Hannah's words had brought to Parry's mind. They were prompting him to examine a quite different trio of friends from Perdita, himself and his late wife.

'Sorry to keep you waiting, Gomer,' said Parry, fifteen minutes later, when he emerged from the lift to find the sergeant waiting outside the front door of his fourth floor flat.

'That's all right, boss. Only just got here. The lady on the ground floor, the one who knows me, she saw me waiting and let me in off the street,' Lloyd replied, glad to have had a moment to get his breath back after climbing the stairs. Someone had left the lattice door of the lift open – and on the fourth floor. The residents of the Edwardian mansion flats along the western side of Westgate Street enjoyed a vintage form of elevation that perfectly equated with the old-fashioned elegance of their quarters.

Parry was renting the flat furnished from the owner, a friend who was working in New York for two years. The rent was low because the friend and his wife favoured having a tenant they could trust to care for their things. The arrangement had been perfect for Parry, at least for the time being. Except for a very few things, he had sold his own furniture with the house in Tawrbach. Both had evoked too many memories for him to want to keep either.

'Glad you didn't mind me fetching you back,' Lloyd said as Parry ushered him through the door and along the hall to the comfortable sitting room. 'What we've got looked too important to wait till morning, and too hot to go into detail on an open line, like,' he went on, 'coming on top of the telephone company report, as well.'

'You said there were two calls to Niedlich from the Coedar Down number?' Parry questioned, pulling the curtains, then dropping in to a chintz-covered armchair across from Lloyd.

'That's right, boss. One of the team checked with Niedlich at home this morning. He thinks he remembers the dates, and the times, and roughly the reasons for both calls. And they were definitely from Mr Griffith. Or someone saying he was Mr Griffith.'

'And it was the same voice on both calls?'

'And the same as on the other calls he'd had from Mr Griffith. He's good at voices, Mr Niedlich.'

'Yes, he told me that when I saw him. But according to Griffith's diary, on the date of the first call he was in London, all day?'

'And not just according to his diary. There's something else now. But I'll come back to that.'

'OK. The first call was made at eleven-forty in the morning?'

'And I'll explain in a sec why we know for certain Mr Griffith couldn't have made it from that number, even if he had access to a phone there other times. There were only the two calls from there to Mr Niedlich in the last six weeks or so, and we're now pretty sure Mr Griffith couldn't have made the other one either.'

'And there were no calls to Niedlich from any of the other lines we've had checked?'

'None. Oh, except five from the rectory. We knew about them, of course.'

Parry frowned. 'Niedlich told me he had a number of calls from Griffith in the last month.'

'Made from lines we couldn't have checked, probably. Call boxes I expect. Safer, that would be, if it was someone impersonating Mr Griffith. If the caller was thinking about security. Except he slipped up over those two. Forgot, probably. Or decided it didn't matter. Funny how clever people can get careless,' Lloyd completed.

'Right, so tell me now what we've got from Griffith's computer that's so revealing.'

Lloyd leaned forward in the chair. 'Mike Price rang me at home this afternoon. You know he took the computer away to work on over the weekend? You said you wanted every document in it read. Well he hasn't finished doing that yet, because of the two books for one thing, but take a look at these.' He handed Parry a print-out of two letters, one of two pages, the other a single sheet which he had just taken from his document case.

Parry scanned the letters quickly. 'Hm. Alters things dramatically, doesn't it?' he said. 'Who is this Dr Literman of Upper Wimpole Street?'

'Until last year he was a consultant at two London hospitals, but he's given that up to concentrate on his private work. More profitable, most likely. He's one of the real international authorities on his subject, boss. Well that's according to Dr Maltravers. I rang him for a view after we'd looked up Dr Literman in the medical directory.'

'Pity we don't have Literman's letter to Griffith.'

'We may be able to get a copy from the doctor himself.'

Parry shook his head. 'Don't count on it, Gomer, not without a court order, and even then some of these top medicos insist the Hippocratic oath protects their dead patients as well as their live ones.'

'We did do another search through the correspondence we took away from the cottage. It's all in the incident room. But there's no sign of anything there from Dr Literman.'

'So either the letter's still at the cottage, or else Griffith destroyed it after he wrote this second sad little note. You noticed he says his local doctor isn't to be told anything?'

'Yes. It's obviously why we got nothing from him on the subject.'

'Right.' Parry reread part of the single sheet letter, and pulled a face. 'Not difficult to understand how Griffith must have felt, is it?' he said.

'And the dates in the first letter, about the two appointments with Dr Literman, they match the diary dates of the trips Mr Griffith made to London in January and February.'

'To see publishers and agents?'

'That's what he'd told Mrs Griffith, boss.'

'While it's clear from both letters that he hadn't told her he was seeing Literman.'

'And the January appointment, which Mr Griffith says in the first letter he's kept already, that was on the day he's supposed to have called Mr Niedlich from Coedar Down at eleven-forty.'

'Ah, I see now why he couldn't possibly have done that. The letters make far better evidence than his diary.'

'While the date and time of the second call from there to Mr Niedlich clashes with the February appointment with the doctor.'

'An appointment it's pretty safe to assume Griffith also kept.' Parry paused. 'Incidentally, it's no wonder he never made appointments with publishers or agents during that time.'

'Like Butler and Robinson, in Baker Street, who said they hadn't seen him for six months?'

'That's right, because when he went to London he spent all the time in Upper Wimpole Street by the look of it. Literman has some kind of day clinic there, does he, as well as consulting rooms?'

'That's what we've been told.' There was silence for a moment, while Lloyd studied Parry's face, then he added: 'Seems we'd been barking up the wrong tree till you went to see Mr Niedlich.'

'And it seems we were meant to, as well. It was a neat plan, and the fall-back plan was even neater, while it held up. D'you want a drink, Gomer?'

'No thanks.'

Parry didn't want a drink either, but he still got up, walked to a side table with bottles on it, touched two of the bottles, then came back again, after glancing at the cello he kept in one corner. The instrument was the largest of the possessions he had brought with him to the flat, though for all the time he had spent playing it he might as well have sold it with his other effects.

'So shall we go and talk to these neat planners, Gomer?' he said, having now made up his mind that they should.

'You want to go to Aberkidy first, boss?'

'No, let's not upset Mrs Griffith until we need to. We'll go to Pitcher's depot at Coedar Down. We may find enough evidence there to justify more than talk. Funny, I've been just up the road from there all day.' He pinched the end of his nose. 'And better call up some willing helpers to come with us,' he added. 'You said Tony Lovelaw was at the depot less than an hour ago?'

'His Land Rover was there yes, boss, and the gates weren't locked.'

When Parry and Lloyd arrived inside Pitcher's isolated depot, Lovelaw's Land Rover was still parked in the outhouse garage that lay on the opposite side of the yard from the small office building. Two detective constables had been riding behind them in a second car. The party had left both cars in the approach road and gone forward on foot through the unlocked gates.

It was nearly seven o'clock, and dark – darker than it would have been if heavy clouds hadn't started forming since sunset. Only the occasional headlight beam from moving vehicles on the main road nearby briefly lit up the mesh fencing, the old farmyard, the gaunt warehouse and the three smaller buildings. Otherwise there was only a little light showing from behind closed venetian blinds in two of the three office windows.

It was Lloyd's torch that had first picked out the Land Rover, and then, when the group got closer, the small Toyota saloon parked beside it. The sliding garage door had been half closed to hide the second car from view.

'I think we know that one, don't we, Gomer?' said Parry, flashing his own torch on the Toyota's number plate.

'Oh, yes. Fancy that being here. I suppose they think the vigilant police force doesn't work on Sundays.'

'More likely passion cannot be denied. Not over the whole of a weekend,' the chief inspector responded with mock gravity.

As the four policemen, each armed with torches, moved inside past the cars there was a sudden rustle of activity in front of them. A moment later, two large black cats and a smaller tabby raced past the intruders and out into the yard.

'Black cats are supposed to be lucky,' said Lloyd.

'If not always for those with asthma,' Parry rejoined. His torch had picked out the object he was looking for ahead of them, amongst what Lovelaw had earlier described to him as 'the leftovers of farming through the ages' stacked against the long rear wall. He doubted his mind had actively registered the same object on his last visit – only vaguely logged it as one of the shapes that made up the amorphous mass of derelict pieces, and then not solidly enough for him to have recalled it without an unknowing prompt from a little girl two hours before. Cats hadn't been in evidence on that visit either. He remembered being about to remark on the absence of them.

When they came right up to it, Parry judged the metal box to be eight feet long, two feet wide and two feet high. It was very nearly an exact match to the box on the back of the early combine harvester in the museum, only this one was painted red inside and out, not black. The box was partly hidden under an upturned wheelbarrow, some wired together, rotting wooden posts, a bundle of sacks, and a dilapidated wooden butter churn with strip metal bindings.

But this cluttered ensemble did not have an ages-old appearance to it. Only its constituent parts were ancient. Altogether their relationship looked contrived by recent arrangement not by the course of time. Most significantly, there was no dust on the box as there was on many of the things around it. It seemed to be in good repair too, and its long top side was open on its hinges, held back by two of the butter churn's splayed feet jammed awkwardly into the gap.

Stepping closer, Parry directed his torch beam to the inside of the box. One end was occupied by apple trays, the middle by two bags of lime, one of them spilled open, but, at the other end, there were six small kittens, three black, two tabby and one mostly white. The kittens were not more than two days old, and they were huddled on a bed of cotton waste. They looked up towards the light, eyes not yet opening properly, but going through the motions of blinking. Their mouths were making more than token efforts at opening though, as they emitted weak mewing bleats.

Parry now moved in closer still, kneeling, and concentrating the light on the box's locking mechanism. There was a keyhole on the outside, but the simple locking catch was inside. He could easily make out pathetic hairline scratches in the paintwork surrounding the bared catch lever.

'That's it then, isn't it, boss?' Lloyd's deep voice sounded quietly from just behind his ear.

'I'm afraid it is,' Parry replied soberly, getting to his feet. 'Tape off the garage, and get a forensic team here on the double, Gomer. Nothing else to be touched till they arrive,' he ordered, turning to the two DCs as Lloyd got out his mobile phone. 'Roberts, you stay here on the door. Hillier, come with us to the offices. Keep it quiet still, till we get there.'

The front door to the office building was locked, with the window beside it dark. DC Hillier's heavy pounding on the door instantly sparked signs of activity from inside the building. An internal door was closed loudly. Light appeared from behind the window blind. Then Lovelaw's voice sounded from immediately beyond the door.

'The depot's closed, I'm afraid. You'll have to come back in the morning,' he called, evidently attempting to inject calmness into his tone.

'Police, Mr Lovelaw. Open up,' Lloyd responded loudly. 'Detective Chief Inspector Parry wants to speak to you.'

'Good God, Merlin. What brings you here?' said the breathless Pitcher's Area Manager, tucking his shirt into his trousers with one hand while doing up a shirt button with the other. He was holding the door open with his foot. 'Do you want to come in?' he added, the invitation short on welcoming warmth.

Inside was a small reception area with a narrow table and a chair on the right, with some cabinets behind these, and an illustrated calendar hanging on the wall still turned to February. On the far wall was a door marked 'Toilet', and beside that a hat stand with two tweed caps and a black rain jacket hanging from it. To the left was a wooden partition wall with a door in the middle marked 'Office' which Lloyd, brushing past Lovelaw, pushed open against some resistance from the other side, accompanied by a woman's muffled cry of protest.

It was Alison Griffith who had stepped back from beyond the door. She was bare legged, wearing a skirt arranged crookedly, the zip still half undone. She was straightening a sweater which clearly she had pulled over her head only a split second before this.

'This is disgusting. Disgraceful,' she protested angrily.

'Yes, ma'am, it is,' Lloyd responded with no attempt at disguising his inborn nonconformist opinion of a young widow caught in the arms of her lover before her husband had even been buried.

The office was as meanly furnished as the vestibule. On the space in front of the desk the cheap carpeting had a tartan rug laid over it with several cushions scattered on top. On the desk there was an open bottle of gin and a half empty one of tonic. There were two glasses on the floor beside the rug. A pair of pantyhose was hanging on the back of a chair with a woman's black handbag open on the seat.

Parry had motioned Lovelaw to follow Lloyd through the door. Now he cleared his throat. 'Anthony Lovelaw and Alison Griffith,' he said. 'I am arresting you on suspicion for conspiring to murder Elwyn Griffith on or after March 17th of this year. You are not obliged to say anything, but anything you do say will be written down and may be used in evidence.'

20

'This is off the record, but once we'd figured the major deceptions, and there were three of them, it was obvious who'd killed Elwyn,' said Parry, as he and Perdita were moving briskly along the beach, a blustery, stimulating west wind in their faces.

It was the following Sunday. They hadn't seen each other since he had dropped her with Hannah after their visit to the Welsh Folk Museum exactly a week before. He would have returned to Tawrbach that evening if it had been possible, but it hadn't been. The first interrogations of Tony Lovelaw and Alison Griffith had not ended until the early hours of the next morning. For the following three days he had been wholly taken up with the case, and, following the confessions, with two new cases.

Today he had collected Perdita mid-morning and driven her along the coast to Ogmore, an elevated seaside village with magnificent views, good beaches and lush rolling downland behind. They were to have lunch there later, but had first crossed the shallow estuary of the Ogmore River, using the centuries-old stepping stones beside the ruined Norman castle. This had brought them on to five unbroken miles of wide deserted sands made the more solitary under a cloudless blue sky. It was the perfect early-spring day to sharpen the appetite with a walk by the seashore.

'And one of the deceptions was Madam Rhonwen never did keep diaries?' said Perdita.

'That's right. The diaries were a total invention. Dreamed up by Tony Lovelaw and Alison Griffith. He'd learned a bit from Reggie Singh about the goings-on at Rhonwen's more exclusive parties, including who'd been principally involved in them. He also got the names of the young performers who'd come for coaching from her agent. Man called Niedlich. Alison got his name from Rhonwen's address book. Lovelaw rang him, pretending to be Elwyn. Said he wanted the information so he could send the people cheques as informal legacies from Rhonwen.'

'But that never happened, did it?'

'No, it didn't. Originally Lovelaw wanted to put some of their names in the memo they sent to Davies, Prothero and Cromwell-Evans.'

'The memo they read out at the inquest on the rector?'

'Afraid so. And I'm sorry that was unavoidable.'

'It was in the paper too. But people seem to have accepted it for what it was – an offer by Elwyn to sell his mother's diaries.'

Parry's lips tightened then relaxed. 'It seems the events the memo suggested the diaries would uncover weren't as steamy as some of us supposed. That's according to Cromwell-Evans anyway. He's now fairly open on the subject.'

'But they were steamy enough to have worried him at the time?'

'And the other two members of the Operatic Committee. It had them all scared stiff. As you suspected, they'd had some fun and games up at Woodstock Grange, all right. If the details had come out it would probably have been damaging, but not terminal to reputations. Cromwell-Evans himself was the most vulnerable, but now this merger of his has gone through he couldn't care less.'

'The rector obviously thought the diaries would be terminal, though?'

'Because his fun and games had been . . . separate and . . . kinky, and, we have reason to believe, illegal. They involved him, Madam Rhonwen, probably Reggie Singh, and certainly a number of the boys who stayed at the Grange.'

'But not the three Tawrbach Godfathers who got the memo?'

'That's right. We'll never know the depth of that one. All

the principals are dead, and the bit players, the young men who came for coaching, they're not owning up to anything. Caradog Watkins panicked, and then acted too impetuously, I'm afraid.'

'He usually did.'

'Yes. But things were compounded this time by the trouble he'd got himself into on the Tuesday afternoon.'

'So did Tony Lovelaw ever use the names of Madam Rhonwen's protégés?'

'No. He may even have been keeping them on ice for a bit of blackmailing on his own account later. At least, that's what Alison is saying now.'

'Alison is saying that?'

'Oh yes. It's been everyone for herself or himself with those two since Monday afternoon.'

'When the coroner's jury decided Elwyn was murdered?'

'By a person or persons unknown.'

'So why did the two of them invent the diaries in the first place?'

'As a safeguard. To throw suspicion on others, if Elwyn's death was treated as murder.'

'But surely they didn't plan it to look like murder?'

'Certainly not. They wanted it to look as if he'd had a bad asthma attack, after he got off the bus. Unfortunately for them, his bruises and the torn fingers, which were definitely not in their plan, told a different story. It meant they had to fall back on their Plan Two.'

'But the memo had already been sent out by then?'

'Before Lovelaw actually did in Elwyn, yes. Pretty cool that was. Of course, if we'd accepted he'd died naturally, no one beyond the first recipients would ever have heard of the memo. Those three would certainly not have mentioned it to anyone else.'

'Wouldn't Megan Davies still have shown it to the rector?'

'Yes. But remember his letter to the coroner didn't refer to any memo. Only Rhonwen's diaries. No one could have figured how he came to know about the diaries, and with the best will in the world, I don't believe the other three, or Mrs Davies, would have done anything to enlighten them.

The police only knew about the memo when I was sent a copy. And that only happened because Alison and Lovelaw were running scared.'

'I suppose the other three might have tried to find the diaries, whatever else happened?'

'Yes. Prothero admitted obliquely he'd had a good look for them in Woodstock Grange, and I'm pretty sure Davies intended to search the Griffith cottage, except the rector did it for him.'

'Alison was so angry about the break-in. But shouldn't she have expected it?'

'She was genuinely angry, yes, because I don't believe she did expect it. Seems it wasn't a feature they'd taken into account in their scenario.'

'And it was Alison who left the memo at Tawrbach Police Station?'

'As soon as they realized we suspected murder. To start the diversion away from the two of them. It was she who wrote the memo on Elwyn's computer, and signed all the original copies. Elwyn's signature was a cinch to forge, especially for her.'

'And Elwyn never did go to London the day he died?'

'No, I'm afraid he didn't.'

'And that was the second major deception?'

'Yes. Lovelaw picked him up earlier than arranged that morning, except Elwyn wasn't too conscious of the time. Or anything else. Late the night before, Alison had laced his tea with three times the normal dose of phenobarb. He was still pretty doped when she got him up at five-thirty and told him Lovelaw was waiting for him. It's why he had no breakfast. He was going to get some on the train.'

'But Lovelaw didn't murder him at the cottage? Not in front of his wife? I can't believe Alison would have –'

'Wanted it done there?' Parry put in. 'That's true, but after everything Lovelaw has said about her, once they were busy grassing on each other, I'm afraid you can believe almost anything else about cool, calculating Alison.'

'They've really incriminated each other?'

'Yes. He was the one who broke first under questioning.

215

But when she was told what he'd admitted, she sang a lot louder than he did. Then it was almost a competition to see who could tell us the most. He said the whole thing was her idea, that she told him she was madly in love with him, hated her husband, but didn't see why she should leave him and lose out on the money he'd inherited, not after all the years she'd waited for it. If Lovelaw helped her murder Elwyn, she promised to marry him. He now insists he was her pawn.'

'And was the whole thing really her idea?'

'Most of it, I think. She's a hell of a lot brighter than he is. He was vulnerable, too. Sure that Pitcher's were going to close their Welsh operation. That that would make him redundant. He had no money apart from the bit he'd put in the design shop. He'd become crazy about Alison, of course.'

'His wife's closest friend,' said Perdita flatly.

'It happens,' he offered, without emotion. 'Only in this case I believe she lured him on for entirely selfish reasons. He was flattered. She's very attractive –'

'And very sexy. And poor Sally Lovelaw's merely worthy. And deeply faithful.' Perdita kicked the sand in front of her. 'So Tony drove Elwyn to Cardiff Central –'

'No. He told Elwyn he'd decided to go to London too. That Elwyn could drive up with him and save the train fare. Elwyn agreed.'

'Elwyn would have,' said Perdita.

'Yes, anything to save money, I'm afraid. Pity. Refusing the ride might have saved his life. Lovelaw said they'd have to go via Pitcher's depot to switch from the Land Rover to another car. Once they were in the garage there, he wrestled Elwyn into a big metal box by brute force. It was a struggle that Elwyn couldn't have won, of course. He hit his head when he fell against the box, Lovelaw says, and ended up unconscious.'

'He must have known he was fighting for his life?'

'I expect so.'

'And the knock on the head wasn't in the scenario?'

'Definitely not. But once Lovelaw got him locked up in that box, he left him there to die.' He paused, then added

216

quietly: 'They think he must have gone into a coma quite soon.'

'The box wasn't airtight?'

'Oh no. He could breath. But it was full of cat bedding. Sacks and cotton waste the depot cats slept on. That was the killer. They both knew it, also that it would seem to be death from natural causes.'

'And that's really how he died?'

'Not before he'd done his best to bust out.'

Perdita stopped and drew in a breath that broke into a sob. 'How could Tony Lovelaw have done anything so bloody callous?'

'I'm afraid because his girlfriend made him.'

She shook her head slowly, and pulled a tissue out of her pocket. 'Couldn't Elwyn even have shouted for help?'

'Probably he did. But there was no one to hear. He was in a box in a locked garage at a depot that was unmanned for the whole day. Lovelaw had arranged that, of course. He then took the train to London, dressed in Elwyn's hat, coat and glasses, and making sure plenty of people would remember him. He went to the station manager's office at Paddington in answer to an emergency broadcast for him. At first he believed it was from Alison to say something had gone wrong. When he realized it wasn't, he thought the whole thing was providential, of course.'

Perdita had wiped her eyes, and the two were moving forward again. 'And it was Evan Cromwell-Evans who put in the message? Did Tony ring him?'

'No, once he knew it couldn't be from Alison, he assumed it was a message for the genuine Elwyn. Soon after though, he introduced himself as Elwyn to a temp outside the offices of his literary agents in Baker Street.'

'But Tony Lovelaw doesn't look in the least like Elwyn?'

'For people who'd never met Elwyn before, he did. Or rather that's what the hat, and the rest of the get-up did for him, plus the Welsh accent – even for people who were shown Elwyn's picture later. Funny though, it was Niedlich who first put us on to the idea of the impersonation.'

'And he'd never met Elwyn?'

'Only spoken to Lovelaw imitating Elwyn on the phone. But Niedlich described Elwyn as always cheerful.'

'And that was as wrong for Elwyn as it was right for Tony?'

'Absolutely. Tony Lovelaw simply couldn't disguise a natural ebullience.'

'And did he wait in London and catch one of the late trains back on Wednesday night?'

'No. He got the next express back to Cardiff, with Elwyn's stuff in a bag. He was with a farmer in Caerphilly by late morning.' Parry sniffed. 'We should have known how late, long before we did. He'd implied to me he'd seen that farmer first thing. Very matter of fact he was about it, and there seemed no reason to check it out.'

Perdita looked puzzled. 'But Alison told me Elwyn was seen coming out of Cardiff Station at eleven on Wednesday night?'

'Yes, but that was Lovelaw again. He spent the evening with his wife, then left the house around ten. Said he'd suddenly remembered he had to prepare the depot for a big delivery early in the morning. He took Elwyn's body from the box, covered it up in the Land Rover, then drove to Cardiff. He parked in a side street near the first bus stop on the Aberkidy route.'

'With the body still in the Land Rover?'

'That's right. Then he walked back to the station carrying the hat and overcoat in the bag again. He waited in the loo on the right platform. When the train came in he appeared to have got off it —'

'Dressed as Elwyn again?'

'Yes. And caught the Aberkidy bus. The driver remembered selling him a ticket, and a passenger remembers he went to the top deck which was empty except for him. He put the disguise back in the bag, and slipped off the bus during the mêlée at the first stop.'

'And nobody noticed?'

'Nobody. Of course, at that point he was actually aiming not to be noticed. He went back to the Land Rover, and drove fast to Aberkidy, beating the bus there by at least half an hour. He put his bus ticket in the dead man's pocket, dumped the body where it was found in the morning, and drove like hell for home. He was there just before midnight, a good fifteen minutes before the bus got to Aberkidy, and with his unsuspecting wife to provide an alibi. He joined her in the bedroom as she was watching the end of a TV movie that finished at midnight.'

'So everything went as planned for Tony?'

'Not quite. Because the body was still stiff with rigor mortis, he couldn't dress it in the overcoat. That didn't matter too much, but he was so concerned about it at the time it was probably why he forgot to leave the right fedora.'

'There was more than one?'

'Yes, two. One that fitted Elwyn, and one that fitted Lovelaw. He left the wrong one by the body. We found the other stuffed behind the junk in the garage at Pitcher's. He'd put it there Thursday morning, probably meaning to get rid of it permanently later.'

Perdita frowned. 'But Alison couldn't have been involved in any of the Wednesday night business? Not at all? I remember she told me Sheila Cromwell-Evans was with her till very late.'

'Yes, till twelve-thirty. And if Elwyn had been on that bus he'd have been home before Sheila left. That was what kept Alison out of the frame. Up to the point we uncovered the third deception.'

'And that involved her?'

'It involved her pregnancy. They'd been trying for a baby for ages with no result. Like a lot of men, Elwyn had refused to submit himself for tests in case it showed the failure was his fault. I suppose he'd had enough failure. Except, without telling Alison or their doctor, he'd been consulting a private fertility specialist in London. We found the correspondence on his computer. And his worst fears were realized. He was quite definitely and permanently incapable of fathering a child. Sperm count of zero, apparently. Something to do with a childhood illness.'

'So the baby she's having can't be his?'

'Afraid not.'

'The third deception?'

'Yes, and the most telling. It meant she'd lied to the police about her relations with her husband. She gave us quite a story about how much the baby would mean to them both, especially Elwyn. It made her grief over his death a good deal more convincing.'

'And the baby is Tony Lovelaw's?'

Parry smiled ruefully. 'Yes. It was what it took to make him go through with the murder conspiracy. His own marriage is childless too –'

'But Sally's never wanted children,' Perdita interrupted.

'But he has. Rather fancies himself in the procreation department. Prize bull material, he thinks he is. Comes with his farming background. Anyway, having his child meant Alison controlled him for as long as she was likely to need him.'

'I still think her money, or rather Rhonwen's money, was Tony's biggest incentive,' said Perdita glibly.

'A different kind of incentive. But it was the pregnancy that made us turn the spotlight on Alison. And it revealed a lot.'

'In what way?'

'Mostly things she'd said that were meant to colour our thinking. She overdid them. It showed up when we analysed our reports. For instance, Elwyn and his mother couldn't have disliked each other that much. Well certainly not as much as Alison wanted us to think. Otherwise Rhonwen wouldn't have treated Elwyn so well in her lifetime, and left him everything. Alison also encouraged us to believe the worst implications in the memo were accurate.'

'That the Operatic Committee had been having orgies in Rhonwen's Jacuzzi?' Perdita gave a quizzical look. 'I think I told you the same thing, didn't I?'

'Not with malice or intent, you didn't. There were parties all right, but it's doubtful they were total orgies.'

'And if they were, no one's going to admit it?'

'No. Not even Cromwell-Evans would go that far. Anyway, no one needs to admit it. It has no real bearing on what happened to Elwyn.' He looked at his watch. 'Perhaps we should turn back, or we'll be having lunch in Porthcawl.'

Perdita nodded as he added: 'Are you warm enough in that raincoat?'

'Too warm,' she said, undoing the buttons as they turned about.

Parry watched her action. 'Alison borrowed Sally Lovelaw's trenchcoat when she went to buy a fedora for Lovelaw,' he said, frowning.

'Without Sally knowing.'

'That's right. I can't explain why, but I found that somehow obscene. Irrational of me, I suppose.' He shrugged. 'She wore one of Rhonwen's wigs for the same event. All helped in the confusion. Led us up one very wrong path.' He took a deep breath, and then exhaled sharply. 'Anyway, it's all over now. They've both confessed. He to the murder, she to conspiracy. Both were hoping they'd get shorter sentences by shopping the other one.'

'Will they?'

'That's up to the judge,' he replied sternly. 'One thing's for sure, I'm afraid. Their love was mainly lust embroidered by avarice.'

She moved closer to him, taking one of his hands in both of hers, and slowing their pace. 'You know, it wasn't irrational of you to think that. About Alison and the trenchcoat,' she said, her eyes searching the sand in front of her. 'Alison and Sally were such close friends. I'm sure Alison borrowed plenty of things from her. It only feels obscene when you know she ended up borrowing Sally's husband.' Then she stopped altogether, turned to face him, and reaching, put her arms around his neck. 'I really think you're beginning to understand how I feel still about Rosemary.'

'Still?' he asked, bringing her closer to him.

Her eyes opened wider. 'Still, but . . . but it's getting easier,' she answered, kissing him very lightly on the lips, then turning to race ahead of him along the beach.